Also by Daniel Klein

Kill Me Tender

Blue Suede Clues

"Where's Elvis?" (with Hans Teesma)

Beauty Sleep

Embryo

Wavelengths

Magic Time

Viva Las Vengeance

Daniel Klein

St. Martin's Minotaur

New York

www.minotaurbooks.com

Library of Congress Cataloging-in-Publication Data

Klein, Daniel M.
    Viva las vengeance : a murder mystery featuring Elvis Presley / Daniel Klein.—1st ed.
        p. cm.
    ISBN 0-312-28806-9
    1. Presley, Elvis, 1935–1977—Fiction. 2. Tourists—Crimes against— Fiction. 3. Las Vegas (Nev.)—Fiction. 4. Rock musicians—Fiction. I. Title.

PS3561.L344 V58 2003
813'.54—dc21

2002035761

First Edition: March 2003

10 9 8 7 6 5 4 3 2 1

For Freke, my love

Acknowledgments

This one took a number of drafts before I was completely happy with it, and I really need to thank those friends who stuck with me through them all, supplying encouragement from draft to draft: my pal Tom Cathcart; my sweet daughter, Samara; that Elvis maven, David Neal of Elvis in Print; the incomparable Lex and Kees, of Elvisnews; and above all, my brilliant wife, Freke. A special thanks to John Pizzichemi for his personal inspiration.

Hats off also to Kim Vickery for this book's title: she was the winner of our title contest. And a bow to the runners-up: Archimedes Lee and Glen Bowles for *Follow That Scream;* Rick Horvath for *Lethal Las Vegas;* Laura McCabe for *Return to End Her;* and Jack Nessel for *Such Vicious Minds.*

As always, I am deeply indebted to the work of Peter Guralnick, whose sensitive and thoughtful biographies of Elvis, *Last Train from Memphis* and *Careless Love,* I reread constantly. In addition, Larry Geller's memoir, *If I Can Dream,* about Elvis's spiritual life, was particularly helpful to me this time around, as was the memoir *Fly on the Wall: Recollections of Las Vegas' Good Old, Bad Old Days,* about "Sin City" in its early 1960s incarnation, by the former *Las Vegas Sun* reporter Dick Odessky.

D. M. K.
elvisdetective.com

Part 1
The Seeker

1

A Foul-Mouthed Breath of Fresh Air

*W*e've got an incredible audience here tonight, folks. Like this lady right over here—she's so fat she's sitting next to *everybody*! I mean, she could take a twenty-minute shower and still not get her feet wet. You should see her driver's license—it says, 'Picture continued on other side.' "

As the crowd howled, Howie Pickles took a couple of mincing steps to the front of the stage and peered down at his target, a hefty bleached-blonde at a table for two.

"Nice makeup job, dear," Pickles gurgled with an adolescent leer in his googly eyes. "How'd you put on your lipstick—with a paint roller? At least that must be easier than putting on your belt—you need a boomerang for that, right? So tell me, is this gentleman your husband?"

The big blonde nodded excitedly. She was clearly having the time of her life, a bona fide Las Vegas story to bring back with her to Ohio.

"That must've been the only wedding in history where the bride and groom had to walk down the aisle single file," Pickles intoned.

He scratched his bald dome with a mock-puzzled expression on his rubbery face. "It's one of the great mysteries of life that these mammoth broads always end up with skinny guys. Right, folks? Look at this guy—he's so thin, he's wearing a pinstriped suit and it only has one stripe! So tell me, pal, when you take her to bed, do you bring a compass with you?"

Elvis laughed in spite of himself. He and the gang had arrived in Vegas late that night and the 2 A.M. show at the Sahara was their first stop. After a month-long Christmas vacation at Graceland, Elvis needed a good dose of Howie Pickles to clear his system of all the fake good cheer he had endured at home. Especially from Priscilla. She'd presented him with a whole pile of insinuations about his relationship with Ann-Margret all wrapped up in glittery paper and shiny bows. Pickles was the antidote, all right—a foul-mouthed breath of fresh air.

"So, why is it all you G-cup gals wear those Hawaiian jobbies?" Pickles was saying to the blonde. "What's that you call them?"

"A muumuu," the woman tittered.

"A muuuuuumuuuuuu?" Pickles crooned, rolling his eyes. He gazed solemnly at the lady in question's husband. "Sounds like it's milking time, pal. Better get her back to the barn."

The whole room erupted, Elvis right along with them. Sure, Pickles's gags were mean, but all the comedian was doing was saying out loud what everybody else was thinking silently. That's why he could get away with it.

"Listen, folks, unless you were led in here by a Seeing Eye dog, you probably noticed that we have in our midst the biggest star in the universe—*The King himself, Mr. Elvis Presley!*"

Pickles pointed, the spotlight swiveled to Elvis's table, the crowd cheered, and Elvis waved back, smiling shyly.

"I see you brought the Memphis Mafia with you, Elvis," Pickles went on, the spot back on him. "They're kinda like Sinatra's Rat Pack, except they only drink moonshine. . . . Just a minute, I take that back. Dean Martin drinks moonshine too—as a chaser."

Pickles strolled across the stage until he was directly in front of Elvis's table.

"These guys are actually Elvis's disciples. I mean that in the biblical sense, folks." Pickles folded his stubby arms across his chest like a professor. "Think about it—Jesus said, 'Love thy neighbor.' And Elvis says, 'Don't be cruel.' See what I'm talking about?"

The audience giggled tentatively, all eyes on Elvis. Elvis offered a brave smile. *If you laugh at other people, you've got to be able to take it yourself, right?*

"I'm not kidding, folks. The similarities are too close to be coincidental," Pickles continued. "Like Jesus was the lamb of God, and Elvis wears mutton chops. See what I'm saying? And listen to this—Jesus lived in a state of grace in a Near Eastern land. And Elvis lives in Graceland in a near eastern state!"

The laughter was rolling now, really picking up steam. But Elvis was finding it increasingly difficult to hang on to his smile.

"It goes on," Pickles said. "Jesus walked on water. And in 'Blue Hawaii,' Elvis went surfing. *Coincidence*? I don't think so."

Howls of laughter. Elvis's smile had completely evaporated.

"Think about it," Pickles was saying. "The most important woman in Jesus' life was born of Immaculate Conception. And the girl Elvis lives with goes to Immaculate Conception High School!"

Suddenly, Elvis was on his feet. The crowd went dead quiet. Pickles froze. Everyone was staring at Elvis.

"I'm a big fan of yours, Mr. Pickles," Elvis said, looking warmly at the comedian. "That's the God's honest truth. And I like to think I can take a ribbing like anybody else. It's just that stuff about, you know, my Lord and Savior. It don't sit right, not with the way I was brought up."

Pickles chewed on his lip for a long moment, the audience growing increasingly anxious.

"O forgive me, my King," Pickles said finally, somehow managing to sound both repentant and mocking at the same time. "Didn't mean to offend."

About half the audience laughed while the other half stared apprehensively at Elvis who was unsure how to respond. Finally, Elvis just mumbled, "Appreciate that," and sat back down. The audience let out a collective sigh of relief.

Pickles paced back to the center of the stage. He stood perfectly still for a couple of seconds, then abruptly pointed a finger at a white-haired man in the audience who was sipping a martini.

"Look at this guy," Pickles crowed. "A real Las Vegas loser. I bet he even loses money on the stamp machines."

The audience roared.

2

The Peaceable Kingdom

lvis didn't let himself off as easily as Howie Pickles had. Was it really the sanctity of Jesus he was protecting? Or was it his own thin skin? God knows, that line about Priscilla still being in high school had rankled. It wasn't even true—she'd graduated a few months ago. Still, it was humiliating, everybody having a big laugh about him living with a teenager. No, maybe his little outburst hadn't had that much to do with his Lord and Savior after all.

On the stage, a bearded young man in a flowing white robe was now sitting cross-legged, playing some kind of Oriental instrument. It looked like a pot-bellied, long-armed guitar, and the sound that came out of it was whiny, like an electric saw or a Hawaiian guitar, but sweeter—much sweeter. The beat was nearly impossible to locate, always lagging way behind itself like a syncopation on top of a syncopation, but that's what made you reach for it, like trying to catch the phantom caboose of a mystery train. All around the nightclub people were laughing and talking, clinking glasses and silverware, and Elvis wanted to shush them so he could concentrate on the music.

That turned out to be unnecessary. The moment the raven-haired young woman emerged from the wings accompanied by a panther on a leather leash, the audience went silent. Whether they were struck dumb by the girl's exotic beauty or by the fact that a jungle animal was just yards away from them, Elvis couldn't say. But about himself, there was no doubt: he was stunned by the girl's loveliness.

She wore a beaded bodice and gauzy harem pants a shade of lavender that made her long legs glow iridescently beneath them. The bare skin of her arms, shoulders, neck, and face were a tawny color, silky smooth, and her long hair had the same luster and blue-black color as the panther's. Her face was a perfect oval, her almond eyes wide-set and slightly tilted, like a Chinese, yet large and diamond bright, and her mouth was full and fleshy and moist—like Selma's, Elvis reflexively thought. Her small, delicate feet were bare but for belled toe rings that chimed with a surprisingly piercing tone every time she bounced. *There* was that elusive beat. She ferreted it out of that sinewy Eastern melody and punctuated it with a slap of her feet and the lucid peal of those tiny bells. A rhythmic revelation.

The girl danced with the panther. She mirrored the animal's stretch and prowl, the languid undulations of its spine, the gentle sway of its long neck, even mimicked the slow roll and whip of its tail with a quiver and snap of her buttocks. Raw and elegant, she both emulated the beast and raised its movements to the level of ballet. Elvis was spellbound.

He had never seen an act like this anywhere, let alone in Vegas. Sure, there had been that Polynesian dance troupe they'd used in *Blue Hawaii*. They were exotic too, in a way, but compared to what he was watching now, they were nothing more than a grass-skirted conga line in slow motion. But who was this woman? And how the heck had she ended up in the Sahara's floorshow? Elvis had been too busy beating himself up for interrupting Howie Pickles to catch her name when the comedian introduced her. Elvis leaned across the table and whispered to Freddy, "Who is she?"

"Sheema? Shirla? . . . No, I remember—Shiva Ree," Freddy whispered back. Then he pumped his eyebrows lecherously a couple of times and added, "Man, how'd you like to be that panther?"

Elvis shot him a scolding glare and turned back to the stage. The dancer had straddled the black beast and was now undulating her hips in an echo of the rise and fall of the animal's back. No, this was beyond erotic. It was sublime, the dance of a priestess. Not something that Freddy or any of the other guys could even begin to understand.

Suddenly, the panther bared its teeth and whipped back its head. It snapped at the girl's thigh, catching the gauzy fabric of a pant leg on one of its canines. The fabric ripped. The audience gasped. Elvis jumped out of his seat, his heart thumping. *How the heck do you wrassle a panther?*

The dancer's shining eyes locked onto Elvis's, halting him. *"I'm okay"*—she mouthed the words to him, smiled radiantly. The panther swung back its head and the girl went on dancing, one of her legs now flashing nakedly under the tatters of ripped cloth. Elvis sat down slowly, not taking his eyes off her. His heart was still pounding. He felt light-headed, dizzy, like some part of him was spinning out of his skull.

Both music and dance gradually slowed. The girl dropped onto her knees and palms, facing the panther, only their heads moving, swaying languidly, feline eye to feline eye. And finally no movement at all, both frozen, silent, an enchanted tableau of the Peaceable Kingdom.

For several seconds, the audience was quiet. Then Elvis began to applaud and everyone joined in, although not nearly enthusiastically enough, he thought. They had probably been expecting a frenzied climax, something torrid and crass—sex, not serenity. This was, after all, Las Vegas. As the dancer rose and took a graceful bow, her eyes again met Elvis's. *"Thank you,"* her lips said.

Elvis tried to watch television in his suite, but he couldn't keep his mind on the *Late Late Show*'s offering, *Ma and Pa Kettle at Waikiki*. That movie hadn't been much good the first time he saw it, and the second time around it seemed uncomfortably close to his own Hawaiian opus. Heck, this Kettle comedy was probably the Colonel's original inspiration for *Blue Hawaii*. The man had a real artistic eye.

Fact is, no movie would have had much luck keeping Elvis's attention this night. He had listened to a couple of songs of the next act, a bony-faced crooner named Tony Amato, but the image of Shiva Ree had prodded Elvis out of his seat and up to his Sahara suite, leaving the boys on their own to prowl the Strip until daybreak. For Elvis, there wasn't an act in all of Vegas that could have followed Shiva's.

Elvis was about to snap off the hillbillies-in-Hawaii flick when he heard some kind of ruckus outside. He walked over to the glass door that opened onto an outdoor balcony, stepped out, and looked down. He was only three floors up and could see immediately where the racket was coming from: a group of about a dozen people standing in a semicircle at the casino's entrance, chanting, *"Cursed be/Blasphemy!"*

They appeared to be dressed in the kind of suits and dresses that folks wore on Sundays back in Tennessee—dark colors, fabrics way too hot for the desert climate, every button buttoned up. Church folk. A couple were holding picket signs that cited Bible

10

chapters and verses—none that rang a bell with Elvis. And some appeared to be throwing something—tomatoes, it looked like—at a small figure in their midst.

Elvis grasped the balcony rail and leaned down as far as he could. Finally, he made out that small figure: it was Howie Pickles. The comedian was cowering, his arms folded in front of his face. It seemed pretty clear that Pickles was the church folk's blasphemer.

A trio of brawny Sahara doormen suddenly appeared and formed a little phalanx around Pickles, steering him into a waiting cab. It looked like they'd been through this drill before. Just before Pickles ducked into the cab, he turned back to his tormentors and shouted, "Jesus is coming! Quick, look busy!" Cackling, he jumped into the car and was whisked away as one last tomato splattered the cab's rear window.

Elvis shook his head. Man, what an idiot that Pickles was. Still, you'd think that good Christian men and women would have more important things to do than pour out their wrath on a pathetic, foul-mouthed clown. Although, come to think of it, Elvis had come pretty close to doing the same thing during Pickles's performance. A lesson there.

From his perch on the balcony, Elvis could see all the way up the Strip to where the constellation of colorful flashing lights ended and the shadowless desert began. Those lights surely were a wonder to behold—the Golden Nugget, the Sands, the Hacienda. This was the Las Vegas that Elvis loved, the one he had come here for: the sparkling dream world that blotted out everything you'd left behind.

Back inside, Elvis popped a sleeping pill and sat down again in front of the clamoring TV. Almost instantly, he fell into a deep, dream-filled sleep. Shiva Ree was doing an erotic encore. No panther this time—that was Elvis, himself, snapping at her pant leg.

11

*   *   *

He woke up in a hot sweat, his ears ringing:

"Mrs. Donaldsen's body was discovered early this morning by a motorist on Route 15 just three miles beyond the Las Vegas city limits. She apparently had been choked to death before being impaled on the Little Chapel of the West billboard."

Elvis bolted upright, stared at the TV screen. Behind the newscaster was the shadowy image of a huge woman, her arms and legs splayed, her wrists and ankles hammered onto a highway billboard.

Elvis gasped. She looked grotesque, terrifying, awful, yet there was also something obscenely comic about her: she hung there like a loathsome parody of the holiest image of them all. The woman's head dangled like a floppy doll's, her thick, light-colored hair obscuring her features. But Elvis did not need to see her face to recognize her. Her oversize muumuu was all the identification he needed.

3

The Dancer from the Dance

A rap at the door.

Elvis did not respond. The local news had moved on to the next order of business, what Herb Alan, the shiny-faced anchor, called, "The Numbers": hotels were at 92 percent capacity; last night's combined casino take was $4 million-plus, a record for the first week of January; and a total of 187 marriage ceremonies had been performed in the Strip's walk-in chapels in the past twenty-four hours, just two weddings short of another record. Herb Alan smiled broadly, as if to say that when you added all those numbers up, the murder of one overweight tourist didn't really amount to much, did it? And that right there was the Las Vegas that made Elvis's insides cringe.

Another rap at the door. Then a woman's voice, "Breakfast, Mr. Presley."

Elvis looked at his watch: a few minutes past eleven. Early, by Las Vegas standards, but his stomach was still on Memphis time and it was two hours later there. Elvis snapped off the TV. "Come on in," he called.

He walked over to the sofa, sat down, and cleared the magazines off the tile-topped coffee table. Behind him, he heard a key turn in the lock and the door open. Something smelled good—*real* good and familiar.

"You can set it right here," Elvis said, not even glancing at the service girl. It may be time to eat, but it was way too early in his day for small talk.

Elvis stared hungrily at the tabletop as to his left the girl set down a silver tray crowded with plates: one holding a big mound of scrambled eggs, one with a half-dozen sausage patties, another loaded with bacon, and the last—the one that was giving off that familiar delicious fragrance—piled high with butter-fried corn biscuits. From the smell, Elvis could have sworn those biscuits had been made by Cook Mary herself back at Graceland. The room-service girl hovered behind his left shoulder, just out of sight.

"Much obliged, ma'am," Elvis said. She was probably waiting for a tip, but his wallet was in his jacket hanging in the closet and he couldn't wait to pop one of those biscuits into his mouth; he'd leave her a double tip next time. He grabbed one of the corn biscuits off the plate and slid it whole into his mouth. Incredible—it was *exactly* like Mary's!

"Is there anything else I can do for you, Mr. Presley?"

Man, this was getting annoying. His mouth full and his brow puckered, Elvis leaned his head back and squinted up at the pesky woman.

Miss Shiva Ree smiled down at him.

Elvis just about choked on his biscuit.

Shiva was wearing one of the Sahara's service outfits, a khaki blazer and skirt strung with gold braid that was probably supposed to look like a French Foreign Legion uniform. Every Vegas hotel had a theme and the Sahara's was a desert fantasy straight out of *Casablanca*. The outfit was topped off with a short-billed military cap that Shiva was now gracefully removing. Her lustrous, blue-black hair tumbled down to below her shoulders.

Elvis stared at her, dumbfounded. One reason he couldn't speak was that his mouth was full of corn biscuit, so he chawed it down as fast as he could. "I didn't recognize you right off," he said, finally.

"I'm a master of disguise." Shiva laughed. She came around in front of the coffee table and lowered herself onto the floor in a single, fluid motion. She sat there, cross-legged, smiling radiantly at Elvis.

"I had a dream about you," Elvis blurted out. He hadn't meant to say that, not first thing.

"I know," Shiva replied softly. "I sent it."

"Sent me a dream?"

"That's right," Shiva laughed. "Special delivery."

"Well, I got it all right."

The dancer's black eyes glowed like gemstone. "You traded places with my panther, didn't you?" she said.

Elvis felt a shiver ripple down his spine. "Beg pardon?"

"In your dream," Shiva said, still smiling beautifully.

Elvis wiped some butter off his mouth with his sleeve. "I imagine a lot of men had that dream last night," he said.

"Perhaps. But I only sent it to you." She tilted her head to one side, her hair glancing against the floor. "Your breakfast is getting cold, Mr. Presley."

"I kinda lost my appetite, ma'am," Elvis replied.

For a long minute, the two just gazed at one another. Then Shiva said, "You're a seeker, aren't you?"

"How do you mean?"

"You know—you look for the meaning behind things," Shiva said. "I can see that in your eyes. That beautiful look of wonderment."

"Right now, all that wonderment is about you, Miss Shiva," Elvis said. "I'm wondering how any woman can look so darned pretty."

The young woman pursed her lips. She seemed disappointed in his reply. "I'm talking about things that go beyond the physical," she said. "To the higher levels."

"Like that dance you do," Elvis said. Shiva's face brightened again and Elvis felt as pleased as a schoolboy who'd come up with the right answer on a pop quiz. "It's two dances, isn't it? Two dances in one."

"Exactly!" Shiva cried. She spiraled up onto her feet again and executed a slithery shimmy thing that made her breasts bounce up like helium balloons. By God, she put Ann-Margret—the Shimmy Queen herself—to shame. "The tourists only see my body. My bosom, my hips, my legs—*my sex*. They can't begin to see the meaning behind that—my vision, my divine inspiration. It's tragic, really, but I don't mind. As long as I reach just one person out there. Someone like you."

Elvis nodded seriously. The God's honest truth was that he'd only seen what the tourists saw: Shiva's body, pretty much to the exclusion of anything else. Maybe her message of divine inspiration was still on its way.

"It's like that poem," Shiva went on. " 'O body swayed to music, O brightening glance, How can we know the dancer from the dance?' "

"That sure is pretty, ma'am," Elvis said.

"It's impossible, you know," Shiva continued. "You can never tell the dancer from the dance. It's all one thing. The truth is, everything in the universe is all one thing."

Elvis nodded again. He wasn't exactly sure what she was saying, but he sure as heck liked the way she said it. And he did have some kind of *feel* for what she was talking about. Although he had never heard the word used that way before, he did think of himself as a "seeker," a man who looked for the meaning behind the way things happened in your life. There had to be some kind of design, some master plan lurking behind the everyday world you lived in. Like one question that had been bothering him a lot lately was: Why had he been chosen to be Elvis Presley? Surely, there must be some soul out there who was more deserving of all the gifts that God had bestowed upon him.

"What about, you know, a man and a woman together?" Elvis said, not quite raising his eyes to Shiva's. "How can you tell the lover from the lovin'?"

"Are you saying that you would like to make love to me, Mr. Presley?"

Elvis's face flushed in spite of himself. "I guess that's so, Miss Shiva."

Suddenly, the young woman began dancing again. Not her panther dance—something even more exotic. She hiked up her skirt and balanced on one bare leg, her other foot folded snugly against the inside of her thigh. Her arms stood straight out from her shoulders, then swung down from her elbows like a pair of pendulums. Her forearms swept back and forth in a staccato so fast that it looked like she had four arms ... then eight ... then a blur of dozens of arms and hands and slender fingers. All the while, she emitted a sing-songy hum that sounded like the Oriental guitar that had accompanied her the night before. For the first few minutes, Shiva's dark eyes remained fixed on Elvis's, but then they rolled back into her head, leaving the glistening whites to fill the almond spaces between her eyelids.

Elvis stared at her, transfixed. He felt dizzy and more than a little frightened, especially by that crazy thing with her eyes. Like the night before, some part of him felt like it was trying to spin out of his skull, leaving his burning body below.

The dance ended as abruptly as it had begun and Miss Shiva Ree was again sitting in front of Elvis, perched on a corner of the coffee table, shyly smiling.

"That was a wonder to behold," Elvis said.

"We were making love, you know," the girl said.

Elvis lifted his eyebrows. "Really?"

"Tantric sex," Shiva said. "Making love outside of our bodies."

"How about that?" Elvis said. He bit down on his lower lip. "I thought my body felt kinda left out."

"Its time will come," she said, laughing. She abruptly stood, planted a moist kiss on Elvis's forehead, and started for the door.

"Hey!" Elvis called after her. "Where are you going?"

"Home to feed Abu," she said, leaning alluringly against the door frame. "My panther."

Elvis stood and started for her. His body felt like it was on fire. Two steps and he could have his arms around her, his mouth on her sweet lips.

"I, uh, I need to ask you something," he stammered.

"Yes?"

Elvis hesitated, trying to think of what to say. Finally, he blurted, "How come you know I like butter-fried biscuits?"

"It came to me in a dream."

"Really?"

Shiva let loose a full-throated laugh. Elvis reached for her waist.

"Actually, I read about it in a movie magazine," Shiva said. And with that, she lightly slipped away from his grasp and was out the door. Gone.

Elvis just stood there, sweat dripping down his brow. Then he stomped back to the coffee table and reached down for a corn biscuit. It was cold and sticky with congealed butter. Elvis flung it against the wall.

"Darned woman! Ruined my breakfast!"

4

Ipso, Fatso

*T*he only breakfast they served at the VIP pool was a gummy Danish with some kind of yellow cheese stuffed inside it. Elvis munched around its edges, washing down the goop with iced pineapple juice.

He had his own table by the teardrop-shaped pool, complete with his own personal potted palm and white plaster foot stool, all courtesy of the Sahara's manager, Luke de Luca. In keeping with the hotel's Mid-Eastern theme, miniature replicas of the pyramids dotted the perimeter of the pool, some now unceremoniously draped with hotel bath towels. This walled enclave sat smack in the center of the Sahara complex, hidden from general view. It was reserved for visiting celebrities, the cast of the floor show, and a select group of high rollers who got everything in the hotel free as long as they dropped a few hundred thou in the casino every night. There were only a handful of people here now, three Japanese men in identical, short-sleeved, white nylon shirts—*very* high rollers, no doubt—and a couple of bikinied chorus girls splashing around in the pool like teenagers, which is probably exactly what they were.

Elvis flipped through the first few pages of the script he'd brought down with him: *Roustabout,* his upcoming picture. This one was Colonel Parker's special baby, based on his own experiences as a carny who painted sparrows yellow and hawked them as canaries, and who dropped chickens on hot plates making them dance to "Turkey in the Straw." Elvis had always enjoyed the Colonel's carnival stories—the flim-flams, the life of the road, the freaks and geeks who dreamed of nothing more than a home and family to call their own. But by the time he got to page six, Elvis's hope for a movie with any real substance was already slipping away. *Roustabout* had the same, tired, boy-meets-two-girls plot and the same studio song-mill ditties as all the others. Just one more cornball comedy starring the King of Corn himself. It filled Elvis with shame just to think about those pictures. Sometimes it almost seemed like a blessing that Mamma hadn't lived long enough to see the worst of them.

"Well, piss in my ear and call me Johnny Weissmuller, if it ain't King Creole himself!"

Elvis looked up. Casting a wide and wobbly shadow on his table was a thick-set young man in a neon-red Hawaiian shirt that stopped short of his waistband, revealing a hairy mound of belly and a navel that looked like a swollen black eye. His face looked twenty-five, but that belly looked like it was going on forty. He was carrying a beer mug full of scotch with a pair of ice cubes floating on top. Elvis nodded to him, then quickly looked back at the script. The VIP pool was supposed to be a sanctuary from intruding tourists.

"I guess you don't know who I am, do you, King?" The wobbly shadow had not moved.

"No, sir," Elvis sighed. "Afraid I can't place your face." Or your belly button either, for that matter.

"Digby Ferguson," the young man said, grabbing a chair from a neighboring table, dragging it over, and seating himself across from Elvis. "The writer, you know."

"Sorry, Mr. Ferguson, but you're the writer I don't know," Elvis said, looking back down at the script. He was here on vacation, darn it! He could be hassled by all the obnoxious tourists he wanted in Hollywood or Nashville. Probably the best thing to do now would be to just get up and go back to his room.

"Good reason for that, Elvis," Ferguson said, grinning. "I haven't published anything yet."

"That so?" Elvis said, then added automatically, "Well, maybe things will pick up for you, son." Man, how famous did you have to get before you stopped worrying about the feelings of every single person you met?

"Oh, they're picking up already," Ferguson said. He took a long swallow of scotch, then fished one of the ice cubes out of his mug and rubbed it all over his face before plopping it back into his drink. "Picking up and taking you and me along with them."

Elvis stood, slipping the script under his arm. Yup, it was definitely time to go.

"Last night, I was driving around the desert, reciting the Twenty-third Psalm, when I saw Jesus Christ himself," Ferguson went on, talking fast. "He was hanging on the cross for all my sins—and yours too, Elvis, yours too. Except on closer inspection, it wasn't Our Savior after all. No siree, it was the fat lady. Tacked up to the Little Chapel billboard like a bountiful breakfast for a whole squadron of vultures."

"You're the one who found her?"

"None other than. I am the mysterious passing motorist. And

being the ever-prepared professional that I am, I immediately snatched my trusty Polaroid out of my bag and took several artful shots of Miss Bountiful. Well, not immediately. Rifling around in my bag, I also came upon a salt shaker which was miraculously filled with pure Columbian cocaine, so I snorted a line to improve my visual perception. I am nothing if not an artist."

Elvis hesitated. This Ferguson fellow was one unhealthy presence, inside and out, but there was no way Elvis could go back to his room without hearing the rest of his story. Elvis lowered himself back into his chair. "What'd you do then?"

Ferguson grinned, showing a row of surprisingly bright white teeth.

"I called the constabulary, of course," he said. "I am nothing if not a law-abiding citizen. To the sheriff's credit, he was out there in five minutes flat. And in appreciation of my good citizenship, he allowed me to follow him while he solved the case."

"He solved it already?" Elvis said.

"With pig certainty," Ferguson said. "After calling in backup to handle the messy details—and hauling down two-hundred-and-fifty pounds of gelatinous flesh from a billboard is one hell of a messy detail—Sheriff Turtleff and I drove straight to the Silver Mine Motel to inform Mr. Bruce Donaldsen that he was a bachelor again."

"Poor guy," Elvis murmured.

"That's one way of looking at it," Ferguson said. "I have to say, the newly minted widower seemed less than shocked by the news. Not exactly overwhelmed with sorrow either. His first words were—" Ferguson withdrew a small spiral notebook from his back pocket, flipped a few pages, then read, " 'Gee whiz!' That's an exact quote, Elvis, 'Gee whiz!' I should add here that Mr. Donaldsen appeared to be several bricks short of a load. As dim as a crescent moon, as my good mother says."

"Maybe he was in shock."

"That very well could be," Ferguson said. He patted the pocket of his Day-Glo shirt, pulled out a red capsule, popped it in his mouth, and washed it down with another gulp of scotch. "However, that was not the way Turtleff interpreted his behavior. The sheriff initiated a strenuous interview at this point. I believe it would have been considerably more strenuous if yours truly hadn't been there. He wanted to know where the little hubby had been for the past twenty-four hours. In his motel room, Donaldsen said, where he'd been since he and his wife left the Sahara at around three-thirty. And how long was his wife with him? She was there until he fell asleep, the man said. They'd climbed into bed together at around five A.M. And when did he observe that she was no longer in bed with him? When he woke up, which was when we came knocking on his door. Fact is, Donaldsen did look like a man who had just emerged from a deep sleep."

"What time was that?"

"Eight-thirty, give or take," Ferguson said.

"It doesn't seem likely that a man would murder his wife and then just crawl back into bed and go to sleep, does it?"

Ferguson laughed. "Well, well, Elvis, you're way ahead of me, aren't you? I heard you had a flair for crime detection. Read all about your role in that Squirm Littlejon case in Hollywood last year. That's how I knew you'd be hot for this one."

Elvis didn't feel hot for anything other than Miss Shiva just now, but that didn't stop him from asking, "What else did the sheriff ask Donaldsen?"

"His next question was not exactly delicate. The sheriff said, and I quote, 'Even if your wife got out of bed on her own, how the hell could a two-ton woman clamber out of your bed without waking you up?' "

"And what did Donaldsen say to that?"

"He said it happened all the time. They'd been married for five years. She'd always been an early riser. He was just used to it."

"Sounds believable." Elvis had slept through worse commotion in his day, like that time he had dozed off in a fox hole during a rifle-and-machine-gun exercise over in Germany.

"And that's when Donaldsen flipped his gourd," Ferguson said, grinning again. "Starts babbling like a baby. The man has a high-pitched voice to begin with, but now it's goosed up to the soprano register. 'Poor Bonnie'—that was his wife's name—'Poor *fat* Bonnie. I was the only one who truly loved her. Loved every *inch* of her.' That is also an exact quote, Elvis."

"It'd finally struck him," Elvis said. "The reality. That she was dead."

"Could be. But then his rant takes up a new direction. 'She's so fat she's sitting next to *everybody*!' he howls. 'You should see her driver's license—it says, picture continued on other side.' "

"Howie Pickles's routine. I was there when he did his number on her," Elvis said.

"So I learned later, Elvis," Ferguson said. "Both about the routine and that you were in the audience. That's when I knew you and I were onto some serious serendipity-doo."

Elvis had no idea what the man was talking about.

"It didn't seem to bother the fat lady at the time," Elvis said. "Or maybe she was just putting on a brave face."

"It was skinny Bruce who was bothered," Ferguson said. " 'Tortured' may be a better word. The guy starts shrieking like a banshee about what a dip-head Pickles is. Insulting his wife the same way she'd been insulted her whole life. *'It's not funny!'* he screams. *'Not funny!'* And then he comes up with the pièce de résistance. 'Pickles killed her!' he shrieks. 'Pickles insulted her to death!' By this time, he is jumping around like he's on a pogo stick. Clawing the air. Tearing at his pajamas. Tears streaming

24

down his face. Sheriff Turtleff grabbed him and put him in a full nelson. He must have held him like that for a good five minutes before Donaldsen finally settled down. Actually, he did more than settle down—he passed out in Turtleff's arms. Turtleff put him in handcuffs and carried him, fireman-style, out to his car. Impressive. I took a Polaroid of that too."

"He arrested him?"

"That's right. Took him to the station house where he booked him for first-degree murder."

"On what grounds?"

"Come on, Elvis, this is Vegas. They don't have grounds here, just desert. You've got to look at this from a pig's-eye view. The fat lady's husband acts like a certifiable nut case, so, ipso fatso, he's the murderer."

"How about crucifying her on that billboard?" Elvis asked. "What's the sheriff's theory for why he did that?"

"The thing about craziness is that it's an all-encompassing theory. Simplifies things. A crazy man does crazy things, end of theory." Ferguson looked at his watch. "Bail hearing starts in twenty minutes. I assume you'll be coming with me."

"Why the heck would you assume something like that?" Elvis had other plans for the afternoon, chiefly trying to locate where in Las Vegas a lady could keep a panther as a roommate.

"Because you know as well as I do that the husband didn't do it." Ferguson quaffed down the rest of his scotch and rose unsteadily to his feet. "Wonderful combo, little red devils and scotch. Clarifies the mystery."

"Who do you figure did it?" Elvis asked.

"Like I said, Elvis, this is Las Vegas. I grew up here. And I was a mere tot when I realized that the place operates on a very simple principle. Anywhere else in the world, I'd say the cop was right—another routine crime of marital passion. But in Vegas there is only one suspect for every crime, small or large—the Mafia. The question here is never, *Who*? It's, *Why*?" Ferguson steadied himself against the table with one hand. "We better get a move on, Elvis. Time's a-wasting."

"Good to meet you, Mr. Ferguson," Elvis said, remaining seated. He was on vacation, damn it. "Maybe see you around the pool sometime."

"Okay, Presley, but while you're lolling around the pool, you might want to take a gander at the local rag," Ferguson said, rooting around in his back pocket. He pulled out a wad of newsprint, then carefully unfolded it and set it on the table in front of Elvis. It was the front page of the local tabloid, the *Las Vegas Sun*. A banner headline read, "INSULT TO INJURY." Under that, the sub-head: "Comedian Howie Pickles Leaves 'em Dead." And under that, two side-by-side photographs: the first of Howie Pickles in performance, pointing a finger pistol-like at someone in the audience; the second of Bonnie Donaldsen crucified on the Sahara billboard.

Incredible. Contrary to anything remotely resembling logic, the biggest newspaper in town was pushing the murder-by-insult angle for all it was worth.

Elvis started to rise, but stopped halfway out of his seat. Just one second here. He'd come to Vegas to take a step back from the world, not to jump feet first into it. And he sure as heck wasn't about to jump into anything with a doped-up delinquent. He sat back down. "Like I say, see you around the pool, Digby."

Ferguson peered down at him imperiously. "You know what your problem is, Elvis? You're under-medicated."

5

Red Tips

The Sahara nightclub was deserted save for a Mexican custodian who was guiding a waxing machine over the floor while singing "O Sole Mio" in a fetching falsetto. He didn't notice Elvis climbing onto the stage and through the wing drop-curtain into the backstage area. Not much doing back here in the middle of the day either, just a flinty-eyed electrician fiddling with the light board. The electrician waved at Elvis like they were old buddies, then went back to his fiddling. There probably weren't many starstruck stagehands in Las Vegas.

"Hot damn! My lucky day!" A woman's voice behind Elvis.

He turned around to see a six-foot-tall redheaded chorus girl wearing an elaborate feather headdress and gold lamé pumps. Between these two items, all she wore was a buttocks-length dressing gown that she had neglected to tie closed, revealing a hilly expanse of pink skin. Elvis stared down at her pumps uncomfortably.

"Excuse me, ma'am," he mumbled. "I'm looking for—"

"You like my shoes, Elvis?" the redhead tittered.

"Very nice, ma'am."

The girl took a couple of steps toward Elvis. That was all it took for her dressing gown to flutter open completely. Her pointy, red-tipped breasts were now just inches away from his chest. There was no sense in even trying to look at her pumps now—the view had been obscured.

"Elvis, you have the most beautiful eyes I have ever seen on any man, woman, or child," the redhead cooed. Behind her, the electrician was obliviously rooting around in his toolbox.

"Thank you," Elvis said, trying to look at the girl's eyes, which were a pale blue. Man, it wasn't even two o'clock in the afternoon and his body had already been squeezed through the wringer once; he still hadn't settled down from his out-of-body sexual encounter with Miss Shiva Ree.

"My dressing room is right over there," the chorus girl whispered, pointing with her eyes to an open door down the darkened hallway.

"I see," Elvis whispered back. For the past few years, he had been getting offers like this almost daily—from starlets and showgirls and, often as not, from perfect strangers who would roll down their car windows in the middle of the street and inform Elvis that they were his for the asking. Most times, he didn't give a second thought to saying, "Thanks, but no thanks, ma'am," but heaven knows, it sure would be a release to have a little *in*-body sexual encounter right about now. Still, that felt kind of disloyal, although he wasn't exactly sure who it would be disloyal to. Priscilla? Ann-Margret? *Shiva Ree?*

The electrician had packed up his tools and was heading out, whistling tunelessly. The redhead smiled, waiting. She stutter-stepped even closer to Elvis, those red tips now touching the front of his shirt.

"I, uh, I was wondering if you could tell me how to get ahold of Miss Shiva Ree," Elvis said suddenly, much louder than he had intended.

"Not *another* one!" the redhead yelped. She spun around and indignantly strode down the hallway to her dressing room.

Man, she was as delicious-looking going as coming! Elvis mopped the sweat off his forehead with the back of his shirtsleeve. Maybe he should have gone to that bail hearing after all; it probably would have been less straining on his nerves.

He had just decided to return to his suite when he heard Howie Pickles's unmistakable voice screeching from the end of the back-stage hallway: *"What the hell do you want me to do? Turn into Doris Day and do a dramatic reading of Hallmark cards?"*

"Keep it down for Christ's sake, will ya, Howie?" Another unmistakable voice, that of "Lucky" Luke de Luca, the hotel's manager. De Luca may have left Brooklyn a decade ago, but he'd brought the nasal diction of Flatbush Avenue out to the Sagebrush State with him. Rumor had it that he had brought some other quaint hometown customs along with him too.

Pickles: *"Jesus, Lucky, you wouldn't ask Frankie to sing 'Ring Around the Rosie,' would ya?"*

Elvis took a couple of steps closer to the voices—they were coming from the half-opened door of de Luca's office at the far end of the hall. Elvis slipped behind a plywood flat in the shape of a giant ice cream cone—scenery for the chorus girls' "Scoopy Doop" number.

De Luca: *"Come on, we're just talking a couple of days here, right? Four shows, tops. Just until this blows over. Until the chat-ter stops. You saw the papers. The Sands is milking this for all it's worth. They're telling everybody who'll listen that you're a dangerous man. Your jokes are* fatal. *A deadly hex. They figure the tourists will stay away in droves. Their casino's been half-*

empty for a year now. It's just the break they've been looking for."

Pickles: *"Damn it, Lucky, I didn't have a thing to do with the fat lady's death."*

De Luca: *"Of course, not. Only an idiot would think you did. But you know this town is built on superstition. It's what gambling's all about, lucky streaks and hexes. And nobody comes to a casino that's got a hex on it."*

Pickles: *"So I gotta turn into Pat Boone to take the hex off."*

De Luca: *"What can I tell you, Howie? We all know who's behind this."*

Pickles: *"We do?"*

Elvis leaned forward, listening intently.

De Luca: *"Let's just say that their timing is too coincidental. Joey Filbert is opening at the Sands tonight. He's the third comic they've put up against you, Howie. Filbert's their last chance to cut their losses."*

Pickles: *"Come on, Lucky, you don't think they'd actually—"*

De Luca cut him with a snicker: *"Don't be an idiot, Howie!"*

Elvis heard footsteps behind him. He peeped out from the edge of the plywood ice cream cone. It was the redheaded chorus girl, now dressed in jeans, cowboy shirt, wide-brimmed straw hat, and harlequin sunglasses. But Elvis's brain was playing X-ray tricks on him: he could still see every inch of her pink body and it made him all hot and bothered again. Man, it was just like that crazy insight he'd had when he was only fourteen years old: *underneath their clothes, everybody's naked.* She walked to the exit and disappeared into the glaring, midday sun. Elvis again cocked his ear toward de Luca's office.

Pickles: *"Look, why don't I just skip a few shows?"*

De Luca: *"Nope, too fishy. Looks like you're feeling guilty. Like you're responsible in some way. The hex won't go away."*

Pickles: *"So what am I supposed to do? Recite nursery rhymes?"*

De Luca: *"No, keep making jokes. Just nothing personal."*

Pickles: *"Nothing personal? I'm Howie Pickles, for crissake!"*

De Luca: *"Call your writers. Tell 'em what you need."*

Pickles: *"I can't do it, Lucky. No can do, comprende? It'll ruin me. I'll never work again."*

De Luca, his voice pitched way down now: *"I'm asking you nice, Howie. Don't make me angry. Please."*

A long silence. Finally, Pickles piped up again, his voice more subdued this time: *"Okay, Lucky, I'll see what I can do. But this kills me, ya know."*

De Luca: *"I know that, Howie. It'll all be over in a couple of days."*

A moment later, Pickles came shuffling out of de Luca's office, his balloon head bobbing as he mumbled a string of four-letter words. Elvis remained hidden behind the scenery as Pickles stumbled into his dressing room where he immediately began whining: *"Look at you, you're living proof of reincarnation—nobody could get that dumb in just one lifetime!"*

Elvis slipped silently down the hallway, his back against the wall, until he was just outside Pickles's dressing room. He peered inside. Pickles was standing in front of a full-length mirror, beads of sweat on his bulbous face, saliva dripping from one corner of his mouth.

"Man, you're so ugly, your dog closes his eyes when he humps your leg!" Pickles spat the words out at his image in the mirror. "You ought to join the Ku Klux Klan—you'd look better with a hood over your head!"

Pickles sniffled. Elvis saw tears in the corners of the comedian's eyes.

"You know, Howie?" Pickles whined at his reflection. "You just haven't been yourself lately—and everybody's noticed the improvement!"

Pickles was now blubbering like a schoolyard bully's victim. That's probably just what Pickles had been—a schoolyard scapegoat—and ever since, he'd made a career out of getting his savage, jokey revenge.

Elvis turned, took a few quick steps, and slipped through the wing curtain back onto the Sahara's stage. The stage electrician was sitting on the edge of the proscenium, apparently waiting for him.

"The Center of the Light," the electrician said, rising. "Up in Indian Springs."

"Beg pardon?"

"Shiva Ree," the electrician said. "That's where she lives. Straight up one forty-six. Can't miss it."

"Thank you," Elvis said.

"No, thank *you*, Elvis," the man said. "We really appreciate the way you stood up to Pickles last night. Him taking our Lord's name in vain and all. The man's an abomination, like all them Hebes. No wonder his wife ran out on him."

6

Exploding with Gladness

*T*he Sahara garage attendant handed Elvis a note from Freddy. Late last night, the whole gang had been invited by some dancer to be judges at a bikini contest up at Lake Tahoe. Freddy wrote that it was a "once in a lifetime opportunity" and that it looked like Elvis had plenty to keep him busy anyhow. As a postscript he added, "Hope you don't mind we took the Caddy. Be back in a few days."

Elvis was about to blow his top when he realized that he was actually relieved to have them out of his hair. For a long time, the old hometown gang had helped him keep his head on straight, especially out in Hollywood. The boys kept him honest with himself—walking, joking reminders of who he really was and where he'd really come from. But lately, the gang had begun to feel more like baggage than ballast. Half the time, it seemed like they were only playacting at being his friends; heck, maybe that just happens when you put your pals on the payroll: friendship turns into a job. But there was something else about them that was beginning to grate on Elvis—the boys were almost thirty now and not a one of them showed any signs of growing up or of trying anything new in life, anything different from high school. And that built a little wall around Elvis's own mind; it held it back from venturing into new territory. No wonder the boys taking off made him feel so freed-up just now.

The garage guy said he would be happy to give Elvis a loaner— a foreign coupe convertible with the top already down. Elvis handed him a fifty and slid behind the wheel. He found Route 146 easily and headed north toward Indian Springs and the Center of the Light, whatever the heck that was.

Man, it felt good to be racing along the desert highway with the wind in his hair. It brought back memories of playing hookey with Ann-Margret when they were shooting *Viva Las Vegas*— taking off for the mountains, swimming in a secluded lake, having dinner in a roadside barbecue where the locals left them alone in a corner booth. Happy times. At least until word leaked back to Memphis and Priscilla got all cranked up. What the heck, the Ann-Margret thing was over. Sort of.

So what the devil was he doing now tracking down this Shiva Ree woman? Just this New Year's he had resolved to simplify his life. Keep things cool and uncomplicated so he could do some serious thinking. Heaven knows, he had some important decisions to make. About Priscilla, about Ann-Margret, about these god-awful movies he kept cranking out. And about—well, *about what a man should do with his life*. Lately, the fact that success had come so easily to him was starting to feel like a burden. All that money and fame threw up a smokescreen around his soul. It was like his life was rolling along without him, without any connection to who he really was. Only at times like this, with nobody around to pay attention to him—nobody screaming out his name—did he feel that center of yearning buried inside him. Maybe Shiva was right, maybe he was a seeker. And maybe that is why he was seeking after her.

Elvis snapped on the radio. James Brown was hooting, "I'll Go Crazy." Talk about the soul—this one came straightaway from that buried place. A howl of bewilderment. Pure yearning. When was the last time Elvis pulled a song from that deep inside himself? He started to sing along with Brown, but he couldn't get the right feeling into it—he was just playacting at soulfulness—so he stopped.

A minute later, the AP three o'clock news came on. Over in Israel, the Palestinians had formed some kind of freedom group. And in Baltimore, a "passionate atheist" named Madalyn Murray was suing the government for exempting places of worship from taxation. "Why should I pay taxes," Murray demanded, "while religious leaders, as they call themselves, get off tax-free?" Maybe she had a point, but how in the name of God could anybody be *passionate* about atheism? Seems like you should save your passion for things you believed in, not for things you thought were foolish.

The lead item in the local news was the bail hearing for the deceased tourist's widower, Bruce Donaldsen. The judge had set the bail at a hundred thousand dollars because, he said, Donaldsen posed a serious threat to society. Apparently if Donaldsen could come up with that kind of money, he would be considered less of a threat to his fellow man and woman. But the accused murderer was a door-to-door vacuum cleaner salesman who had spent his entire savings on this once-in-a-lifetime trip to Vegas, so he was staying put in the county jail. One thing was certain: the trip to Vegas had been a once-in-a-lifetime deal for his wife.

The newscaster reported the whole Pickles connection, repeating the comedian's fat-lady routine word for word and then cutting to an exclusive interview with Donaldsen in his cell, where the alleged wife-killer ranted in his high-pitched voice about how Pickles had insulted his beloved to death. The man sounded absolutely certifiable. Finishing up his report, the newsman mentioned that crowds had been gathering around the Little Chapel of the West billboard where the victim had been impaled. And that Reverend Tyrone Sweetser, the Little Chapel's man of the cloth, had stated that he was going to tear the billboard down as soon as the authorities would permit him to.

Tyrone Sweetser. Elvis remembered meeting the good reverend when they shot the wedding scene at the Little Chapel for the wrap of *Viva Las Vegas*. Sweetser had wanted to play the role of the minister himself, but George Sidney, the director, had told Elvis that Sweetser was "way too creepy" for the job.

Elvis had been climbing the Spring Mountains for about fifteen minutes when he saw a hand-painted sign leaning against a Christmas cactus that read, WELCOME TO SHOSHONE TERRITORY. A couple of miles after that, a tin sign said, INDIAN SPRINGS, NEVADA, THE PLACE WHERE HEAVEN AND EARTH MEET. Elvis slowed down. That busybody electrician had said he couldn't miss Shiva's place. Sure enough, a mile later another sign appeared, this one in carved redwood, featuring a colossal, five-pointed star painted silver: ENTRANCE, THE CENTER OF THE LIGHT.

Elvis hung a right onto a dirt road, drove a half-mile, then came to a halt at an iron gate that blocked his way. Instantly, two large bearded men in white robes appeared on either side of his open car. The man on Elvis's side grasped the top of the car door and leaned down until his fuzzy face was just inches away from Elvis's.

"You're beautiful, man," he said.

Elvis stifled a giddy laugh. Seems everybody was telling him how beautiful he was today.

"He's talking about your soul, Elvis," the other man said, winking. He, too, had leaned his head down level with Elvis's.

"Well, thank you. Thank you very much," Elvis said. "I'm looking for—"

"Shiva," the man next to him murmured.

"That's right," Elvis said. "Is she, uh, expecting me?"

"Of course," the man said.

Elvis smiled nervously. He waited for the men to swing open the gate, but neither man moved. A cyclone fence topped with barbed wire stretched as far as the eye could see from each side of the gate. Maybe Elvis should just throw the car into reverse and get the heck out of here.

"I'll take you to her," the man who had admired the beauty of Elvis's soul said finally. He opened the door on Elvis's side. "Please leave your keys in the car," he said.

Elvis hesitated. "Can't do that. It's not my car."

Both men erupted into laughter, as if Elvis had gotten off a Pickles-worthy zinger. These guys sure were tuned to some weird frequency.

"The car doesn't belong to *anybody*, Elvis," the man at his side explained in a tone that most people reserve for explaining right and wrong to kindergartners.

"Nothing does," the other man elucidated. "Who are we to own the Earth's objects?"

"I see what you're saying," Elvis said, nodding understandingly. "But the thing is, it's a loaner."

The man next to Elvis shot out his hand and snagged the keys from the ignition. "Shiva is waiting for you," he said.

Elvis didn't budge. It wasn't the car he was worried about—he could always buy the Sahara a new one—but he sure didn't like being ordered around like this.

"It's holy ground, you see, Elvis," the man who'd grabbed the keys said soothingly. "No cars. Not even shoes."

Maybe nobody really owned anything, but these guys certainly were taking a proprietary interest in their barbed wire–encircled plot of land.

"Shiva will be real happy to see you," the other chimed.

Elvis took a deep breath and let it out slowly. Fact was, these guys were more peculiar than scary. And what the heck, he'd driven this far already. He removed his shoes and socks inside the car, then opened the door and stepped out onto the road. It was prickly with sharp pebbles and cactus spines. Elvis bounced from one foot to the other like a chicken on a hot plate.

"Follow me," the second man said. He twirled a combination lock on the gate, pulled it open, and waited for Elvis to pass through. His partner was already in the car, backing it down the dirt road, then disappearing with it into a stand of spruce. Elvis danced gingerly through the gate. Then the gate swung closed, the lock snapping loudly into place.

"It is one peaceful day on God's green earth, isn't it, Elvis?" his escort said.

Elvis said nothing, minding the flat rocks that formed a path through the cacti and scrub pine.

"I apologize for my friend," his escort went on. "He's a little uptight these days. We've had a few ugly run-ins lately. Folks trying to break in and do us harm. We've got some pretty hostile neighbors who don't like what we do in here."

"Who *do* you do in here?" Elvis asked.

The man stopped and turned around to look directly into Elvis's eyes. "*Love*," he explained.

Moments later, they emerged onto a sandy clearing, a large circle bordered by reddish-brown stone ledges. To Elvis's right were about ten army bivouac tents, a couple with smoke swirling out their front flaps. Straight ahead, about thirty yards away, were a good twenty men and women in Levi's and bib overalls and straw hats. Half were coming and going from the woods, hauling in wheelbarrows filled with fresh red clay soil, while the other half were spreading the soil on a raised plot bordered by rocks. Desert farming. Back-breaking work, but they seemed to be enjoying themselves, whistling and laughing while they shoveled and raked. To Elvis's left, fed by a mountain stream, was a glacier-scooped pond where a dozen men, women, and children, all naked, were splashing and washing each other's hair.

"I could use a little wash-up myself. How about you, Elvis?" the man said, grinning. He instantly shed his robe. He wasn't wearing undershorts.

Elvis gazed off uneasily toward the tepees. There seemed to be a lot of naked people in Nevada today.

"You go ahead," Elvis said. "I'm still getting my bearings."

"Whatever you like, Elvis," the man said. "No rules. I'll tell Shiva you're here." With that, the man skipped off toward the bathers, singing a wordless song, his member flopping in front of him like a tassel on a fez.

Elvis smiled. This had to be one of those hippie communes he'd read about in *Life* magazine. A place where folks came together to make a new life after dropping out of their regular lives. The *Life* article had made it sound like these commune types were soft in the head, people who were afraid to grow up and face responsibilities so they ran around smoking marijuana and babbling nonsense, like kids throwing a wild party in their basement while their parents were out of town. That could be, but the article hadn't mentioned anything about them being so natural and hardworking and full of life.

A couple emerged from one of the army surplus tents, the woman carrying a steaming bowl, and began walking slowly to-

ward Elvis. They were clothed, thankfully, in shorts and T-shirts—
it was going to take a while to get used to the casual nudity around
here. They smiled warmly as they approached.

"Wonderful to see you again, Elvis," the man said. He was
about Elvis's age, tall, slim, bearded, and he had blue-green eyes
that looked out from under his dark brows so intensely that it was
hard to look at anything else.

"We've met before?" Elvis said.

"Not formally," the man said. "But I saw you from the stage
last night. We appreciated your enthusiasm."

Now Elvis recognized him—he was Shiva's musical accompanist. "I truly liked it," Elvis said. "Your music too. Got to say,
I never heard anything like it before."

"Well, I'd never heard anything like 'Mystery Train' when I
first heard you sing it on the radio," the man replied. "And I've
got to tell you, it changed my life."

"You're kidding me."

"It's true, Elvis. I wasn't that far away from where you recorded it. Up at Vanderbilt University studying poetry. Fascinating
stuff, but it didn't touch me where I live. Not the way 'Mystery
Train' did. I couldn't keep my head buried in the books after that.
Dropped right out of college and started on my quest."

"What kind of quest?"

"The same one we all go on sooner or later," the young man
said earnestly. "You know, to find out what I was really meant to
do with my life. To find out where that mystery train is heading."

While the man spoke, the young woman watched him intently,
as if every word he said was a quote from the Bible.

" 'Mystery Train' is just a rockabilly blues song," Elvis said.
"I'm no poet."

"Oh, it's more than just a song and you know it," the man said,

40

looking seriously into Elvis's eyes. "It's an entire attitude. An attitude toward all of life."

Right or wrong about "Mystery Train," this fella sure didn't talk the way Elvis expected a hippie to. He sounded more like a college boy—a serious and confident college boy—which is apparently what he had been, at least until he started listening to rock and roll. Elvis often wondered whether educated people dug his music or if they thought it was beneath them. He had to admit that it was gratifying to hear one of them say that he appreciated his work, especially a song like "Mystery Train." That song had sung itself in the old Sun studio, erupted out of him like hot lava.

The woman spread a cloth on the sand, set down her bowl, then twirled down to a sitting position with the same fluid ease as Shiva. She was a large girl, big-boned and fleshy, and she had long stringy hair that framed a plain face that was scattered with acne scars. There was something about her narrow-set eyes that made Elvis think she'd been through some rough times in her life. The *Life* magazine article had mentioned that too—that some kids had escaped to these communes from awfully ugly home situations.

"I thought you might be hungry after your drive," the young woman said, gesturing to the bowl.

She was surely right about that. Neither of Elvis's breakfasts this day had worked out and he hadn't stopped for lunch. But the murky gray appearance of the bowl's contents didn't exactly quicken his appetite.

"Blue corn porridge. Indian grub," the fellow said, laughing. He, too, twirled down and sat cross-legged. "I'm afraid it's an acquired taste. But it gives your body exactly what it craves."

Elvis lowered himself onto his knees, then sat back on his heels. It wasn't very comfortable, but you had to be double-jointed to do that cross-legged thing. The young woman dipped a large wooden spoon into the bowl, blew on it, then held it out to Elvis's mouth.

"There's nothing—nothing in it, is there?" Elvis said.

"Just corn meal, water, and a little cactus-flower honey," the girl replied, still holding out the spoon.

"I mean, nothing that messes with your head," Elvis said.

"You mean like LSD or magic mushrooms?" the bearded man laughed.

"Well, yes, like that," Elvis said.

"Not a chance," the man said. "We don't have many rules out here, but that's one of them. No drugs of any kind. The truth is, we don't need them. I don't think we could get any higher if we took every drug there was."

Elvis could see that the girl's outstretched arm was tiring. He closed his eyes, took the spoon into his mouth, and slurped the muddy brew down.

"What do you think?" the young woman asked eagerly.

What Elvis thought is that it tasted like nothing so much as a mouthful of Mississippi swamp water. But the girl looked at him so expectantly with those hurt brown eyes that he said, "It tastes just like home, ma'am."

The girl immediately scooped up another big spoonful of the stuff and was offering it to Elvis when he saw Shiva striding toward him, the panther trotting obediently beside her on its leash. They were coming from the bathing pool, Shiva's long, blue-black hair wet and shining. She had apparently slipped into her clothes without drying herself off: her fine, firm breasts were virtually visible through her water-blotched T-shirt. By God, the woman was a wonder to behold—long and lithe and copper-colored, a luminous smile on her lips. Elvis's mouth fell open. The hippie girl inserted the spoon.

"Elvis!" Shiva cried. "I'm so happy you came!"

Elvis just about choked on a lump of corn meal. "Hi . . . Hi . . . there," he sputtered.

"Welcome to my family," Shiva said. "I see you've met Tzar and Manovah. And this is Abu." She patted the panther's head as he snuggled against her thighs.

"How d'ya do, Abu," Elvis nodded at the panther. Man, whenever he was around this woman, everything that came out of his mouth sounded like baby talk.

"I'm glad you're finally getting some breakfast," Shiva said, reeling down onto the cloth. "And that porridge has got to be a whole lot healthier than your old butter-fried corn biscuits."

"So, this is where you live," Elvis said. More fool-sounding words coming out of his mouth.

"It sure is," Shiva replied. "A little bit of heaven on earth, don't you think?"

Elvis's eyes kept drifting down to the front of Shiva's T-shirt, so he made himself look beyond her toward the garden. A couple of the wheelbarrow pushers were doing a little dosado as they passed by one another and some of the rakers just dropped their tools and started clapping in square-dance rhythm. "Well, everybody seems to be having a right good time," Elvis said.

"That's the whole idea, Elvis," Tzar said. "To celebrate life. Enjoy every minute of the here and now. Accept the whole world as your family. Pretty simple concept when you get down to it. But it's amazing how many people miss it. Get distracted by silly things like money and fame. Their vanity blinds them."

Elvis suddenly dropped his gaze to the ground between them. Tzar's words had caught him in the gut like a sucker punch. For a long moment, Elvis had to tighten every muscle in his body to keep from lashing back at the young man. But while he held himself in, Elvis found himself wondering just why those words had stung so much.

"I never could understand why you can't have it all, Tzar," Shiva said with a little laugh. "Fame, money, *and* a pure love of life too. Seems like those could all go together if you had your heart in the right place and your head screwed on straight."

Man, Elvis couldn't have said it better himself! Fact is, he hadn't even thought it yet before she said it. But Shiva was surely right—you *could* be rich and famous as long as you didn't let that distract you from the more important things in life. Maybe it wasn't easy, but it was possible. From the corner of his eye, Elvis saw Manovah pucker her brow, like she thought Shiva had spoken out of turn or something. But Tzar was laughing and clapping his hands together.

"You said a mouthful, woman!" Tzar said, winking at Shiva with those high-beam eyes of his. He smiled at Elvis. "I sure am glad we have some smart people around here to keep me honest," he said.

"So, why don't I show you my little home, Elvis?" Shiva said, rising. Holding Abu's leash with one hand, Shiva held out her other hand to help Elvis to his feet. Once Elvis was up she didn't let go.

As they started for the furthest stone ledge, Elvis took a deep breath. By God, it *was* a joy to be alive today. To be strolling in this hidden hollow holding hands with this divine-looking woman who could speak his mind better than he could himself. Truth to tell, Elvis couldn't remember the last time he felt so light and happy and full of love for life.

Just beyond the last tent, Shiva stepped into the pine woods, the panther straining at its leash ahead of her. Elvis followed. A few feet into the thicket stood an ornate cage on wheels, the kind you sometimes saw in traveling circuses. Abu's private room and the animal seemed happy to be back there. Shiva locked the cage door with a key, hung the leash around the lock, then took Elvis's hand again and led him back into the clearing.

"I prayed for you to come out here," Shiva said, finally.

"Coulda just asked me," Elvis said, smiling. "You didn't need a middleman."

Shiva burst out with the most musical laugh Elvis had ever heard, like the chime of those toe-bells when she danced. Yes, indeed, *a celebration of life!* Without really thinking about it, Elvis executed a little buck-and-wing in his bare feet. Still laughing, Shiva matched it step for step, then added in some frisky business with her hips. Elvis matched that too, whirling his hips, laughing like he was sixteen years old and had just discovered that he was his own man. Now they were both improvising a crazy, joyous, ecstatic dance on the sand under the Nevada sun. Elvis felt like he was going to explode with gladness.

The moment Shiva led Elvis into her tent, they clutched each other and kissed. And oh my God, what a kiss it was—succulent, rapturous, and yet somehow so very young and innocent. Elvis started to unbutton his shirt.

"Hi, Mommy!"

Elvis froze. A little girl appeared just inside the tent's entrance. She had dark bright eyes and shimmering black hair just like Shiva's. She couldn't have been more than five years old. Shiva was a mother? That made kissing her feel kind of strange.

"Hi, Kali," Shiva said. "I want you to meet my friend, Elvis."

"Elvis?" the child said. "That's a funny name."

"It surely is," Elvis said. "And not just in this place either, Kali." He quickly rebuttoned his shirt, although he wasn't exactly sure why.

"Kali doesn't know who you are, Elvis," Shiva said. "We don't listen to radio or TV out here."

"I can understand why," Elvis said. "It just clutters up your mind with nonsense anyhow."

"Exactly!" Shiva said. She planted a kiss on his cheek. Relatively speaking, it was a pretty chaste kiss, but that didn't stop Elvis from feeling her young breasts pressing against him through her damp T-shirt. God help him, it was one trying situation for both body *and* spirit, whether or not she was a mother.

"I'm afraid I have to give the children their lessons now," Shiva said. "Looks like our timing is off again, but no matter. We have all the time in the world." She laughed that musical laugh again. "I mean, we have our whole lives, don't we, Elvis?"

Our whole lives? Elvis had already been feeling light-headed, but now he felt downright dizzy. Things sure were moving quickly for a place where they'd forsaken life in the fast lane. But maybe living naturally meant that you didn't waste time chewing your feelings over and over again. You just followed your heart.

"How about if I meet you backstage after tonight's show?" Shiva went on. She stooped down and picked a small book off of a cushion. "Here. I think you might like this."

The book was titled *The Autobiography of a Yogi*, and it looked as if it had been thumbed through hundreds of times.

Now Shiva lifted Kali into her arms and stood in front of Elvis, smiling deliciously. Lord, they were a sight to see, like one of those South Sea paintings that Frenchman did. How could he *not* follow his heart?

Shiva walked Elvis to the path that led back to the road. Still holding the child, she quickly kissed him on the lips.

"Elvis," she said, "you make me happy I was born."

7

Don't Be Cruel

By the time he hit North Las Vegas, the churning in Elvis's body and soul had simplified itself into pure acute hunger. After all the jumbled thoughts that had been bouncing in his brain since leaving the commune, it was a relief to have something clear and definite to focus on, especially an animal need that could be satisfied without personal complications. So when he saw a sign for GUIDO'S DRIVE-IN DOUBLE-BURGERS at an intersection, he took a left onto Route 15 and headed straight for it.

A perky blond teenager decked out in a cheerleader outfit rollerskated to the car to take his order. She, apparently, *had* been exposed to the corrupting influences of radio and television, and recognized Elvis instantly, but she managed to keep her composure. She insisted on paying for Elvis's two double-burgers with chili sauce out of her own purse; in return, all she requested was that he give her his autograph. She handed Elvis her ballpoint pen.

"Put it on my skin, Elvis," she cooed.

For a dizzying moment, Elvis thought the girl was going to pirouette on her skates and expose her pert bum for his signature.

In that same moment, he considered immediately leaving Las Vegas and driving straight back to Memphis, not stopping anywhere unless he happened across a monastery that took in guests. But the girl simply extended her open palm. Relieved, Elvis signed it and threw the car into reverse.

"I'll never wash it again!" the girl called as Elvis sped back onto the highway.

Elvis gobbled down the burgers in three bites each. They were definitely an improvement on swamp stew. Maybe next time he paid a visit to the Center of the Light, he'd stock up on Guido's double-burgers on the way up. Except next time, for sanitary reasons, he'd pass on doing business with the teenager who'd sworn off washing her hands.

Half a mile ahead of him, Elvis saw a few cars parked willy-nilly on the sandy shoulder of the highway. He slowed down. On the right stood a colorful billboard picturing the Little Chapel of the West. The way the chapel was rendered, it looked like a prairie church, while in actuality it was crowded between the glossy structures of the Hacienda Hotel. In big red letters, the sign declared, FASTEST WEDDINGS ON THE STRIP! Elvis had to smile at that: only in Las Vegas would a marriage ceremony be clocked like a horse race.

On the billboard, a happy couple was puckering up for a post-vows kiss in front of the chapel. Elvis squinted. By Golly, that happy couple was none other than Ann-Margret and himself! No doubt, the Colonel had presented the chapel with a still from *Viva Las Vegas* and his blessing to use it in their ads—anything to build up box office interest for the film's upcoming release. Of course, Parker hadn't asked Elvis's permission to use the photo that way; he'd probably say he couldn't bother Elvis with trivialities like that. But at this moment, seeing Ann-Margret and himself kissing up there, Elvis felt guilty for more reasons than he cared to count.

A stepladder stood in front of the billboard. Balanced on the top rung was a stoop-shouldered man in a black frock coat with frizzy hair jutting out from under a panama hat, and horn-rimmed glasses on his long, sallow face. Reverend Sweetser. He held an axe in his hand. Elvis parked behind a pickup truck and got out, but he kept his distance, hoping that nobody would notice him.

A half-dozen men and women stood in a semicircle around Sweetser, chanting something Elvis couldn't quite hear. He took a few steps closer, remaining in the shadow of the pickup truck. The onlookers were chanting, "Judas! Judas! Judas!" And in between ferocious swings at the billboard with his axe, the good Reverend Sweetser was shouting back, "Go screw yourself!"

Elvis couldn't help smiling at Sweetser's comeback. It was pretty much what these people deserved, but only in this town would you hear a preacher saying it straight out like that. This crowd had to be the same church folk who had fired tomatoes at Howie Pickles last night. Man, they were one busy bunch. And they seemed to have enough fire and brimstone to go around for just about everybody. What the heck had Sweetser done to incur their holy wrath?

Suddenly, one of the churchmen grabbed the side of the stepladder and began shaking it. Sweetser tottered on top, terrified, his axe swinging wildly as he tried to keep his balance. Elvis sprinted toward him. The church folk separated, gawking at Elvis with their mouths open.

"Come on, friends, don't be cruel," Elvis said.

"It's a shrine, Elvis! A holy shrine! And he's destroying it!" said the churchman who had been rocking the stepladder.

"What are you talking about?" Elvis said.

"Look!" The churchman took a step toward the billboard. With an outstretched finger, he traced the nail holes where Bonnie Donaldsen's big body had been hammered to the sign. It formed a perfect cross.

"Listen, friends, a poor woman has lost her life." Elvis's voice was low and clear and soothing. Sunlight reflecting off the billboard's blue-tinted lamps fringed Elvis's head like an azure halo. He had that feeling he used to get while singing to a spellbound audience, the feeling that he was reaching deep inside each and every one them. "It doesn't seem like the right time to be pointing fingers. Or throwing tomatoes for that matter. It's like Jesus said, 'Let he who is without sin cast the first . . .' well, you know."

The whole group stared at Elvis with rapt expressions on their faces. "Look! The blue light!" one of the men suddenly cried. "It's the sign!" one of the women echoed after him. Then another woman said, "Praise be!" and a whole chorus of "amens" followed. Just one moment later, the entire group began to retreat to their cars, some sort of bowing. Elvis peered after them in bewilderment.

"Screw 'em!" Pastor Sweetser snarled. He again raised his axe and took a mighty swing. It sliced right through Elvis's lip-puckered face on the billboard.

"Why *are* you destroying it, Reverend?" Elvis called up to him.

"Why do you think, Presley?" Sweetser snapped back, then slammed his axe through the steeple of the Little Chapel's image. Elvis had to admit that George Sidney had made the right decision when he'd passed on Sweetser for the role of the minister in *Viva Las Vegas*. It was a wonder any betrothed couple would choose this creep for that role in real life.

"Bad for business—is that it, Reverend?" Elvis said. Heaven knows, a crucified fat lady on your billboard probably wasn't good publicity.

"You got it," Sweetser said. "And that's just what they want."

"Who wants?"

"The Good Samaritan Chapel," Sweetser said.

The Good Samaritan Chapel was new on the Strip since Elvis

had last been in Vegas. It was a futuristic structure with a steeple resembling a rocket ship. Elvis had noticed a long line of couples outside it when he'd rode into town the night before.

"What are you getting at, Sweetser?"

"Oh, come on, Presley. Don't be naive. We're their main competition. They'd do anything to get our business. Including this little stunt."

"This wasn't a stunt, Reverend," Elvis said. "It was murder."

"It wouldn't be the first time somebody broke the Sixth Commandment to get ahead in business."

Man, there sure were a lot of conspiracy theories about Bonnie Donaldsen's murder floating around Las Vegas, almost as many as were floating around Washington D.C. about JFK's assassination. And most of the Donaldsen murder theories were pinned to cutthroat business practices. Of course, in Las Vegas business operated at a whole different level of intensity from anywhere else in the country. Competition-wise, Las Vegas made Hollywood look like, well, a hippie commune.

"I can't believe anybody who calls himself a good Samaritan could do something like that," Elvis said.

"Well, who the hell do you think did do it, Presley? The lady's husband? That skinny bastard couldn't have hoisted her up here if he'd wanted to."

Sweetser had a point. And he punctuated it with an axe swat through Ann-Margret's happy face. Elvis turned and started back to his car.

"Hey, Presley!" Sweetser called.

"What?"

"You should've given me that part in your movie."

"No, Reverend," Elvis said, shaking his head. "It woulda been bad for business."

8

Flop Sweat

$\mathcal{S}$o little Johnny comes home after his very first day of school and his mother asks, 'Well, what did you learn today?' And Johnny replies, 'Not enough. They want me to come back tomorrow.' "

Not a single laugh. Not even a titter. Howie Pickles paced to the other side of the Sahara nightclub stage, a Bozo smile frozen on his face. The good news was that the club was more than half full in spite of all the hex publicity. The bad news was that Pickles was dying up there.

"So on Sunday, little Johnny goes to Sunday school, and the teacher asks him who the first man in the Bible was. 'Hoss,' says Johnny. 'Wrong,' says the teacher. 'It was Adam.' 'Shucks!' says Johnny. 'I knew it was one of them Cartwrights.' "

More silence, only broken by a few coughs and some fidgety feet. Flop sweat poured off of Pickles's forehead. Elvis felt for the guy. He couldn't help thinking about his own Las Vegas flop at the New Frontier Hotel less than eight years ago. For two whole weeks, he had fizzled like a faulty firecracker in front of one audience after another of middle-aged middle-Americans who'd much rather been seeing Liberace.

"So Johnny's little sister, Lulu, goes up to a policeman who's directing traffic at a busy intersection and she says, 'My mommy said that if I ever needed help, I should ask a policeman.' And the cop says, 'That's right, little girl.' And Lulu says, 'Well, would you tie my shoelace then?' "

Not a sound. Pickles looked beseechingly at Elvis. Elvis forced out a little croak of appreciation that sounded less like a laugh than a belch.

"Hey, Pickles!" someone called out from a back table. "My mother-in-law's funnier than you!"

The audience tittered nervously. Pickles stared down at his shoe tips.

"What's a'matter, Pickles?" the heckler went on. "Cat got your tongue? Or have you gone all squishy from reading about your deadly powers in the newspapers?"

This line elicited a bigger laugh than Pickles had gotten all night. Elvis was close enough to see the comedian's knuckles turn white from clenching his fists. Pickles raised his head and glared out at the heckler. That's when Elvis saw Lucky de Luca in the stage wing no more than ten feet away from Pickles. Lucky raised his forefinger in a stern warning and said, "Don't bite, Howie," loud enough for the people at the front tables to hear. Pickles turned to de Luca, then stared back at the audience.

"So," Pickles went on in a near monotone. "Did you hear the one about the weatherman who got fired for always getting his predictions wrong? He moved clear across the country and applied for a job with another TV station. On the application it asked why he'd left his previous place of employment and he wrote, 'The weather didn't agree with me.' "

A beat of silence. Then, from the heckler: "Hey, Pickles, if I really wanted to hear from an asshole, I'd fart!"

Pickles was visibly trembling now. Spittle appeared in the corners of his rubbery lips—he was literally frothing at the mouth.

"Franco!" Pickles suddenly called up to the light booth. "Give this guy a spot, wouldja? He deserves it."

"Don't!" de Luca warned again from the wings.

Apparently the lighting guy didn't hear de Luca because a spotlight swiveled to the back of the nightclub and found the heckler. He was a big man with a round florid face and Brylcreemed sandy hair. He wore a plaid sports jacket and chartreuse golf slacks. As the spot picked him out, he stood and raised both arms in the air like a winning prizefighter.

"So there you are, sweetheart," Pickles crooned. "Finally getting the attention you crave, eh, buddy? I bet when you go to a funeral, you're even jealous of the corpse!"

The audience giggled tentatively. The heckler began sputtering back, "Listen, Pickles, I—"

"Shut up!" Pickles shouted. "I'm trying to see things from your point of view, but I can't get my head that far up my ass."

The audience erupted in laughter, some of them breaking into applause. Elvis saw Lucky de Luca take a step out from the wings onto the stage. Pickles ignored him.

"Buddy, I've come across decomposing bodies that are less offensive than you are! You're a regular poster child for birth control! You've got the IQ of lint!"

Raucous laughter. Pickles was grinning like a cat, his small eyes dancing in his head. De Luca came up behind him and firmly clasped his right shoulder. Pickles shrugged off his hand.

"I'm doing a public service here, Mr. de Luca," Pickles wailed. "There's some village out there that's lost its idiot!"

The audience roared. Some spontaneously rose to their feet and began cheering. Pickles screeched over the din: "This guy's so stupid, he—"

But de Luca had enlisted the help of a few stagehands, including the flinty-eyed electrician, and they were dragging Pickles offstage before he could continue.

A thunderous chorus of boos. And then Tzar stumbled on stage carrying his Oriental guitar, followed immediately by Shiva and her panther. The audience was still booing, but Elvis half rose from his seat and held out his palms for them to quiet down. Shiva smiled bewitchingly at Elvis. Tzar began to play, Shiva began to dance. Elvis gazed at her like a bear gawking at a full moon.

The audience quieted a bit, although some still tittered and whispered among themselves. Elvis was thinking of shushing them again when he saw a large man with slicked-back black hair lean over the heckler's table, apparently whispering something to him. The heckler looked flustered. He shrugged, but the man kept on yakking in his ear. The heckler pushed him away, but the big man responded by grabbing the heckler by the back of his neck. The heckler looked terrified. Finally, he got to his feet and, with the black-haired man still clamping his neck, headed for the nightclub's exit.

By God, maybe de Luca's theory wasn't so crazy after all! Pickles's latest insult target was in jeopardy, all right. Elvis stood and started after them. From the corner of his eye, Elvis saw Shiva momentarily pause in her dance to look questioningly at him. Elvis kept moving.

Emerging into the casino, Elvis spotted the heckler's green pants as he disappeared down an aisle of one-armed bandits. His muscular escort was just behind him, one hand still clutching him tightly by the neck. Elvis broke into a trot after them.

"Oh my God! It's Elvis!" A trio of middle-aged women in tight, short-sleeved nylon sweaters fanned out from the slot machines, blocking Elvis's way.

"I heard you were here!" one of them cried.

"Please, ma'am—"

Another of the women thrust a pen and a piece of paper out at Elvis. "Nobody will believe this back home!"

Elvis charged right through them, spinning one of the ladies into a slot machine which immediately began to honk its "tilt" alarm.

"Mr. Big Shot!" the woman screamed after him, probably brazen words where she came from.

Elvis raced down the aisle just in time to see the heckler being hustled out the casino's front door by the muscular man joined by another swarthy man. Elvis pushed through the door. The men were shoving the heckler into the back of a black sedan.

"Stop!" Elvis shouted.

One of the men glanced back at Elvis. "Why, it's Elvis the Pelvis!" he laughed, then jumped into the car beside the heckler. The sedan burned rubber lurching away from the curb and onto the Strip. Elvis waved urgently at a cab that was idling under the casino's awning.

"What's happening, baby?" Digby Ferguson. The would-be writer had appeared from out of nowhere behind the wheel of an open-topped, bloodred Olds convertible just a few yards to Elvis's right. Elvis dashed to the car, vaulted over the door like a stuntman, landing beside Ferguson with a squish.

"Go!" Elvis snapped, pointing over the windscreen. "That car! There! Follow it!"

Ferguson chortled. "Are we the cowboys or the Indians?"

Elvis socked him in the biceps. "Go! *Now!*"

Ferguson took off with a screech. "Hiho Silver!" he cheered.

"They grabbed the heckler!" Elvis shouted to Ferguson as they sped after the sedan.

"What?"

"Pickles's target tonight," Elvis hollered over the engine. "Like the fat lady last night. Two guys grabbed him. Kidnapped him. They're in that car!"

"Whoopee!" Ferguson yodeled, yanking the wheel sharply to the right as the black sedan careened onto Encarta Drive. No matter what this guy was on—Red devils? Scotch? LSD?—he drove this baby with the finesse of Graham Hill. The sedan veered right again on North Ninth Street with Elvis and Ferguson less than a block and a half behind. But at the intersection with Wilson Avenue, they lost it. Ferguson let the car idle in the middle of the street, cars whipping by them on either side, drivers cursing at them through their open windows.

"Get stuffed!" Ferguson screamed back at them, grinning.

Elvis stood on the floorboard, peering up and down Wilson Avenue. "There!" he shouted, pointing to the right. Ferguson lurched the car around the corner, toppling Elvis back into his seat.

The black sedan was parked in front of a pink stucco ranch house. Ferguson pulled up behind it and parked. Elvis jumped out, dashed to the sedan: it was empty and locked. From out of the open windows of the pink house came a shriek of high-pitched laughter. Elvis gestured to the front door, put a finger to his lips, and signaled Ferguson to follow him, which he did in an exaggerated tiptoe, like the Jolly Green Giant sneaking up on a hidden pea patch.

At the front stoop, Elvis hesitated. These men were undoubtedly armed and he was not. What's more, Ferguson was useless in this situation. Less than useless, actually—he'd probably dance the Watusi to the tune of gunfire. Best to call the police.

Another shriek from the open window, followed by a deep groan. No time for phone calls. Elvis shot his hand to the doorknob. The door was unlocked. He flung it open and jumped inside, both hands raised in karate attack position.

"Beautiful!" a woman cried.

"My hero!" another woman laughed.

"Come to Mamma, Elvis," cooed a third.

Elvis was immediately surrounded by a half-dozen women in see-through negligees, bikini panties, half-bras, and fishnet stockings attached to lacy garter belts. They ranged in age from late teens to late thirties; two were colored, one Chinese, the other three bleached blondes.

"This is a raid!" Ferguson whooped behind Elvis. "Line up, ladies—we're doing a strip search!"

The ladies giggled. Two of them—the Chinese teenager and the bustiest of the blondes—draped themselves over Elvis's shoulders. The blonde whispered, "Wanna do a double with Cindy and me? It's heaven, Elvis."

Elvis shook himself loose. "Where's the guy in the green pants?"

"He's not wearing them now," the busty blonde tittered.

"Where is he?" Elvis barked.

The women backed away from him, intimidated. Finally, one of the colored girls pointed up the stairs. "Third . . . third door on the left," she stammered.

Elvis ran to the stairs.

"Ding! Ding! Ding!" Ferguson yelped after him. "False alarm!"

Elvis bounded up to the second floor, dashed down the hallway, skidded to a halt in front of the third door on the left. He did not knock before entering.

"Jesus!" This from the heckler, naked, lying on his back on a water bed.

"Elvis!" crooned a scrawny brunette, also naked, riding on top of the heckler.

Reflexively, Elvis cupped a hand over his eyes. It was not a pretty sight.

"You're—you're all right?" Elvis mumbled.

"I *was*, asshole!" the heckler shouted back.

"Hey, you can't talk that way to Elvis," the brunette said, not missing a beat of her ministrations.

"But those men—the kidnappers!" Through his fingers, Elvis saw the heckler push the young woman off him and sit up against the headboard.

"They're my buddies, for crissake!" the heckler yelled. "It's my birthday and this was supposed to be my present, you idiot!"

"But it looked like they—" Elvis cut himself off.

"One of them's with Helene now and the other's with Peonie," the brunette explained dutifully.

"What the hell's happened to this town?" the heckler snapped. "People used to mind their own business."

"I'm sorry," Elvis mumbled. He started out the door, then stopped and, without turning, said, "Anyway, happy birthday."

9

Ain't Nothin' but a Dead Man

here were you, Elvis? I waited as long as I could. When will I see you again? Forever, Shiva."

Elvis yanked the note off the door and slunk into his Sahara suite. This had to be the perfect ending to a perfectly ridiculous night. The idiot flies off on a wild goose chase and returns to find that he's lost his dream girl. How's that for a plot turn, Colonel? Why not go the whole route and make yours truly into a *total* buffoon in the next picture?

It sure as heck had amused Digby Ferguson. He'd cackled like a hen for the entire ride back to the hotel. "It sounds just like a joke, eh? Elvis Presley walks into a whorehouse and asks if they've seen anybody wearing green pants. A surreal gag. Pure Dada. You ought to give it to Pickles. God knows, he needs new material."

It was a joke, all right. The same old one—Elvis decides to ride into town on a white horse and save the day. *The singing sleuth*. Damnation! He'd been watching too many foolish movies lately, including his own.

Man, if he'd just minded his own business, he'd be sitting here right now with the most enchanting woman he'd ever laid eyes on. Probably more than just sitting. Maybe it wasn't too late. Elvis paced toward the phone, then abruptly stopped. He hadn't seen any telephone lines at the Center of the Light. Of course not. It was an oasis from all the intrusions of the modern world. Nobody's going to stop communing with nature to answer the telephone.

Sitting on the telephone table was the book Shiva had lent him, *The Autobiography of a Yogi*, by one Parmahansa Yogananda. Another one of those vowel-heavy names like the folks at the Center had. Elvis picked the book up, sat down on the sofa, and began to look through it.

It was just like the title said, the autobiography of an Indian man who'd spent his whole life trying to figure out what life was all about. Like what sense did life make if you're only going to die anyhow? And when you're feeling lost, how do you get the spirit of God inside you? And above all, *what should a man do with his life?*

Elvis had never read anything like it in his life. The book was written in simple words and sentences, almost like a child had composed it. But this yogi man was asking questions and saying things about life and God that Elvis thought nobody but he had ever wondered about. Or *dared* to wonder about. These weren't questions he could have asked in Sunday school in Tupelo without getting his knuckles rapped, but that hadn't kept him from pondering about them even as a boy. Like why had he lived while his twin brother, Jesse Garon, had died at birth? Was it just some fluke? Or did it mean something, like that he had to do something special with his life to make up for Jesse's not having one?

A tranquil feeling began to settle over Elvis as he read on. The path to God's spirit, or God Consciousness, as Yogananda called it, was through perfect stillness. Just sitting quietly and emptying your mind of all the stuff that clutters it up all the time. That didn't just mean turning off TV and radio, it meant turning off the world. And then this life force—*"prana,"* he called it—would zap into you like a charge from a cosmic battery. Fill you right up with energy and hope and love. That part sure sounded weird. It made him think about those colored ladies in that gospel church he'd gone to in Memphis—they got zapped, all right, and then started shimmying and shaking and jabbering in tongues until they fell back unconscious into their pastor's arms.

Still, there was no denying that serene feeling he had right now. Fact is, he hadn't felt so peaceful in a long, long time. It was a combination of feeling all alone, yet feeling connected to everything at the same time. Elvis set the book onto the table, then reached up to turn off the reading lamp, but at that moment the light—in fact, all the lights in his room—blinked out. *Like magic. Like a cosmic sign.* Elvis leaned back in the sofa, closing his eyes.

The first thing he saw in his mind's eye was Howie Pickles being hustled offstage by de Luca and the stagehands. Then the heckler lying back in the bed with the brunette doing him. *Man, talk about mind clutter!* Elvis tried to push these images away, but they just did a U-turn and marched back into his mind. The yogi had written that you shouldn't shove away thoughts, just gradually let them go.

Now Elvis saw the teenager on roller skates sailing toward him carrying two double-burgers with chili sauce. That one was pretty easy to let go of, but it was immediately replaced by an image of a steaming bowl of blue corn porridge which, for some unknown reason, was harder to let go of. Next he saw Shiva—glorious Shiva—dancing with him on the desert sand. This was not an image he wanted to part with, at least not right away, yet as Shiva whirled before his mind's eye, he started to see pure motion, like a swirling white tornado, now turning opaque, now lifting into the sky. By golly, there *was* no way you could tell the dancer from the dance.

Now nothing. Nothing at all. Stillness. Perfect stillness. A warm glow pulsing up his spine, then bursting with white light in his brain and emanating out of the top of his skull. He was hardly breathing at all. He did not need to—the universe was breathing for him. Peace. Perfect peacefulness. And now the energy came— the *prana*—a subtle stream of strength that was life itself. Elvis felt his body drinking it in.

"Presley! You in there?"

Elvis remained still, kept his eyes closed. He tried to gently push the voice away.

"Hey, pal! It's magic time!" It was Digby Ferguson.

Go away! Please, please, go away!

"Open up, buddy boy! You were right on the money! The heckler is all heckled out! He ain't nothing but a dead man!"

10

Droopy Little Thing

 *T*he stillness vanished as swiftly as it had come. The lights were on again. Elvis rubbed his eyes, stood, walked to the door, and opened it.

"They're getting more creative." Ferguson was babbling at full throttle as he stumbled through the door. "The heckler was found on top of that new chapel, the Good Samaritan's. Pierced through his guts by that rocket steeple of theirs. Looked like a puke-green distress flag."

Elvis squinted at Ferguson. Maybe that stillness was gone, but he couldn't quite take in the real world yet.

"Hey, you're stoned, aren't you, Presley?" Ferguson grinned. "Terrific. Now we can communicate on the same wavelength."

"No drugs," Elvis mumbled. "Don't need 'em."

"Whatever you say, Big Guy," Ferguson said. "Anyway, the victim's name is J. P. Whaley. *Was*, that is. A cop from Atlanta, here with his wife for his birthday celebration."

"His wife?"

"That's the cute part, isn't it, Presley? He's off to the whorehouse while the little woman stays behind to watch the floorshow. In Vegas, there's entertainment for everybody, right?"

Elvis closed his eyes again, sucked in his breath. That *prana* energy was still pulsing up and down his spine. It tingled.

"You saw him?" Elvis said. "On the steeple?"

"Yup." Ferguson stuck a hand inside his shirt and scratched his armpit vigorously.

"You're always the man on the scene, aren't you, Digby?" Elvis said. His mind was crisp and clear, as if it were still illuminated by that white light.

"That's me, all right," Ferguson replied blithely. "I'm driving up and down the Strip, saying the Lord's Prayer, when I see this crowd gathered in front of the Samaritan Chapel. A small crowd— it's four in the morning, trickle hour in the wedding biz. Of course, there's always those folks who only get up the nerve to get hitched after a long night of drinking."

"So you just happened to be driving by when you saw him up there," Elvis interrupted.

"Makes a man wonder, doesn't it? Maybe they planned it that way so they'd get the best writer in the business to cover it." Ferguson beamed at Elvis. "Anyway, when I saw those chartreuse pants flapping up there, I called Sheriff Turtleff right away. But by the time he arrived, the Good Samaritans had unsteepled the body and brought it down. Disturbing the crime scene, as Turtleff put it. The man talks like a police academy textbook. No matter, I'd already documented the scene with my trusty Polaroid."

"How could you get a body all the way up there without anybody seeing?" Elvis said. "Maybe it's the middle of the night, but there's people all over the Strip. People and bright lights."

"Must've done it during the blackout," Ferguson said.

"Blackout?"

"Did you sleep through that one, pal?" Ferguson said. "The

whole city went dark for about fifteen minutes. Transformer problems, Turtleff said. Well, it certainly transformed the Strip. For fifteen minutes, it was the sleepy little prairie town I grew up in. Peaceful and quiet. Except, of course, if you were lugging a dead man up to a steeple top."

"Doesn't sound like a coincidence, does it? The cover of darkness just when they needed it?"

"Not to the well-trained legal mind," Ferguson giggled. "Of course, Turtleff has his own theory. He thinks the culprits are those Jesus freaks who have been hounding Pickles for his blasphemy. Using the steeple to make a point, as it were."

"So the sheriff's letting Bruce Donaldsen go?"

"Of course not," Ferguson said. "Turtleff's of the jail-'em-all-first, ask-questions-later school of law enforcement. Takes them one case at a time. Can't be bothered with theoretical consistency. Anyway, the constabulary around here only does what its bosses tell them to do."

"What bosses?"

"The *Mafia*, Presley," Ferguson said. "I don't think you've been listening. Maybe you should be taking notes."

"Sounds like a lot of folks are jumping to conclusions," Elvis said. "That'd be you too."

"All I'm doing is jumping on this story, Elvis," Ferguson said. "And I do believe I've jumped on the story of a lifetime—the one that's going to make my career."

"It's not a *story*, Digby!" Elvis snapped, suddenly furious without really knowing why. "It's two real folks dead for no good reason. And one man in jail just for being dim and goofy."

"Well, well, aren't we touchy?" Ferguson sat down heavily on the sofa and propped his legs up on the coffee table. "I thought you were too busy unwinding from the stress of stardom to worry about the mortality of common folk. That and chasing moonbeams up at the Center of the Light."

Elvis felt like punching Ferguson right in his fat, simpering face. Everything was a joke to this guy, an *insult* joke. But unlike Howie Pickles's zingers that were aimed at people's little foibles— their fatness, their pompousness—Ferguson's were aimed at absolutely *everything* that was human. People weren't just funny to him, they were utterly absurd through and through, good for nothing except a gonzo story that would finally get him in print. A flabby tourist's death, her husband's unfair imprisonment, a philandering cop's birthday murder, a sheriff who takes his orders from Mafia bosses—all big gags, all fodder for his irony mill.

But Elvis did not punch Digby Ferguson. No, he sat down across from him in a Sahara safari chair and bit down on his lower lip. What exactly was he, himself, doing about all this rampant injustice and sloppy police work? Nothing except dipping his little toe in it, shaking his head in dismay, and then backing away for fear of making a fool of himself. Was that any different from laughing at it? Or from turning it into a juicy story?

And if Elvis really wanted to be honest with himself, what *was* his excuse for not getting more involved? For not taking it upon himself to do the right thing when it looked like nobody else around here was going to do it? The truth was, he had convinced himself that he had far more important things on his mind. And just what would those important things be? Which godforsaken motion picture he should make next? What woman he should make love to?

Yes, Elvis's mind was crisp and clear, all right. And resolute too. Maybe it was that *prana* stuff, but whatever it was, he was certain of one thing: Digby Ferguson may be a drug-addled madman, but right now he was the one person Elvis knew in this town who could help him do what had to be done.

But first things first. "How'd you know I went up to the Center of the Light?"

"A little bird told me," Ferguson said. "A very tall, redheaded bird who takes rejection badly, especially when she's in full display mode, all feathers and tits."

"You get around, don't you?"

"It's my business," Ferguson said proudly.

"And where do I figure in your business, Digby?"

"Hey, you're the celebrity hook for my big story!" Ferguson said. "All I have to do is put Elvis Presley in the first chapter and, presto change-o, a local murder becomes a national epic."

Well, at least the man was honest; that was more than Elvis could say about most of his friends these days. "Where do we start, Digby?"

"The place where all good things start," Ferguson said, struggling to pull his corpulent body up from the sofa. "At the whorehouse."

In Ferguson's car, Elvis tallied up the hit parade of murder theories: Lucky de Luca's supposition that the Sands management was murdering Pickles's insult victims so they could put a deadly curse on the Sahara and thus drum up business for their own failing floorshow and casino business; Reverend Sweetser's notion that the Good Samaritan Chapel was pulling the same number to drum up more wedding business; and if that was so, then maybe the Atlanta cop's steeple-top spearing was payback by Sweetser himself; Turtleff's theories that Bonnie Donaldsen was done in by her psycho hubby or that both murders were perpetrated by the holy roller contingent in town, depending on what mood you caught the sheriff in; and finally, Ferguson's own, all-inclusive Mafia theory. Ferguson laughed when Elvis finished his litany.

"They *all* sound true to me," Ferguson said, gunning down the

Strip. "It's like that story about the rabbi holding court. Shmuel tells the rabbi that his neighbor, Moishe, is ruining his crops by running his sheep across his land. He says Moishe should be stopped and the rabbi says, 'You're right.' Then Moishe says that he *has* to run his sheep across Shmuel's land because it blocks the path to the watering hole. And the rabbi says, 'You're right.' So somebody in the back of the synagogue says, 'They *both* can't be right, Rabbi.' And the rabbi says, *'You're right!'* "

Elvis smiled. "You Jewish, Digby?"

"Right, my real name's *Dubbie Fergessen*," Ferguson replied, grinning.

"Me, too, way back somewhere on my mother's side," Elvis said. He'd only heard a few years ago that he had a Jewish great-grandmother.

"I'm just kidding, Presley," Ferguson said. "I'm Episcopalian to the core, except for the fact that there's no core left. Even took communion right here in town at St. James Church. But thank God, I'm rid of all that now."

"Rid of what?"

"Religion, God, the holy ball of wax," Ferguson said, turning the Olds onto Encarta Drive. "Religion's bad for the spirit. Bad for digestion too, for that matter. And it sure as hell is bad for civilized behavior. I'm living proof of that."

"How do you figure?"

"I'm a divinity school dropout," Ferguson said, staring straight ahead. "I know that doesn't have the same zing as 'beauty school dropout,' but that didn't happen to be my calling."

"You were going to be a minister?"

"Or a theologian," Ferguson said.

"What's that?"

Digby laughed. "Basically, it's a man who makes up unbelievable stories about God," he said.

"And you lost it?" Elvis said. "The calling?"

"Oh, I lost it, found it, and lost it all over again," Ferguson said.

"How's that?"

"Long story, Elvis," Ferguson said, waving him off. "We've got more important things to think about."

"They can spare a minute," Elvis said.

"Whatever you say, Big Guy," Ferguson said. He glanced at Elvis a moment before continuing. "Okay, I went to Harvard Divinity School, if you can believe it. That was when I was still smart. Or thought I was. Anyhow, I went straight from the University of Nevada to Harvard Divinity. Suddenly, the smartest kid in Nevada was a certified moron. First course I took was Comparative Religions—Hinduism, Islam, Zen Buddhism, the primitive religions of the South Sea Islanders. Mind-boggling stuff, Elvis. People like to tell you that every religion basically believes in the same thing, but that's bull. I'll tell you how they are the same—everybody's god says, 'Let there be no other god before me.' Every religion insists that it's the *one* true religion."

"I've been wondering about that myself," Elvis said. "If you can go out and pick and choose a religion that suits you."

"Well, how about *that*?" Ferguson said. "You're a lot further along than I was at the time, Elvis."

"So what do you think? *Can* you pick and choose?" Elvis asked.

"Not a chance," Ferguson said. "At first, that seems like an improvement over just believing in the religion you were born into. But then it gets tricky. Because they're right, you know— you've got to believe that yours is the one true religion in order to *really* believe in it. Otherwise, you're saying that one thing is true for the Hindu and another thing is true for the Episcopalian.

And that never did make any sense to me. It's like that rabbi story. 'They can't *all* be right, Rabbi.' "

Elvis wasn't sure that he'd followed everything Ferguson had said, but he got the gist of it.

"So that's what made you lose your faith?" Elvis said.

"Yes indeedily-doo, cowboy," Ferguson said, suddenly giggling and rooting around in his shirt pocket.

Elvis shook his head. There sure was more to this Digby fellow than Elvis had thought there was. In fact, recently Elvis had begun to think that there was a whole lot more going on inside most people once you got a genuine peek into their lives.

"But a man has to believe in something, Digby," Elvis said finally.

"Oh, I believe in something, all right," Ferguson said, withdrawing a white capsule from his pocket and popping it into his mouth. "My personal Eucharist, straight from the laboratory. Want some, Elvis? It helps you sort through your options."

"No, thanks."

Ferguson took the turn onto Wilson Avenue and coasted to a halt in front of the pink whorehouse. A trio of new girls in see-through gowns greeted them at the door—the day shift.

"Elvis!" the tallest of them cried. "We heard you'd been here and we prayed you'd come back."

"Make no mistake this time, Elvis, any little thing you want is on the house," another girl said. "Your friend too, of course."

"Joy to the world!" Ferguson chimed, immediately starting to unbutton his Hawaiian shirt. "Makes a man believe in Christian charity all over again."

"No thank you, ma'am," Elvis said. "No offense, but we're in kind of a hurry. We're trying to find out about three gentlemen who came here last night. One had on green pants when he walked in. And he spent some time with a brunette. Skinny gal, about twenty or so."

"Tiny Tits," the tall woman said.

"They were kinda small," Elvis said, his face coloring.

"That's her nickname," the woman said. "Real name is Kathy, Kathy Lemon."

"Can I talk to her?"

"That's up to her," the woman replied. "She's home now. Has to get back in time to make breakfast for her husband and kid."

It was just like Mamma used to say: no matter what they are—bankers, crooks, or fallen women—all most folks want is a home and family to call their own.

"Could you give me Miss Kathy's address?" Elvis said.

"I guess so," the woman said, "but maybe you ought to call her first. Her husband's the jealous type."

Hard to figure a prostitute's husband for the jealous type, but then again, maybe she'd told him she worked nights in a canning factory.

"Okay, write down her phone number too," Elvis said. "Now what about those other two? Dark guys, both of them. Italian or something. They wore shiny suits, midnight blue. And their hair was slicked back. Wait a minute." Elvis scratched his jaw. "One of them was with a girl named Helene, the other with one called Peonie."

"Helene's still here," the woman said. "In the kitchen having breakfast last time I saw her."

She pivoted around and started down the hallway, followed by her two coworkers, then Ferguson, and finally Elvis. Ferguson had left his shirt unbuttoned and now flounced the tails as he mimicked the sway of the woman's hips. The man starred in his own surreal circus.

Helene was a mulatto girl in her thirties with high cheekbones, big brown eyes, and straight black hair; she probably had some Cherokee in her somewhere just like Elvis did. She was wolfing down a plate of chicken-fried steak and burnt peppers, Creole style. Smelled awful good to Elvis. Helene skewered a hunk of steak on her fork and held it out to him by way of a greeting— old time Southern hospitality. Elvis took it in his mouth and chawed it down.

"Thank you kindly, ma'am," Elvis said.

Helene responded by stabbing a slice of pepper and holding it out. "Ya need the full combo, Elvis," she said. "Steak and peppers go together like love and marriage. Can't have one without the other."

Elvis chewed down the burnt pepper too. Best little breakfast he'd had in days.

"I need to find out some things about one of your, you know, customers from last night," Elvis said finally.

" 'Johns' we call 'em," Helene said, mopping up the grease on her plate with her fingers.

"He was a swarthy gentleman," Elvis went on. "Dark suit, hair slicked back."

"I know the one you mean," Helene said, then stuck her fingers in her mouth and sucked them clean. "I was working on him when you came upstairs and made your ruckus."

"I'm sorry about that, ma'am," Elvis said.

"Didn't make any difference nohow," Helene said, sitting back in her chair and pulling her dressing gown tight at the neck in a surprisingly modest gesture. "Bucky—that's what he wanted me to call him—old Bucky wasn't taking care of business anyways."

"Beg pardon?"

"Bucky was a little limp in the dick department," Helene said matter-of-factly. "He claimed that had never happened to him be-

73

fore which is a sure sign that it happens to him all the time."

The tall woman put her forefinger to her lips and made a shushing sound; apparently talk about slack male members was considered bad taste in a brothel, at least when men were listening. Helene ignored her.

"Bucky was in that place between wanting to weep and wanting to knock me around a few times when you popped in the next-door bedroom," she went on. "Then he cursed you, blaming your racket for his droopy little thing. I ought to thank you, Elvis. You probably saved me a couple of slaps."

"Do you know anything else about him, ma'am?" Elvis asked.

"Yes, I do. When he paid up—and he knew he had to pay up even if he didn't do nothing, so you gotta believe this'd happened to him before. Anyhow, when he paid up, I saw a badge pinned in his wallet. Sergeant William "Bucky" Bucowitz from the Atlanta *po*-lice. Vice squad, of course. Good customers, the vice squad. Exceptin' if they're local, they don't pay."

The other women tittered.

"Anyways, he said he was paying for his buddy next door too. His birthday present. He said he and his pal had flown in from Atlanta just for the night. They had a rental car and were going right back to the airport afterward because they had to be on duty there this morning."

"And green pants?" Elvis asked. Clearly, nobody here had heard about Whaley's murder yet. "Did he leave with them?"

"Nope," Helene said. "I saw him standing by the curb after they took off. Waiting for a cab, I figure."

"Thank you, Miss Helene," Elvis said.

"No problem," Helene said. "Listen, Elvis, you mind giving me your autograph?"

"Not at all, ma'am," Elvis said.

Helene dashed out of the kitchen, then returned a moment later holding out a small, red, vinyl-covered autograph book. Pictured on the front was Shirley Temple doing a curtsy. Elvis flipped through the book looking for a blank page; along the way, he spotted the signatures of just about every male headliner in Vegas during the past ten years. Helene handed him a ballpoint pen and he wrote, "Helene, Thanks for taking care of business. I need all the help I can get. Elvis Presley."

It was only when he was getting back into Ferguson's Olds that Elvis wondered how the next man to autograph Helene's book might interpret his little message.

11

Conspiracy Theory Number Six

athy Lemon said, "Call me later," and hung up right after Elvis said hello. He waited a few minutes inside the phone booth next to the Golden Nugget, then dialed her again.

"Sorry about hanging up on you, Elvis," she said this time. "It was not, as they say, a convenient moment. Jude from work told me you'd be calling. How about meeting me at Fritz's Diner up in North Vegas in about fifteen minutes? Just have to drop off Cindy at kindergarten. I think you'll recognize me with my clothes on."

Digby Ferguson drove silently up the Strip to Route 15.

"You seem kinda quiet," Elvis said to him. Ferguson had barely said a word since Elvis began questioning Helene.

"Yup," Ferguson said, staring bug-eyed through the windshield.

"Something on your mind?"

"Absolutely nothing," Ferguson said. "And nothing makes me happier than nothing."

Elvis decided to let it drop there.

They stopped at a gift shop at the far end of the Strip where

Ferguson picked up a sombrero for Elvis to wear hunkered down on his head by way of keeping a low profile. Then they made their way to Fritz's Diner.

With her clothes on, Kathy Lemon looked for all the world like a garden club lady from the good side of Memphis. Her dark brown hair was tied up in back in a velvet ribbon; she wore tortoiseshell reading glasses far down on her narrow nose; and her tailored linen suit emphasized the narrowness of the chest which had given rise to her professional nickname. She immediately waved at Elvis from a corner booth of the diner, apparently unfooled by the sombrero. Ferguson picked a newspaper off the rack next to the cash register and sat down at the counter.

"Sorry about disturbing you last night, Miss Kathy," Elvis said as he slid into the booth across from her.

"Don't be silly, Elvis," she said, smiling. "It broke the monotony."

She not only looked like a garden club lady, she talked like one. Curious how a woman like her ended up in her line of work. Of course, the answer was probably simple: money—better money than she could earn doing just about anything else in this town except being a chorus girl and, God knows, she wasn't built right for that job. Elvis asked her to tell him everything she knew about J. P. Whaley, the customer he had interrupted in mid-act.

"Be happy to, Elvis," Kathy Lemon said. "But how come?"

"He's dead," Elvis answered. "Murdered sometime between the time he left you and four in the morning."

"God almighty!" she said. Then, "But what's that to you?"

Elvis shifted uncomfortably in his seat. "Nothing directly. I just hear that the local police are a little slow on the pick up, so I thought I'd help out."

"Oh, they're slow about some things, quick about others," Kathy said. She then recounted everything she could remember about

77

Whaley's visit. He had come in full of himself for cracking wise at the floorshow at the Sahara, saying that he was funnier than Howie Pickles and everybody knew it. He'd told Kathy that he was thinking of becoming a comedian himself, that he could do a whole stand-up routine about corruption on the Atlanta vice squad. Then he'd told her that she was his birthday present—he'd turned forty that day—and that what he wanted was for her to "ride" him while he lay back on the pillow. He'd said that his wife was too uptight to do it in this position because she didn't like him looking at her while they did it.

Elvis studied the menu nervously while Kathy told this part of her story. These working girls seemed to know more about the inner workings of married life than a whole convention of marriage counselors.

"Do you know what he did after you, you know, finished up?" Elvis asked.

"Just that his wife picked him up out front," Miss Kathy said.

"His wife?"

"That's right. He called her from the house. Told her he was ready, that he'd had a wonderful time. They seemed to share an intimate snicker when he said that. Then he walked out the front door with his buddies."

"Did you see her pick him up?"

"Actually, I did," Kathy said. "I was curious so I watched through the window. I mean, it wasn't the first time a john had his wife pick him up, but this guy didn't seem the type."

"What type is that?"

"You know, the shy type. The kind the wife sends to us to warm him up so he can finally take care of business when she gets him home." Yes, indeed, thorough knowledge of the inner workings of married life.

"Oh, one other thing," Kathy went on. "They had some kind

of row out there, J. P. and his vice-squad pals. A real shouting match. I couldn't hear much of it, but I did hear them say 'I.A.D.' a couple of times. You know, Internal Affairs Department, the people who police the police."

Elvis nodded. "How can you be sure the woman who picked him up was his wife?" he asked.

"It was the way he kissed her when he got in the car," Kathy said. "Familiar. And totally unsexy. If it wasn't his wife, it was his sister."

Elvis started to slide out of the booth.

"Wait until they hear about this out at the Bambi Ranch," Kathy blurted.

Elvis stopped sliding. "What's that—the Bambi Ranch?"

"Whorehouse at the other end of town. The competition." Kathy shook her head. "Oh yes, Bambi's going to throw a party when she hears one of our johns got whacked right after doing business with us."

"How do you figure that?"

"Bambi Hummel—she owns the Ranch. And she runs the place like a movie studio. In fact, she used to work for Paramount. That is, until she saw the opportunity for making some *real* money."

"Slow down, please, ma'am," Elvis said. "I'm still back at that party this Miss Bambi's going to throw."

"A celebration," Kathy said. "Bambi knows she can build this thing up until the talk all over town is that our house is hazardous to your health. Unsavory neighborhood. Incredibly dangerous. Why, just last night one of their johns was murdered. That story should be good enough to take a big chunk of business away from us. A *big* chunk. Maybe it'll even get a few of our girls to switch places of employment."

"I see," Elvis said. Man, even the flesh business was viciously competitive in this town. "Well, thanks for your help, ma'am."

"Actually, I hope this murder isn't what I think it is," Kathy suddenly blurted out.

"What are you saying, Miss Kathy?"

"Bambi could have set it up herself," Kathy said. "You know, set up the murder and had her story about our place being deathly dangerous all ready to fly. I wouldn't put it past her."

"That sounds pretty far-fetched to me."

"Maybe," Kathy said. "But Bambi and Harry—Harry Huff is our owner—they've been going at each other fast and furious lately. Just last week Harry put out the rumor that one of Bambi's customers came down with a bad case of the clap. Bambi needed a counterpunch. She had to top that story and top it fast."

Elvis scratched his jaw. What was this, Conspiracy Theory Number Six? Or was it Number Seven? It was getting hard to keep track.

Ferguson fell in alongside Elvis as they walked out the diner door. He had his newspaper scrolled up under his arm, a cardboard container of coffee in his hand, and was mumbling something about the coming of the apocalypse when a fat fist collided with Elvis's right eye.

"Scum!" the owner of the fist shouted. "You stay away from my woman!"

Elvis stumbled backward against the door, his sombrero tumbling to the ground. The fist tightened, readying for a second smack. Digby flung his container of piping hot coffee into the attacker's face. The assailant was a big man with spiky black hair and he shrieked when the coffee hit his eyes. Elvis's head was spinning. He clutched at his own eye as if he had to keep it from dropping out of his skull.

"Jesus, Gus! What's wrong with you?" Kathy Lemon stepped

out of the diner door, clucking like a schoolmarm surveying the damage of a playground fight.

"What's wrong with *you*, woman?" the man named Gus shouted back, his hands still covering his stinging eyes. "You going uptown on me? Carrying on with a fancy-pants movie star now?"

Apparently Gus was Miss Kathy's jealous husband.

"I'm just doing my job, damn it!" Kathy shot back. "Somebody's got to support our family!"

Elvis was just about to step in here to clarify that he wasn't one of Kathy's usual-type customers when Gus pulled back his fist in preparation for a smack at Elvis's other eye. Elvis stepped back, but Digby stepped forward and whacked Gus on the jaw so hard that you could hear it snap like the thigh bone on a fried chicken. Gus fell to the ground, out cold.

"Oh, dear," Miss Kathy said, kneeling down beside her husband. "I'll take care of this. Anyhow, Gus has a running tab at Memorial Hospital. But you two better get lost now. Be better for all of us."

"You sure there's nothing we can do, ma'am?" Elvis said. He picked up the sombrero.

"Just go, please," Miss Kathy said.

"Thanks, man," Elvis said to Digby when they were back in the car. "You really came through for me back there."

Digby smiled gratefully, for a split second looking for all the world like the Saint James communicant he once had been.

12

Recently Adjusted Underwear

$\mathcal{T}$ he headline in the newspaper Ferguson handed him read: "HOLD THE PICKLES!" The subhead: "Heckler Dead/Comic Defunct." With his handkerchief pressed to his wounded eye and his other eye blinking like crazy, Elvis had some trouble reading the body of the *Las Vegas Sun* story, but he got the main points: Virtually the entire Sahara casino had emptied out the moment word got back to the tourists that Howie Pickles's second insult target had been murdered; Luke de Luca had immediately called a press conference to announce that Pickles was taking an indefinite leave of absence for "health reasons"; both Reverend Sweetser of the Little Chapel and Reverend Lockhart of the Good Samaritan Chapel had publicly accused the other of being involved in the murders; and, finally, Sheriff Reginald Turtleff had told the press he was confident that he would wrap up both cases in a day or two. Elvis read this last part out loud.

"Glory be the constabulary!" Ferguson yodeled. "Doesn't it make you feel all warm and cuddly to know that Turtleff is on the case?"

"Maybe you're selling him short, Digby. Maybe he knows something we don't. Let's go talk to him."

"I got a better idea," Ferguson said. "Let's eat some peyote and *pretend* to talk to him. We'll probably get more coherent answers that way."

Elvis squinted at him with his one good eye. "You know, Digby, you seem too smart a fella to be all tied up in this drug stuff."

For the life of him, Elvis couldn't fathom why anybody would want to mess up his head with any of these new drugs. Sure, Elvis still popped those little energy pills that sergeant over in Germany had put him onto, and he took a painkiller now and then, but those were totally different. Those were to clear his mind, not fog it up.

"I'm not tied up in anything, Elvis," Ferguson said. "I'm just searching for answers."

"Sounds like you're searching in the wrong place."

"Not so. The first time I ate mushrooms I got a closer look at the truth—the Big Truth—than ever before. Or since, for that matter."

"You had a vision?" A Washington Street neighbor in Memphis had had a holy vision once—God spoke to the man right in his garage—and Elvis remembered feeling kind of envious of him.

"You could call it that," Ferguson said.

"How do you know it wasn't a hallucination?" Elvis said.

Ferguson burst out laughing. "How do you know that riding around in this car with me isn't a hallucination?"

"Because it doesn't *feel* like a hallucination," Elvis said.

"The good ones never do," Ferguson replied, grinning.

Elvis scrutinized Ferguson's face. Half the time he couldn't tell whether the man was pulling his leg or spouting some kind of weird wisdom.

"So that's what got you started taking drugs?" Elvis asked. "Searching for answers?"

"That's right," Ferguson said, staring straight ahead. "Started my first year at divinity school. I hadn't had a decent conversation with God since I began reading about all those other religions in the world. And then along came this Harvard professor who said he had just the ticket for me. Man named Timothy Leary. A fellow Irishman, so I thought I was in good hands. He gave some of us peyote mushrooms. He said a shaman—some Indian spiritual type—had turned him onto the stuff in Mexico. He said peyote was a shortcut to God, no matter what your religion was."

"Was it?"

"Seemed that way at the time," Ferguson said.

"And now?"

Ferguson smiled. "There's this Zen saying about spiritual enlightenment, what they call 'satori.' It goes like this: 'Before I had satori, mountains were mountains and rivers were rivers; after I had satori, mountains were no longer mountains, and rivers were no longer rivers; but since I've had satori, mountains are mountains and rivers are rivers.' "

"What the devil does that mean?" Elvis said.

"Damned if I know, Elvis."

For a town as big and brawling as Las Vegas, the sheriff's office and police headquarters had the size and stature of a whistle-stop lock-up on the Rocky Mountain line. Only one squad car was parked in front, empty but the motor was running and the air conditioner was on at full force. Elvis knocked on the single-story building's door. No answer. He knocked again, then let himself in, Ferguson skittering in behind him. Nobody at the front desk. A phone was ringing, then stopped.

"Hello?" Elvis called out.

Nothing. Then some muffled voices behind a glass-topped door labeled SHERIFF REGINALD TURTLEFF.

"Anybody home?" Elvis called again.

"Leave your name and number," a man's voice behind the door called back gruffly. "I'll get back to you."

"You gotta be kidding," Elvis said loudly. "This here's the police station, ain't it?"

"You need an appointment," the man's voice replied. Elvis could hear a woman's stifled laugh behind the door.

"Help!" Ferguson suddenly screeched. *"I'm on fire!"*

The glass-topped door instantly swung open. Stepping through was a short, muscular man with one of those crewcuts that is supposed to disguise a balding head by making you think there's no difference between real short hair and no hair at all. Sheriff Turtleff. His shirt was buttoned crooked and his fly was at half-mast. Inside the office, Elvis glimpsed a plump-cheeked woman who was busy making some kind of underwear adjustment through her cotton skirt.

"Geez, Digby! Nice timing!" Turtleff croaked. Then, seeing Elvis, he said, "Why, hi there, Mr. Presley. I thought you might be dropping by."

"That so?" Elvis said. "What for?"

"A deputy's badge," Turtleff replied in a mocking tone. "I heard you collected 'em wherever you go."

Elvis blushed, embarrassed and riled in equal parts. "Looks like you *could* use a deputy around here. For a man with two unsolved murders, you don't look to be taking care of business."

"My deputies are out combing for clues. Meantime, I'm taking care of business, all right, Elvis," Turtleff said, smirking. "Why just now, I was debriefing the victim's widow, Mrs. J. P. Whaley."

As if this were a formal introduction, the plump-cheeked woman with the recently adjusted underwear came striding out of Turtleff's office door with her hand extended.

"This is such a thrill," she said, heading straight for Elvis. "J. P. and I are your biggest fans in all of Georgia."

Elvis shook her hand uneasily. It felt awful moist for inside an air-conditioned office.

"I should say, *was* your biggest fan," Mrs. Whaley went on buoyantly. "But J. P. would've been pleased to hear you paid your respects. Very pleased."

"Yes, uh, sorry for your loss, ma'am," Elvis mumbled, although it didn't appear that the widow was experiencing much in the way of loss at the moment.

"We had the most wonderful marriage, you know," Mrs. Whaley continued excitedly. "So free. Yet we were always there for each other."

"Just like the sheriff is there for you now, ma'am," Elvis said, looking directly in her eyes.

"Reggie has been a real comfort to me in my time of need," the widow replied.

"Oh yes, Reggie's got a fine coffin-side manner," Digby said, pumping his eyebrows at nobody in particular.

Elvis studied Mrs. Whaley's face. Her late husband was still warm and she's looking all sexed-up. Of course, back in Memphis when Timmy Wilkins helped his mortician daddy pick up fresh corpses, he swore half the widows were in heat by the time he and his daddy arrived. His daddy had said that it was a natural thing, sex being a way of reasserting life in the face of death.

"I just had the most wonderful idea," Mrs. Whaley went on, putting her damp hand on Elvis's shoulder. "We're planning a beautiful funeral back home. Police bagpipe band, twenty-one-gun salute, a requiem mass at Our Lady of Fatima. But you know what would make it absolutely perfect? If you came, Elvis. If you came and sang a hymn for J. P."

"Let me think about it," Elvis said, although the idea wasn't worth a moment's thought. He stepped back so that the woman's hand dropped free of him. "But right now, ma'am, if you don't mind, I'd like to hear everything that happened after you picked your husband up last night."

"Thanks for your interest, son," Turtleff said, winking to Mrs. Whaley. "But why don't you leave this to the professionals?"

"And just where would I find a genuine professional, Sheriff?" Elvis said, looking him hard in the eye. He turned back to Mrs. Whaley. "Whenever you're ready, ma'am."

"Well, you know, I picked him up after his little birthday surprise and we went for a drive in the desert," the woman began. "It was such a nice night and all. You never get to see the moon so clear in Atlanta."

Elvis nodded. Sheriff Turtleff cracked his knuckles peevishly.

"So, you know, we parked the car out there in the moonlight and, well, we did it in the back seat. Made love. Just like kids."

Elvis continued nodding attentively, although he couldn't help thinking that maybe Kathy Lemon was wrong—maybe J. P. *had* been the type who needed to be warmed up by a prostitute in order to take care of business with his wife.

"And then he got out of the car to take a whiz," Mrs. Whaley went on earnestly. "J. P. always has to take a whiz right after, don't you know?"

"Flushing the pipes," Digby chimed. Elvis gave him a stern look, then turned back to the widow.

"And that's when this car came up and stopped right next to him," she said. "A big old Hudson. Couldn't tell what color it was by moonlight, but it was something pale. Blue, maybe."

Elvis glanced at Turtleff as the widow continued. It was pretty clear that the sheriff was hearing this part of her story for the first time.

"So J. P. zips up and leans down to talk to this guy through his car window," Mrs. Whaley said.

"On the passenger side?" Elvis asked.

"Yes."

"Must've been two of them, then. Two, at least," Elvis said.

"Yes, I think that's right," Mrs. Whaley said. "I couldn't hear what they were talking about, but it seemed okay, because J. P. kept laughing. Except, come to think of it, it was kind of a nervous laugh. J. P. does this little hiccuppy laugh when he's nervous about something. And then he just got in the car with them and they drove off."

"Without saying anything to you?" Elvis asked.

"No," Mrs. Whaley said matter-of-factly.

"Did you call the police?" Elvis said. "Or follow them? You at least followed them, didn't you?"

"My husband is . . . was a policeman. A detective," Mrs. Whaley said, shrugging. "That kind of thing happens all the time. We're out at the movies or a picnic or just about anywhere and one of his partners comes driving up and—zip!—off he goes, just like that. He was on the vice squad, you know. A crime buster."

Digby found something inordinately funny in the word "crime buster" and chortled.

"But you're in Vegas, ma'am," Elvis said. "Not Atlanta."

"I know, but the Hudson had Georgia plates. I mentioned that, didn't I?"

Elvis looked at her incredulously. "No, ma'am, you didn't mention anything about Georgia plates."

"I only got the first three numbers," Mrs. Whaley went on. "One-three-six."

Elvis saw Digby write the numbers down in his spiral notebook.

"And then what did you do, ma'am?" Elvis asked her.

"Just drove back to our hotel—the Hacienda—and waited for him," she said. "But, of course, he didn't come back. Next thing I know, Sheriff Reggie here is knocking on my door with the sad news."

For the first time, something resembling genuine sadness appeared in the woman's eyes, but she quickly shoved it away.

"Did you recognize anyone in that Hudson, ma'am?" Elvis asked.

"Couldn't really see them."

"Is there anybody in Georgia who might have wanted your husband dead?" Elvis asked.

"About a million people," Mrs. Whaley said, sounding proud. "In J. P.'s line of work, you make enemies easily."

"How about somebody connected with the Atlanta Internal Affairs?" Elvis asked, trying to make the question sound casual.

The widow looked away, then said, "I wouldn't know what you're referring to, Mr. Presley."

Elvis decided to let it drop, at least for now. "Thank you, Mrs. Whaley," he said. He hesitated a moment, then, "That business with Howie Pickles. Heckling him. You don't think that had anything to do with your husband's death, do you?"

"Don't be ridiculous!" Turtleff snapped. "That's just newspaper crap!" For some reason, that question made him angrier than any other Elvis had asked the widow.

"I don't know," Mrs. Whaley replied. "It did seem like a strange coincidence, didn't it? First that fat lady who Pickles ranked on and then my J. P. after he ranked on Pickles." She smiled satisfiedly. "J. P. really skewered Pickles, didn't he, Elvis?"

Elvis nodded. "Speaking of Mrs. Donaldsen, Sheriff, where are you holding her husband? I'd like to talk to him too."

"Forget it, Elvis," Turtleff said. "You've wasted enough of my time."

"But Donaldsen's right here, isn't he, Sheriff?" Ferguson chirped brightly.

"What if he is? I don't have time for this crap," Turtleff snapped.

"But I'm sure Mrs. Whaley would like to see him," Ferguson said, offering the Widow Whaley a goofy grin. "You know, so they could commiserate about their losses."

"Why, yes, that would be nice," the widow said, as if she were accepting an invitation to a backyard barbecue. She gave the sheriff's hand a quick squeeze. "Maybe just a quick hello, anyhow."

Grumbling, Turtleff led them to the rear of the reception area. Following behind him, Elvis saw a couple of plastic-framed diplomas hanging on the wall, a bachelor's degree and a law degree from the University of Nevada, both endorsed to Reginald P. Turtleff. You had to wonder what kind of university handed out law degrees to the likes of Turtleff. Next to the diplomas was a photograph of the sheriff with Luke de Luca, and beside that, a faded photograph of the sheriff with his arm across the shoulders of Las Vegas's patron saint, that visionary, Bugsy Siegel. Man, Turtleff did get around, just not around to solving murders. The sheriff pulled out a large ring of keys, and opened a steel door. After the three filed through behind him, he locked the door again.

"Holy Mother!" Mrs. Whaley screeched, her knees buckling under her.

She was the first to see Bruce Donaldsen hanging by his belt from a light fixture in the Clark County Jail's sole cell. Elvis caught her around the waist and held onto her like she was a sack of cornmeal. Then Elvis stared full-on at the dangling bony body. Donaldsen's eyes were open, his pupils bugging out of their sockets like a ventriloquist's dummy, his bluish tongue lolling out the side of his mouth. Elvis felt dizzy himself. He set his feet wide to keep both him and his burden from toppling.

Man, it was one thing to talk about dead folk, even to see pictures of them on TV or in the paper. But it was altogether something else to see a dead man hanging by his neck ten feet away from your eyes. There is nothing so plain, so just what it is, as a dead man.

A bulb flashed. Elvis turned. Digby Ferguson was recording the swaying corpse with his trusty Polaroid.

"Guilty as hell," Turtleff grumbled. "An innocent man don't hang himself."

13

The Foretelling

"I'm glad I know who Jesus is.
He's more than just a story."

The church folk began singing the gospel hymn the moment they saw Elvis arriving in the open Olds as Digby drove up the crescent driveway in front of the Sahara. There were a good thirty of them this time, about double the number that had been taunting Reverend Sweetser out on the highway. And although it was the hottest hour of the day, every one of them was decked head to foot in black flannel looking like a posse of pallbearers.

When Elvis stepped out of the car under the hotel awning, several of them cried out, "The king of glory!," followed by a chorus of "Amens." Elvis even saw a couple of them cross themselves as they gawked at him with gooey eyes. What the heck was going on with these folks now?

The tallest of them, a gaunt man with a cowboy complexion, walked straight up to Elvis and bowed his head before speaking.

"I hope you can forgive us, King," the man said, his voice trembling. "We have committed the worst of sins."

"What are you talking about?" Elvis asked. Man, was Sheriff Turtleff's theory actually right? Was this man about to confess that his group was responsible for the murders?

"I'm asking your forgiveness for not recognizing you," the gaunt man said.

"That's all right," Elvis said, although it seemed to him that they'd had no problem recognizing him out by the billboard yesterday. He took a step toward the Sahara's front door.

"The Bible said it wouldn't be easy to recognize you," a pretty young church woman in a wool shawl said.

Elvis turned to her. "Beg pardon?"

"When you came back," the woman said. "You know, in your new form. The King of Kings."

This was worse than a murder confession—it was insanity! Complete and utter insanity! Maybe the whole bunch of them was suffering from mass sunstroke.

Elvis looked the young woman hard in the eye. "Ma'am, I don't know what you can be thinking, but if it's what I believe it is, that's your sin right there. Idol worship. Taking a false god before you."

"But we *know* who you are," the young woman said, smiling happily.

"Listen, woman!" Elvis said gruffly, pointing a finger in her face. "I am just who I've always been, Vernon and Gladys's boy from Tupelo. And for you to think otherwise, well, *that's* a blasphemy."

In his car, Digby Ferguson was laughing like a madman.

"The Bible said that too," the woman went on earnestly. "That you'd deny it. That you wouldn't want anyone to know. So you can wander freely among us. We understand, Elvis."

Man, there was no way to win this argument! The more he

denied he was the Second Coming, the more they'd believe it. And the worst part was, that made him feel like a sinner himself. It made him wonder if deep inside his soul something vain actually did want folks to believe he was holy—and somehow that part of him showed through. Maybe that's what that Tzar fellow meant when he said that being famous keeps you from living a true and meaningful life.

Elvis turned away from the young woman and started for the hotel entrance when he abruptly stopped and turned back to face the entire group. By golly, if these people were going to invest him with all this power, he might as well use it to do some good.

"Listen," he said. "If any of you God-fearing folk know anything about the murders we've had here these last couple days, I want you to step forward right now and tell me about it."

No takers, just downcast eyes. At the rear of the crowd, Elvis saw a dour-faced woman with a child in her arms whispering frantically to the man next to her. Elvis waited a full minute, then strode in the front door of the Sahara, catching his reflection in the glass. Darn if he wasn't developing one heck of a shiner from Gus's punch.

He squinted around the foyer with his good eye. It *was* virtually empty in here—the newspaper hadn't exaggerated about that. Usually by two o'clock in the afternoon the blackjack tables and one-armed bandits would be filling up with the breakfast crowd, the "early risers" in their peddle-pushers or Bermuda shorts with a rum-and-Coke in hand. But this afternoon Elvis could count the number of people he saw gambling in the Casino, almost all of them Orientals. They probably subscribed to a whole different scheme of hexes and bad omens that had nothing to do with Howie Pickles's deadly insult jokes. Or maybe they just didn't read the local newspapers.

Elvis had just pressed the button for the elevator when he saw the woman with the kid in her arms coming through the front door, a man following behind her. That child looked awful big to still be toted by his mamma. The woman was now pushing the man toward Elvis. The man stumbled forward, his eyes blinking a mile a minute.

"Hello, King," the man said. "I'm with the church group."

"I know. Saw you out there," Elvis replied, hoping the elevator would come quick so he could make an escape.

"My name's Joby," the man went on, still blinking. "Agnes— my wife—she said I should tell you what I know. You know, about them murders."

At that moment, the elevator arrived. The operator stepped out and executed a comically elaborate bow-and-scrape to usher Elvis inside. Elvis waved him off. He guided the blinking man to the end of the bank of elevators where they both slipped behind a potted palm.

"So what do you know, son?" Elvis asked softly.

Joby shifted from one foot to the other a couple of times before replying. "I'm born-again, you know, King. I was a sinner and now I've been saved, just like in the song."

Elvis nodded encouragingly.

"Anyways, in my other life—my *bad* life—I did jobs for the big bosses. Nothing important. I'm just a local. Born and raised in Sin City. Not from New York or Miami or nothing, so I was never a contender. No chance of being made."

"Made?"

"You know, made part of the family. The Mafia."

"Go on," Elvis said.

"Anyway, I was basically a Mafia messenger boy, although sometimes the message was with my fists. Collecting outstanding

95

debts, that kind of thing. That was all. I never killed anybody or nothing like that."

Elvis did some more nodding.

"But I did get to know people. Important types. Like 'The Owl.' "

The man looked at Elvis as if that name should mean something to him, but Elvis just shrugged.

"He's a hit man," Joby explained. "You know, a hired killer. Pay as you go. They call him 'The Owl' because of his glasses—big and round and thick as Coke-bottle bottoms. Didn't seem to interfere with his aim though."

Here, Joby issued a roguish laugh—no doubt a laugh left over from his former "bad" life.

"Anyway, I hadn't seen 'The Owl' for a long time, maybe a year or so," he went on. "And then the other night I see him just outside here. Hanging out in front of the Sahara with his hands stuffed in his jacket pockets. The man was definitely packing. Heavy artillery, I'd say by the bulge. I kind of saluted him, like in the old days, but he looked right through me. Maybe he didn't recognize me. You know, I look different now that I'm saved."

"I'm sure you do," Elvis said. For one thing, Joby had probably worn sportier attire in his Mafia days.

"So there I am with the congregation on our Howie Pickles vigil," Joby said.

"Calling him down for being a blasphemer," Elvis said.

"Right. Of course, that was before we realized that Mr. Pickles was a holy harbinger."

"A holy what?"

"Harbinger. Of who you really are. The *foretelling*."

"What are you talking about?" Elvis could feel his flesh starting to crawl around under his shirt.

"You know, Jesus lived in a state of grace in a Near Eastern land. And you live in Graceland in a near eastern state," the man recited earnestly.

"That's a *joke*, darn it!" Elvis snapped. "He's a comedian!" Man, one trouble with religious folk is they had absolutely no sense of humor.

But then Elvis bit down on his lip: he'd taken Pickles's line pretty seriously himself, hadn't he? Truth is, he'd made a real fuss about it. Maybe if he hadn't made that fuss, these people wouldn't now be thinking he was the Son of God. Oh yes, Tzar was surely right: being famous made you do things just for your vanity. And then your vanity turned around and bit back at you like a rattlesnake.

"Maybe it was a joke," Joby said. "But the foretelling comes in mysterious ways."

Elvis took a deep breath. *Remember*, he told himself, *the best thing you can do is wrest something worthwhile out of these people's craziness.* "You were talking about a hit man, Joby," he said.

"Yeh, I was kinda curious. I mean, what's the Owl doing here after all this time? So after the congregation went home, I stuck around across the street. And so did the Owl, right in front. And then about three o'clock or so, out comes the fat lady and her skinny husband, all laughing and excited and everything. The doorman signals a cab for them, but they want to walk. Likely because they're still flying high from Pickles's putting the spotlight on them."

That's probably not the way Bruce Donaldsen would have described his feelings at that moment, but there was no double-checking that now.

"Sure enough, the Owl falls in right behind them," Joby continued. "Follows them about ten feet behind all the way back to their motel. The Silver Mine Motel, up on West Bonanza."

"So you followed him too."

"Yeh, it was a regular parade," Joby said. "And after they go into their room, the Owl hangs around in front and I hang around across the street. In my old life, I did a lot of that, you know. Following people and hiding in shadows." He paused here to steal a furtive glance through the palm fronds at his wife, then added in a confidential voice, "Actually, I kinda miss that stuff sometimes, Elvis—the hide-and-seek stuff. It gives you a little rush, you know."

"I know," Elvis said. Fact was he knew only too well.

"So about an hour or so later, the Owl goes up to the door of their room and knocks. The fat lady answers in her nightgown. They whisper back and forth a bit, then he waits while she goes back inside. A minute later, she's back wearing that tent dress she wore to the floorshow and she tiptoes out the door and closes it softly, like she didn't want to wake her husband. And then, zip-zip, some big old car drives up, they both get in like they're off to a party or something, and that's that."

"You didn't follow them?"

"I can't afford a cab in this town, King," Joby said.

"Did you call the police when you heard she'd been murdered?"

"Of course not!" Joby said. "I've been going straight for three years now."

Elvis couldn't begin to follow the logic in that excuse. "You figure the Owl knew Mrs. Donaldsen from somewhere and that's how he got her to come out with him?"

"I doubt it," Joby said. He had ceased blinking for a while now. "Old Owl has a way with folks, women and men alike. When he looks at you through those specs of his, he seems so harmless and trustworthy. Like an uncle. And he's got this down-home voice that makes you think he's your next-door neighbor dropping by to help you set out your garbage instead of dropping by to help you put a noose around your neck. I figure he told Mrs. Donaldsen some flattering bit of garbage, like Howie Pickles was dying to meet her in person and he'd been sent to fetch her. That's the way the Owl operates. With a gift like that, you could be blind as a bat and still be a top-dollar hit man."

Elvis had to smile. It surely was a marvel how animated this holy roller became when he got up to full steam talking about criminal talent.

"Who does the Owl work for?" Elvis asked.

The man let loose one of his naughty-boy laughs. "The highest bidder," he said. "The Owl is strictly freelance."

"So who do you figure was the highest bidder this time?" Elvis asked.

"You got me," Joby whispered.

Two white-haired couples had made their way to the elevator door on the other side of the potted palm and now one of the old women winked at Elvis through the plant's fronds as if they were playing a private game of peekaboo. A moment later, the elevator arrived and both couples disappeared into it.

Joby leaned his head close to Elvis. "King, I got a special favor to ask of you."

"Sure," Elvis replied, although he got a panicky feeling the moment he said it. Still, he owed this young man.

Joby stepped out from behind the palm and waved his wife over to them.

"This here's Agnes and our boy, Timmy," Joby said after they arrived.

"Pleased to meet you, ma'am," Elvis said.

Agnes performed a little curtsy that looked distressingly like she was genuflecting. The woman had unhealthy-looking skin and tiny eyes. "My King," she said softly. She had one of those sing-songy Southern voices like back home.

Elvis ruffled the boy's hair. "Hi, there, Timmy."

The freckle-faced boy gazed at Elvis with big, eager eyes. He moved his lips, but no sound came out. Then he looked expectantly at his father, as if waiting for approval.

"Timmy can't talk," Joby said. "Can't walk right either."

"I'm sorry to hear that," Elvis said.

"We've brought him to all kinds of doctors," Joby went on. "Even drove all the way down to Tucson where they got a specialist. But not one of them can figure how to fix it."

"Really sorry," Elvis murmured.

"Heal him!" Miss Agnes suddenly blurted out. "Please heal him, King!"

Elvis felt the blood drain from his face. He stepped back against the wall, his head reeling.

"Ma'am, p-p-please," he stammered. "I can't do that. I'm no healer."

"I'm begging you," she said, tears in her eyes.

"I wish I could, Miss Agnes," Elvis said softly. "I really do. But I'm not who you think I am. I'm just not and that's the God's honest truth."

"Please, Elvis," Joby pleaded. "Just try. No harm in trying, is there?"

"But I—"

"Please, King," the woman whispered urgently. She was weeping freely now.

Elvis sucked in his breath. He closed his eyes, then let his breath out slowly.

By golly, there it was again! That stillness, that peacefulness. And that warm glow pulsing up his spine. The life energy, that *prana* stuff. Elvis could feel it tingle in his hands. He slowly opened his eyes and placed both his palms on the boy's head.

"Bless you, my son," Elvis whispered.

14

The Beagles of Liverpool

illy? It's me, Elvis."

Elvis had phoned his best friend, Dr. Billy Jackson, at his Alamo, Tennessee, clinic the moment he got back to his hotel room. Billy's new assistant and wife, Connie Spinelli Jackson, put Elvis right through.

"Something wrong, Mr. P.?" Billy said. "You don't sound too good."

Elvis smiled just to hear his friend's voice. "You making diagnoses over the phone now, Doc?"

"A man's voice tells me more about his vitality than his temperature any day," Billy said.

It sure was comforting to have someone who really understood you. Sometimes Elvis thought that Billy's being colored gave him extra sensitivity in reading other people's feelings.

"I am feeling kind of agitated," Elvis said. "I came out here for some R-and-R before my next picture starts and I find myself in the middle of some real awfulness."

"Those murders I read about in the papers? Something to do with a comedian fella?"

"That's part of it, Billy," Elvis said. "They got a sheriff out here who thinks he can solve crimes with his eyes closed."

"So you're keeping your eyes open to make up for it," Billy said.

"Trying to," Elvis said. One eye, anyhow. Billy was the only person in the world who understood Elvis's need to see justice done even if he fell on his face now and then in the process. "Strange case in a strange town. A hundred leads leading in a hundred directions. And about a hundred suspects too—every one of them with a motive as big as a highway billboard."

"Sounds like you've got your hands full," Billy said. "But you say that's just part of it. Part of your agitation."

Elvis sat down on the sofa. *The Autobiography of a Yogi* still lay open on the telephone table where he had left it early that morning. And now he saw that a sheet of hotel stationery was jutting out from between the pages. He pulled it out. "I brought you breakfast, but you weren't here. I miss you, Elvis. Maybe I can drop by around midnight. Forever, Shiva."

"You still there, Mr. P.?" Billy said.

"I'm here," Elvis said. He suddenly felt a knot of tears tightening behind his eyes. That happened sometimes when he talked with Billy, when he opened up his heart to him. "Billy, the thing is I've been feeling sort of strange lately. Like life is passing me by, you know?"

"Oh, I know all about that feeling," Billy said, with his sweet tenor laugh. "Does yours have anything to do with that new music coming over here from Liverpool, England? Those shaggy-haired boys on the *Ed Sullivan Show*? What're they called—the Beagles?"

"The Beatles. No, that's not it, Billy. Or maybe just part of it.

It's *all* this craziness nowadays. Seems as if everybody's lost their way. Like I met this educated fella who pops hallucination drugs like they're jelly beans. And some hippie kids who run around naked as Injuns. And just this morning I was talking to this lady who was a day-old widow and she was carrying on like a sow in heat. I don't know, it all makes me feel like a stranger in my own time."

"The times are changing, all right," Billy said. "But I got to say, a lot of those changes are turning out to be a good thing for colored people."

"And I surely do appreciate that," Elvis said. He paused a moment, gathering up his gumption. "But I haven't told you the worst of it, Billy. There's this holy roller bunch out here. And they've got it into their heads that I'm . . . I'm the—" He couldn't say it.

"That you're the Second Coming, right?" Billy said.

"How'd you know that?"

"I didn't," Billy said. "But I could see it coming. On the air the other day, a deejay said that if Jesus were around today, he'd be a rock 'n' roll superstar."

"That's blasphemy," Elvis said. It seemed he'd been saying that word an awful lot lately.

"True enough," Billy said. "But then somebody called in and said that if anybody's Jesus today, it's Elvis. And pretty soon a whole bunch of people are calling in and saying the same thing."

"I can't tell you how awful that makes me feel," Elvis said.

"I'm afraid it just comes with the territory, Mr. P.," Billy said. "When they project your face up there on that movie screen, it's bigger than life. So folks just naturally come around to believing you really *are* bigger than life. That you are more than just a human being."

Elvis closed his eyes. God help him, if he was going to say it—to *confess* it to his friend—he'd best do it right now.

"I . . . I did something today that's making me feel awful ashamed, Billy," Elvis said. He took a long breath and then told Billy about laying his hands on the sick boy downstairs.

"You can't hold yourself responsible for what other people believe, Elvis," Billy said.

"That's not the all of it, Billy," Elvis said. He swallowed hard before continuing. "The thing is, for just one minute there, I felt like I was really doing it."

"Doing what?"

"I felt it in my hands," Elvis said softly. "Like maybe I really was—you know, healing him."

For a long moment, Billy did not make a sound. And then he burst into an uproarious laugh.

"Well, well, maybe you've found yourself a new calling," Billy said, still laughing. "But time will tell. Time will tell what kind of healer you turn out to be, won't it, Mr. P.?"

And suddenly Elvis was laughing too, laughing with relief. Man, there was nothing in the world like talking to Billy Jackson to cleanse his mind of foolishness. "Hey, I'm just a country singer, don't you know?" he cried.

"When you aren't being a detective," Billy said. "So tell me, Mr. P., any way we can help you down here with this new case of yours?"

"There is," Elvis said, thankful to move on. He told Billy about the late J. P. Whaley of the Atlanta vice squad, his possible involvement with an I.A.D. investigation, and a pale blue Hudson with Georgia plates that began with the numbers 1-3-6. Billy said he had a friend who worked for the colored newspaper over in Atlanta and he'd ask him to find out what he could.

Elvis heard someone at the clinic calling to Billy. He would have liked to sing a couple of choruses of gospel with him, the way they usually signed off their phone calls, but that voice calling Billy sounded pretty urgent. There was work to be done at the William Jackson Clinic, God love them all.

"You take care, Billy," Elvis said.

"You too, brother," Billy said and he hung up.

Elvis just sat there for several minutes, fighting back a feeling of desolation. Neither he nor Billy had even mentioned Selma Du Pres's name this time. Not a word about putting flowers on the Alamo grave of the love of Elvis's life. Nor had Elvis mentioned Shiva, whose dark eyes and tawny skin so reminded him of Selma. That would have to wait for next time.

Elvis swung his feet up on the sofa, boots and all. He had not slept a minute in the past twenty-four hours. He immediately drifted off into a dreamless sleep.

"Knock! Knock!"

Elvis clamped a pillow over his head.

"Hey, Elvis! Knock! Knock!"

No pillow was thick enough to block out the whiny voice on the other side of his hotel room door. Elvis sat up and started rubbing his eyes before he remembered that his right eye was in no condition for rubbing.

"Who the heck is there?" Elvis called.

"Wurlitzer!"

"Wurlitzer? *Who?*"

A high-pitched giggle and then, in a note-perfect imitation of Elvis, *"Wurlitzer one for the money, two for the show, three to get ready . . ."*

Elvis groaned, then got up, turned on the lights, and walked to the door. Howie Pickles was still giggling when Elvis opened it.

"You don't know how long I've waited to use that gag," Pickles said.

"You could've waited longer," Elvis said. He glanced at his

105

watch: it was past eleven. He'd slept longer than he would have guessed.

Pickles was studying Elvis's face. "Are you wearing eye shadow or is that a shiner?"

"A shiner."

"Well, on you it looks good, Elvis," Pickles said. "In fact, it looks *smashing!*" He paused a beat, then, "Just made that up. Not bad, huh?"

"It was nice to meet you, Mr. Pickles," Elvis said. "But if you don't mind, I'm expecting company."

Pickles shrugged and shuffled past Elvis to the balcony window where for a long moment he stared out at the bright lights. Then he slowly turned around and faced Elvis.

"The doorman told me that he heard you asking some people out front if they knew anything about the murders we've been having," Pickles said quietly.

"You know something about them?" Elvis said.

"Nope. Not a single thing about any murder that's happened. Not *yet.*"

It sounded like a setup for another one of Pickles's lame jokes. Elvis looked hard into the comedian's face. His rubbery lips were turned down at the corners like a clown's impression of the mask of tragedy. That probably said it all: the man had been making fun of the tragedy in people's lives for so long that he didn't know the difference anymore. For him, tragedy *was* a comedy.

"Good night, Mr. Pickles," Elvis said.

"It's an emergency, Elvis," Pickles said, almost whispering. For once, he did not look like he was working on a gag. In fact, he looked like he was about to crumble before Elvis's eyes. "The life-or-death kind."

"Whose life or death?"

"Joey Filbert's," Pickles said, his shoulders quivering. "The new comic at the Sands."

"Somebody going to kill him?" Elvis said.

Pickles nodded.

"Who? Who's going to kill him, Pickles?" Elvis took a step toward the trembling comedian.

Pickles stared down at the rug and shrugged.

"I can't hear you, Howie," Elvis said.

"But I . . . I . . . I'll never work again if I ta-ta-tattle," Pickles stammered. "And telling jokes is the only thing I do. It's either that or pumping gas."

"The way I hear it, you aren't working now," Elvis said. He walked up to Pickles and put an arm across his shoulders. "Tell me what you know, Howie. You said it's an emergency."

"Lucky," Pickles whispered.

"De Luca?"

"I heard him on the phone. Talking to New York. They're down a million bucks in just one day. The casino's deserted. And the Sands is suddenly full."

"So I hear," Elvis said.

"And then I heard him say the word," Pickles said. "*Payback*. He said, 'It's payback time.' And then he told the guy in New York that he'd take care of it tonight. Make a public example that will put them out of business for good. And that he'd find the best person for the job."

"He mentioned Joey Filbert by name?"

"Yes. He said that at tonight's show Joey's going to tell his last joke."

Elvis scratched his jaw. He hadn't shaved in a couple of days now. He looked at his watch. It was almost midnight. Shiva should be arriving any minute now.

"What time does Filbert go on?" Elvis asked.

"Midnight," Pickles said.

The Dummy

"*G*oin' my way?" Digby Ferguson was idling by the curb in his
Olds convertible at the Sahara's entrance when Elvis and Pickles
came rushing out.

Elvis stared at him. It was a good eight hours since Ferguson
had dropped him off at the same spot. "You been here all this
time?"

"Time flies when you're writing the great American crime
story," Ferguson replied. He flipped closed his spiral notebook,
stuck a ballpoint pen behind his ear, and pushed open the door on
the passenger side.

Elvis clambered into the backseat, then gestured for Howie
Pickles to get in front beside Digby. "Digby Ferguson meet Howie
Pickles," he said.

"Why, you're Paddy Ferguson's little boy, aren't you?" Pickles
said sarcastically. "Your dad still work in the kitchen here? Dish-
washer, right?"

"That's right," Digby replied defensively. "But *he's* managed to
keep his job."

The two hadn't exactly gotten off to a great start, but it didn't matter—Elvis wasn't starting a church fellowship here.

"The Sands. Step on it," Elvis said, and once again Digby lurched onto the Strip and sped to their destination in Indie 500 time. Not another word was spoken—heck, barely enough time elapsed to utter two syllables—until Digby tossed the keys to a Sands valet and the three men sauntered into the hotel.

"What's up, Presley?" Ferguson said, clearly enjoying the impression this improbable trio was making on the casino's guests: the King of rock and roll flanked on one side by a rubbery-faced comedian who was currently notorious for his deadly insult jokes and on the other side by a Hawaiian-shirted druggie with his belly button on full display.

"Joey Filbert," Elvis muttered. "He's the next target. Need to keep an eye on him."

"Yippidity-dippity," Ferguson replied, grinning.

They were just approaching the nightclub reservations desk when another trio of men cut them off. The flanking members of this group were obviously security guards; they made no effort to conceal the bulges of shoulder-holsters under their suit jackets. And front and center, wearing a silk-lapelled tux, was obviously executive management in the form of a craggy-faced man with bushy eyebrows and diamond-hard eyes.

"What an honor," this man said, extending his hand to Elvis. "Sol Epstein. I run this little bed and breakfast."

"A pleasure, Mr. Epstein," Elvis said, shaking his hand. "These here are friends of mine, Howie Pickles and Digby Ferguson."

Epstein gave the two a cursory glance, not offering either of them his hand. Epstein's manners reminded Elvis a little too much of Colonel Tom's: he switched from hot to cold faster than an army barracks shower.

"We wanted to catch Filbert's show," Elvis said.

Epstein nodded deliberately before he replied. "I'm afraid we just have room for one, Mr. Presley. For *you*, of course."

"We're a party of three," Elvis said, looking Epstein straight in his dark eyes.

A group of eager tourists had already formed a circle around Elvis and Epstein and their respective escorts. Obviously, Epstein didn't want Pickles anywhere near his casino—his very presence could send the Sands's newfound gamblers scurrying in superstitious panic. But on the other hand, publicly refusing Elvis Presley just about anything could be even worse for business.

"All right," Epstein said, sighing. "But—you know—keep a low profile, okay, boys?"

"Thank you, Mr. Epstein," Elvis said.

A moment later, a buxom blonde wearing some kind of French maid uniform two sizes too small led Elvis and his sidekicks to a front table in the nightclub. The place was packed, all right. On stage, a ghoulish-looking magician was in the process of sawing a cringing chorus girl in half. She lay in a coffin-like wooden box with her head sticking out one end, her feet out the other. Luckily, few in the rapt audience noticed Elvis's arrival.

"You wouldn't think sawing through a broad would be such hard work," the magician crooned to the audience, pausing to make a big show of mopping sweat from his forehead with a handkerchief. "But it's their gristle that gets you every time!"

The crowd snickered nervously, their eyes glued to the horrified expression on the saw-victim's face. Strange how much entertainment features a victim, Elvis thought. That didn't say a lot for human nature, did it? Then again, Elvis's last few movies were virtually victim-free and they were about as entertaining as lunch in a cafeteria.

As the magician continued to saw away, grunting and cursing,

Elvis scanned the audience. They looked like any Vegas crowd—middle-aged, earnest, and overweight. Most were couples, but some appeared to be conventioneers, men in dark business suits with name tags pinned to their breast pockets. Not a hard-bitten face among them. Of course, over the last couple of years Elvis had learned that killers came in all kinds of faces, both hard and soft. He peered into the stage wings, but all he could make out was a stage manager holding a clipboard and pencil, and a pair of chorus girls in high-heeled shoes, feather headdresses, and skimpy underwear—apparently the standard dancer's uniform in this town. It would be hard to conceal a lethal weapon in that getup.

The audience emitted a collective gasp as the magician separated the two halves of the coffin—the victim's screaming head in one half, a pair of twitching feet in the other. The smirking magician spread his cape in front of the whole business and then, *presto*, stepped aside to reveal the chorus girl standing in one bikini-clad piece. Applause, applause.

"Just goes to prove, the whole is greater than the sum of its parts," Digby said.

Now, none other than Sol Epstein himself appeared onstage at the microphone. "Ladies and gentlemen, it is my great pleasure to present the Sands's new comedy sensation, the man whose comic talent and *congenial* personality has virtually put the Sahara out of business—*Joey Filbert!*"

Elvis saw Pickles grimace at that "congenial personality" line. No doubt about it, Epstein was milking the "insult murders" for all they were worth. And they were currently worth about a million bucks a day in casino revenue.

Joey Filbert was innocent looking, all right. A small, bird-like man with timid, wide-set eyes, he shuffled on stage in a baggy suit carrying a tattered suitcase. He set the suitcase down and blinked out at the audience as if the whole bunch of them had suddenly appeared in his bedroom.

"Oh, hi," he said, shyly.

The audience giggled.

"Hey, Joey! I'm dying in here!" A squeaky voice. It seemed to come from the suitcase. More audience giggles.

"Take it easy, Howie, we've got company," Filbert pleaded, addressing the suitcase.

"Company-shmumpity, I can't breathe in here!" the squeaky voice replied. *"Let me out or I'm telling Mommy!"*

Elvis smiled; nobody had told him that Filbert's routine was a comic ventriloquist act.

"Come on, Howie, these folks came here for a wholesome, good time," Filbert said to the suitcase. "They don't want any of your lip."

"My *lip? Listen to yourself, Joey. Shouldn't a guy with your I.Q. have a low voice too?"*

Big laugh.

"This guy's good," Ferguson whispered.

"A good *thief*," Pickles whispered back, scowling. "That 'I.Q.' line is mine."

"Okay, okay, I'll let you out, Howie," Filbert said to the suitcase. "But you've got to promise to mind your manners, okay?"

"Okay, Joey, I promise," the squeaky voice replied meekly.

Filbert set the suitcase flat on the stage floor and opened it slowly. Suddenly, flying out on the end of his hand was the dummy. It was a miniature caricature of Howie Pickles.

The audience howled.

"I'll sue the bastard!" Howie Pickles, the human being, said in a hoarse whisper.

"Whew! I was getting sick of my own stench!" the dummy exclaimed, his bulging, Picklesesque eyes revolving in his head. *"Who says flop sweat doesn't reek? No wonder I emptied out the Sahara!"*

The audience screamed with laughter. Howie Pickles was trembling with fury, his round face visibly red in the dimly lit room. He started to rise from his seat, but Elvis clamped a hand on his shoulder and pulled him back down.

"Stay cool, Howie," Elvis whispered urgently.

"Cool it!" Joey Filbert snapped at the dummy. "Don't you want to make a nice impression on these people?"

"I'll leave that to you, Joey," the dummy replied, his head revolving in a full circle before it faced Filbert again. *"You have such a sympathetic face. Goodness knows, it has* my *sympathy!"*

"That's *my* line!" Howie Pickles hissed. Fortunately, the dummy's line got such a loud laugh that nobody heard him.

"You've got to hand it to this guy, he's clever," Ferguson whispered to Elvis.

Oh, he was clever, all right, Elvis thought. Filbert turned the victim thing around so that he was attacking the attacker while remaining an innocent fool. It was a crafty way to let the audience have their cake and eat it too: they felt safe laughing at the insult jokes because they were directed at Filbert himself, but at the same time Filbert was tearing Howie Pickles to shreds. Tricky. And very effective. But you had to wonder how Filbert had put together his act so fast, complete with a feature-perfect Howie Pickles dummy. He'd had less than a day's lead time, that is unless he had been prepared long before Pickles was fired. Or maybe even before Bonnie Donaldsen's murder. Elvis darted his eyes toward the wings again. Nothing suspicious going on there.

"Geez, they call me a dummy, but what about this guy?" The

Pickles dummy gaped googly-eyed at Filbert. *"This morning Joey spent a half-hour staring at an orange juice can because it said, 'Concentrate.' "*

The audience roared. "Mine!" Howie Pickles hissed. *"My joke!"*

"I mean, Joey's so dumb, he thinks the St. Louis Cardinals are appointed by the pope!" the dummy went on. *"Just yesterday, he missed the forty-four bus, so he took the twenty-two twice!"*

"Mine! Mine! Mine!" Howie Pickles chanted furiously. Some members of the audience had started to notice and were pointing at him and laughing.

But the dummy was on a roll. *"Man, if you give Joey a penny for his thoughts, you get change!"*

Once again, Elvis flicked his eyes to the stage wing. At that moment he saw the man with the clipboard reach into his shirt pocket and remove a pair of glasses. He put them on—big round glasses with lenses thick as Coke bottle bottoms. *He looked like an owl.* And he was slipping one hand into the back of his waistband.

"Filbert! Duck!" Elvis screamed, jumping from his chair.

The audience stared at Elvis, then burst into uproarious laughter as Howie Pickles, in the flesh, popped up beside him. Onstage, Pickles-the-dummy rolled his eyes and yodeled, *"Filbert's a duck? Hey, who am I to argue with Elvis?"*

Elvis jumped onto the stage and took a flying leap at Filbert, tackling the ventriloquist at the knees and toppling him onto his back. A single muffled shot burst from the wings. It zinged just inches above the two of them and smashed into the dummy's head with a surprisingly dull sound, like an egg cracking against the side of a bowl. But it splintered into hundreds of plaster particles that sprayed straight into the audience. They screamed. Most of them dropped to the floor and crawled under their martini-laden tables.

Elvis looked up. The Owl was cocking his pistol. He put the rear sight against one lens of his glasses. Elvis grabbed the ventriloquist's tattered suitcase off the stage floor, hoisted himself up with one arm, and flung it side-arm at the Owl. It was a perfect throw. The hinged edge of the suitcase smacked the barrel of the gun and sent it flying from the hit man's hand.

The Owl froze, baffled, disoriented. Then, with astonishingly deliberate care, he removed his glasses and returned them to his pocket before retrieving his gun and dashing into the dark depths of the backstage area.

Elvis was on his feet immediately, racing after him. He saw the Owl careen around a corner past frightened chorus girls who flattened themselves—as much as their well-rounded bodies permitted—against the corridor walls. Elvis was gaining on him.

"Stop!" Elvis shouted.

The Owl turned, pointed his pistol unsteadily at Elvis. But it was obvious that without his glasses on the Owl was half blind, so Elvis kept coming at him. The Owl spun back around and continued running. He pushed at a door marked EXIT. It flung open onto a parking lot at the back of the building. Elvis jumped through the door only a couple of yards behind him.

Suddenly, a car screeched between them, knocking hard against the elbow of Elvis's outstretched arm. The Owl jumped into the back of the car and it sped off. Elvis stood there, cradling his stinging elbow in the cup of his other hand, staring at the receding car. It was a Hudson. Pale blue. He could not make out the numbers on the license plate, just the legend: GEORGIA—THE PEACH STATE.

16

One Body

*Y*ou shoulda let him kill that vicious joke thief!" Howie Pickles barked when they were back in Digby's car. It had taken them close to an hour to plow through the frenzied crowd at the Sands and retrieve their car. By then it was far too late to even think about pursuing the Hudson. It was now past three in the morning.

"At least his dummy's out of business," Digby said, pulling onto the main drag. "So tell me, Howie, did you feel any referred pain when the dummy's head exploded?"

"Har! Har!" Pickles croaked. Not his best rejoinder; Digby Ferguson was a higher level heckler than Pickles was used to.

"Hey, you did good, Howie," Elvis said from the backseat. "You saved a man's life."

"How do you figure that?" Ferguson asked skeptically.

"Howie overheard that there was a contract out on Filbert tonight. Revenge killing by the Sahara management. So he came to me," Elvis said.

"Well, surprise, surprise," Ferguson said, looking impressed in spite of himself. "Underneath that corny exterior lurks balls of steel."

A look of boyish pride flashed across Pickles's face. It probably wasn't often that anyone cited him for masculine courage.

"They call him 'the Owl,' the guy with the gun." Elvis said, trying to piece things together out loud. "Professional hit man. Works for whoever pays him. Tonight, he was working for de Luca. But I got reason to think the Owl did in Mrs. Donaldsen too and it wouldn't make sense for de Luca to be the paying customer for that job."

"You've been keeping secrets from me," Ferguson said. "Jesus, Elvis, I thought we were partners."

"Don't ever say that!" Elvis snapped.

"Say *what?*"

"Don't ever mention Jesus and me in the same breath," Elvis said.

"Well, *excuse* me," Ferguson said. "What's the matter—you and our Lord and Savior on bad terms these days?"

"Shut up, Digby," Elvis said.

All three remained silent for several moments, then Pickles said, "What if I ask him?"

"Ask who?" Elvis said.

"This Owl guy," Pickles said. "Ask him who he was working for when he murdered the fat lady."

"Now that's really brilliant, Howie," Ferguson said sarcastically. "Or was that the dummy speaking?"

"Shut up, Digby," Pickles said, then turned in his seat to look at Elvis for approval. Indeed, Howie Pickles wasn't himself tonight and Elvis noticed the improvement.

"But really, Howie, it sure don't sound like a question the Owl would likely answer," Elvis said.

"I don't know," Pickles said. "The guy's a whore, right? He'll do anything for money as long as it doesn't cost him anything. And talking can't be any more costly than killing, can it?"

Elvis wasn't so sure. Hit men probably had some kind of code of conduct that kept them from disclosing their clients. A bad reputation in that department could put them out of business. Maybe the Owl was a whore, but Elvis had recently discovered that whores were more complicated than he'd ever thought. Still, at this point they didn't have much else to go on.

"Anyway, you got to find him before you can ask him anything," Elvis said.

"I already thought about that," Pickles said. "What if I put out the word that I'm looking to hire him for a hit? Just another paying customer. God knows, that *momser* will believe that Howie Pickles has some major scores to settle."

Digby Ferguson looked at Pickles incredulously, running a red light in the process. "Man, you are full of surprises, aren't you?" he said.

"You'd make a good detective, Howie," Elvis said.

"Good thing," Pickles replied, grinning. "I've been forced to consider a career change lately."

Elvis laughed. "Okay, let's go for it. I think I know just the guy to put your business proposition on the gangster grapevine."

From the end of the hallway, Elvis saw that his hotel room door was open—just a crack, but open. His heart began pounding. He pressed his back against the wall. *This was it! Payback time again! But this time he was the recipient.* The Owl knew that Elvis could finger him for the attempted murder of Joey Filbert. And he also probably knew that Elvis was one of the few people in Vegas who would be foolish enough to risk his life by going to the press with that information. For a professional killer, there was a simple enough solution to that problem.

His back still pressed to the wall, Elvis edged, crablike, toward his door. A gun certainly would be handy right about now. Like that Luger he'd brought back with him from Germany and was now sitting in his closet at Graceland. If he was going to take this detective thing seriously—especially in Vegas—he couldn't count on his karate moves to handle every situation.

Elvis was at the door now. He stopped, peered with his good eye through the crack. It was dark inside. He cupped his ear to the opening. Staccato steps, a humming sound. Elvis touched the door lightly with his fingertips, then gave it a little shove and swung himself back against the wall. The door creaked open maybe five inches, then stopped. Silence. Or was that heavy breathing he heard just inside the door?

Elvis's heart was banging in his chest. Hadn't he played Superman enough for one night? Why go looking for danger? But what else could he do? Run for the police? Seek help from that model of American law enforcement, Sheriff Turtleff?

Elvis stepped away from the wall and faced the partially opened door. He took a deep breath and braced himself. Then he charged the door, slammed it fully open, and ran inside.

"What's this? *Room service?*" Shiva laughed from Elvis's bed.

Panting for breath, Elvis stared at her. She was sitting cross-legged on top of the covers, her long back straight, her hands in front of her chest with the tips of her fingers touching. Elvis would have liked to laugh, but at the moment he felt too darn foolish to.

"Didn't you think I'd wait for you?" Shiva said, rising and walking barefoot toward him. She was still wearing the gauzy outfit from her dance downstairs.

"Guess I just didn't think," Elvis said.

Shiva came up to Elvis and rested her hands on his shoulders.

"I meditated the whole time," she said. "Nice. It's very tranquil in here."

"I, uh, I'm sorry I'm late, Miss Shiva," Elvis mumbled.

"No matter," Shiva said, kneading the tops of both his shoulders. "Gosh, you feel tense. And where'd you get that black eye? You must have had an awful evening."

"It was strange, all right." Elvis didn't feel like talking about either Miss Kathy's husband or the attempt on Joey Filbert's life at this particular moment.

"Well, why don't we see if we can do something about all that tension, Mr. Presley." Shiva smiled. She took his hand and led him to the bed. "Strip down to something comfortable and I'll give you a special massage."

Elvis sat down on the bed, but he didn't move. He was feeling kind of funny just now. If Miss Shiva was talking about sex, she sure was talking about it in a peculiar way. Sounded almost businesslike. But then again, if she was talking about *really* giving him a massage—well, that felt funny too. Kind of disappointing, actually. But right now the problem was, how much should he strip down? *If she was only talking about a massage, then . . .*

"Just take everything off, Elvis," Shiva said, as if reading his mind. She kneeled down in front of him and began unlacing his shoes. "I don't bite."

Elvis did as he was told. Then, still following Shiva's directions, he spread out on his belly on top of the bed.

"This will feel a little strange, but don't be frightened," Shiva said. She was standing over him, a foot on either side of him. "I'm light on my feet."

And then Miss Shiva Ree stepped onto Elvis's back. It *did* feel peculiar. So light and solid at the same time. And it was amazing how smooth the bottoms of her feet felt, as soft as her hands. Starting on the small of his back, she took a tiny step forward, pressing down forcefully. She took another. A bone in Elvis's spine cracked loud as a finger snap. Another bone snapped, then another. He could feel the muscles in his back loosening up. *Surrendering* is what they were doing. And some of them felt like they hadn't surrendered to anything in years. Elvis felt good, real good.

"This dance have a name?" Elvis said from the corner of his mouth.

"Shush," Shiva whispered. "Just go with it."

Elvis went with it.

But several moments later he said, "It's, uh, it's getting a little painful just now, ma'am."

"Where?"

Elvis didn't feel like saying. "Just from lying on my stomach," he murmured.

Shiva laughed. "Are you saying that your friend down there has no place to go?"

Elvis laughed too. That was it, all right: he'd gotten so excited just thinking about Miss Shiva walking on his back in that gauzy thing that lying facedown on a firm mattress was twisting his "friend" out of shape.

"Why don't you turn over then," Shiva said, stepping off his back.

Elvis hesitated, then did what she suggested. There was no hiding his excitement now.

"I, uh, I thought you weren't supposed to get—you know— during a massage," Elvis said.

"That was no ordinary massage, Elvis," Shiva said. She lay down next to him. "The masseuse happens to be very fond of you and your back could feel that."

121

"Well, I guess it did," Elvis said, smiling over at Shiva. He reached out and touched the side of her face. He couldn't believe how beautiful she looked.

"I feel so happy," Shiva said.

"Me too." Elvis looked deeply into her eyes. "But we hardly know each other, Miss Shiva," he said.

"Of course not," Shiva whispered back, peeling off her dance costume. "It takes a lifetime to really know somebody."

It was like no other lovemaking Elvis had ever experienced.

For the longest time, they just lay on their sides, facing each other, looking into each other's eyes, touching each other lightly with their fingertips. Just when Elvis would feel like he couldn't keep himself from grabbing Shiva to him with all his might, she would gently roll away from him. Lying on her back, she would start humming a zithery-sounding melody. Then she would roll back on her side, gaze wondrously into Elvis's eyes, and begin tracing her fingers across his chest so delicately he had to strain every sense in his body to its breaking point just to feel it. But the wonderful strange thing was, that made him feel Shiva's touch all the more intensely.

Still, at one point, Elvis had to ask, "You teasing me, Miss Shiva?"

"No," Shiva whispered back. "I just want us to savor every minute of this. Every second . . . I want it to last forever."

"Me too," Elvis said, then added softly, "well, *almost* forever."

A moment later, Shiva covered his mouth with hers, tugging his lower lip between her own lips. When she kissed him, her tongue touched his lip, then slipped inside and touched his tongue. Elvis felt as if she could draw the very center of who he was right out of him with that kiss.

The kissing part went on for a long time too. In fact, it went to the point when Elvis felt like he couldn't savor it another second without exploding. Suddenly, Shiva was up, her knees astride him. Slowly—so slowly Elvis felt like they were underwater—Shiva lowered herself onto him, drawing the very center of what made him a man inside her. For one awful moment, the image of Miss Kathy riding on top of J. C. Whaley flashed in his mind, but thankfully it instantly went away.

"We are one body," Shiva was murmuring above him. *"One . . . One . . . One."*

Later, before dozing off in Shiva's arms, Elvis told her about his close call with the Owl at the Sands.

"You're safe now, my sweetness," Shiva whispered, stroking Elvis's forehead. "You're safe now."

17

Viva Las Vengeance

*M*ove it, sweetheart!"

Elvis blinked open his eyes—or rather just his left eye; his shiner was now swollen completely shut. A face hovered above his—a woman's face, a sexy face with a lascivious smile. Not Shiva. No, it was Miss Kathy, the classy-looking prostitute with the tiny bosom. She was in her working clothes—fishnet stockings, garter straps, bikini underpants, and a half-bra, all barely covered by a filmy nightgown. She patted Elvis on the cheek, something between a caress and a wake-up slap.

"Let's go, big boy. London's burning," Kathy said.

Oh no, it was all a dream—that delirious lovemaking with Shiva. Only a glorious dream. And now I'm being rousted from a whore's bed. "Time's up, big boy. Make room for the next paying customer."

"Duty calls, Presley!" Ferguson's voice. "We've got ourselves a brand new crime. Arson."

"Huh?" Elvis sat up in the bed. It was his own bed in his own hotel room. His head was still foggy, but his body felt fantastic, more rested than he could remember it feeling. And younger somehow too. "Where's—?"

"Your girlfriend?" Kathy laughed. "She left in a hurry. Had to see a man about a panther. How about that? I didn't figure you for the kinky type, Elvis."

If Elvis hadn't felt so relieved that his night with Shiva hadn't been a dream after all, he could have given Miss Kathy a little wake-up slap of his own.

"I'm double parked, boss," Ferguson called. He was standing just inside the door with a highball glass in hand. And who was that leaning unsteadily against the doorjamb just behind him holding a bottle of whiskey? None other than a very pickled Howie Pickles.

"Arson?" That part had just registered on Elvis.

"Yes, the Pink Palace," Kathy said. "My place of employment. Blazing. You can see it from here."

She pointed out the balcony window. Elvis could see smoke rising against the rosy dawn several blocks to the east. He started to get out of bed, then stopped, realizing that he was stark naked. "Excuse me, ma'am, but would you mind—you know—turning your back or something?"

All three of Elvis's guests burst into uproarious laughter. Man, didn't anybody believe in modesty anymore?

In the car—Kathy and Pickles in the backseat, Elvis up front with Ferguson—Elvis was filled in on the events of the past few hours. That mulatto working girl, Helene, had been the first to smell the smoke. She had screamed "Raid!" at the top of her lungs. Later she'd told Kathy that she figured if she'd screamed "Fire!" the johns might have been slower getting their bare asses out of there. Scampering out of the burning house, Kathy had spotted a broken window and a flaming gas canister just inside that window. It was arson, all right. The fire department had taken almost an hour to get there and the reason for that was that they had been busy battling a blaze at the Bambi Ranch for the past three hours. Also obviously arson, a fireman had informed Kathy. She had hitched a ride to the Sahara with one of the departing johns. There she'd found Ferguson and Pickles parked at the entrance, well into their second bottle of scotch. Apparently the pair had become overnight drinking buddies.

"Anybody hurt? Anybody killed?" Elvis asked.

"No, thank goodness," Kathy said.

"Any idea who started the fires?" Elvis asked.

"Of course," Kathy said, matter-of-factly. "My boss, Harry Huff, did Bambi. And then Bambi did us."

"What makes you so sure?"

"It's obvious, isn't it?" Kathy said. "First Harry pays back Bambi for killing my customer and making patronage of our house look like risky business. Then Bambi does double-payback for torching her operation. What goes around comes around."

"And around and around and around again," Pickles piped from the backseat.

Kathy laughed appreciatively and gave Pickles an affectionate pat on his balding dome. Oh yes, Howie Pickles was making a lot of friends in the schoolyard today. What puzzled Elvis was why Pickles and Kathy were in such high spirits, considering all the mayhem surrounding them. For starters, each of them had recently lost their respective sources of income. But maybe it wasn't so puzzling. Maybe this morning Digby Ferguson had converted them to his own religion with its laboratory-formulated Eucharist.

The Las Vegas Fire Department had managed to keep the blaze from spreading to the neighboring buildings, but by the time Elvis and company arrived, the Pink Palace was just a steaming pile of embers. About half the firemen were rolling up their hoses while the other half were solicitously comforting the displaced working girls—some even appeared to be going beyond the call of duty in this regard. There were a good fifty onlookers taking in the scene. One near Elvis was lecturing his companion about the exact temperature at which stucco burns. And standing under a flood-light directly in front of the former house of pleasure was Sheriff Reginald Turtleff, all dressed up in a Stetson hat and string tie with his five-point brass badge gleaming on his chest. The sheriff was giving a press conference.

His chin tucked down, Elvis strolled as inconspicuously as possible to the edge of the crowd that was gathered around Turtleff.

"We cannot rule out arson, of course," the sheriff was saying into the outstretched microphone of a TV reporter. "But it wouldn't be responsible to jump to any such conclusion yet. Not until we've done a thorough investigation."

"And the other one? Out at the Bambi Ranch? Was that one arson, Sheriff?" the reporter asked.

"I'd have to say the same thing, Bobby," Turtleff answered in his most earnest voice. "We'll just have to wait on the investigation."

"Thank you, Sheriff Reggie," the reporter said.

"So you're saying maybe it's just coincidence. Our two top brothels going up in flames in the same night. That's just the way the lightning strikes, eh, Sheriff?" It was Kathy Lemon speaking as she strode right up to the sheriff, her flimsy robe fluttering as she turned to face the television camera. Incredible! You wouldn't think Miss Kathy would be accusing Harry Huff—or even the Bambi woman, for that matter—if she wanted to remain in her line of work. And what is more, if she had been trying to keep her night job a secret from her crazy husband, that cover was shot in one TV minute. Hard to figure what could be on Miss Kathy's mind.

Sheriff Turtleff offered her a patronizing smile. In front of a television camera, the man seemed to have more facial expressions than in his entire off-camera life.

"Always good to hear the opinion of another professional—*a working girl*," the sheriff intoned sarcastically.

"At least she's using her head. That gives her a real advantage over you, Sheriff." This from Howie Pickles who had sidled up beside Miss Kathy. Now Pickles swiveled to face the camera as if he were doing a guest shot on the *Ed Sullivan Show*. The surrounding crowd tittered. "Glad you're wearing your Stetson, *pardner*—for once you've got something on your mind. So tell me, Turtleff, is it true that you're the only cop in America who can get stabbed at a shootout?"

The crowd howled. Elvis gaped at the scene incredulously: a comic doing stand-up in front of a crime scene on the morning news. Man, Las Vegas had to be the weirdest town on the planet. Pickles turned to the TV reporter. "Listen, Bobby, I fully understand why you're interviewing the sheriff. Your boss musta told you to go out and get the *real dope!*"

Oh yes, it was weird, all right, but it wasn't getting them any closer to finding out why Vegas was in the midst of a deadly crime spree.

Someone behind Elvis tugged at his shirt. Apparently Elvis hadn't gone unnoticed after all. He turned around slowly, hoping to make a quiet business of signing some tourist's autograph book. For a moment, he could not locate his shirt-tugger, but then a small hand came up and tugged again. Elvis looked down. A freckle-faced boy smiled up at him.

"Thank you, Jesus," the boy said.

The blood drained right out of Elvis's face. Holy Moley, it was Timmy! The crippled son of that holy roller couple. And Timmy was standing there on his own two feet with a proud grin on his animated face.

"What?" Under the circumstances, it was the only word Elvis could get out of his mouth.

"God love you, Elvis." This from Agnes, the boy's mother, who was standing just behind him. "Our Timmy has been born again."

"It really feels that way, Jesus," the boy said, looking rapturously into Elvis's eyes. "I been born again, but normal this time. I can walk and talk and all because of you."

Elvis felt faint. He had to brace his hand on the boy's head to keep his legs from buckling under him. *"Time will tell,"* Billy had said. *"Time will tell what kind of healer you turn out to be, won't it, Mr. P.?"*

"But . . . but I . . . I'm not Jesus, son!" Elvis stammered. "You gotta believe that."

"Please, Elvis," the boy's father, Joby, said urgently. He, too, was standing behind his son. "You healed him, so you *must* be who he says you are."

Elvis looked at Joby. The man's eyes were pleading with him. *"It doesn't matter how it happened or who you really are,"* Joby's eyes seemed to be saying to Elvis. *"All that matters is Timmy is cured. Why shake his faith when that might undo this miracle?"*

Elvis stood there, not moving. It would surely be a sin to allow people to keep thinking he was a man with holy powers. But wouldn't it be another kind of sin to risk the boy's cure just to prove Elvis's humility? Especially just to prove it to himself? Pride was a master of disguise.

"I'm . . . I'm glad to see you doing so well, son," Elvis finally said to the boy.

"Hallelujah!" came a chorus of a good fifteen men and women.

The congregation. So help Elvis, *his* congregation in their long black coats and skirts and buttoned-up shirts, looking for all the world like a convention of grave diggers gathering around him. Elvis's eyes darted, looking for an escape route.

But it was too late. Bobby from the morning news had heard the Hallelujah chorus. And when the reporter saw Elvis Presley at the center of this crowd, he dropped Howie Pickles and his Sheriff Turtleff insult routine as fast as Luke de Luca had dropped Pickles the day before yesterday. This had to be Bobby's lucky day: he was getting more stories just hanging out in front of a burnt-out whorehouse than in a year of stakeouts at the county courthouse. Before Elvis could make his escape, the camera was on him and little Timmy. And the little boy who had been utterly mute a day earlier was now blabbing a mile a minute into Bobby's outstretched microphone about his miraculous recovery under the healing hands of Elvis Aron Presley.

"You must be very proud, Mr. Presley. Or should I say, *Jesus* Presley?" Bobby said sardonically, thrusting his microphone in front of Elvis.

Elvis froze like a trapped beast. This was TV, darn it, the kind of TV story that went national faster than a train wreck in Appalachia. And the story could put a deadly hex on Elvis's career in about two minutes flat. Elvis could just hear the Colonel screaming at him: "*Now you've done it, son!* Calling yourself a holy man. *In one minute you've destroyed everything I created for you!*"

Little Timmy reached out and took Elvis's left hand in both of his, gawking up at him with worshipful eyes. Elvis trembled. *God help me, if I shake this poor child's faith, will he become a cripple again?* Elvis was trapped, all right.

Suddenly Digby Ferguson stumbled in front of the camera,

blocking out both Elvis and Timmy, then grabbed the microphone out of Bobby's hand.

"Jesus lives inside us all!" Ferguson declared in the sonorous tones of a Bible-belt preacher man. "He lives in Elvis, in this little boy here, and in you and me, brother. Oh, yes, Lord, his spirit dwells in you and me too. Say, 'Amen,' somebody."

The entire crowd of firemen, whores, holy rollers, and fire-truck chasers now surrounded him. Some mouths dropped open, but no one spoke. Even Bobby, the newsman, seemed stumped for words. And then a loud, bellowing, "Amen, brother!" It was the voice of Howie Pickles, who now stepped out of the crowd and took his place alongside Ferguson, doubling the screen in front of Elvis.

"Jesus is everybody! Everybody who's been saved!" came another voice. It was Kathy Lemon as she came up on the other side of Ferguson in her fluttering gown and long bare legs. "Believe me, friends, I know. For I am a sinner. A whore. That's right, just like the whore of Babylon. But Jesus does not discriminate. He's inside me too. Slipped his soul inside me so that I could see the light and find the way. Oh yes, I am Jesus too, my friends. We *all* are Jesus!"

"Amen!" Pickles said. Then another "Amen" echoed from the edge of the crowd. And another and another until "Amens" were popping off like firecrackers at a Fourth of July picnic.

Elvis disengaged his hand from Timmy's, patted the boy on top of his head, and stepped backward into the crowd. In less than a minute, he had slipped all the way back to Digby Ferguson's car where he jumped into the backseat and, slumped down low, waited for his friends to finish testifying.

It took longer than he expected. Elvis heard another woman follow Kathy with a few personal words about sin and redemption. Next, a man with a fine baritone sang, "What a Friend I Have in

Jesus." Peering over the car door, Elvis saw that it was one of the firemen. After that, Ferguson took over again in his most resonant voice with a free-associating homily that jumped from the gospel according to St. Mark to "Mary Had a Little Lamb" to a word-for-word recitation of his favorite Pogo comic strip. Elvis had to admit that there was even some kind of logic to it, a plea not to prejudge God's manifestations, to let Him take you by surprise. And the strangest part of all was that Elvis could not detect an ounce of irony in Ferguson's sermon.

Elvis saw Bobby retire to his van with his TV crew. The reporter looked seriously frustrated. What at first had seemed like a once-in-a-lifetime exposé had turned into a surreal revival meeting; the story had finally gone beyond the bounds of weirdness of even Las Vegas TV. But the deed was already done, thank God—Timmy's testimonial about Elvis curing him had been completely diluted by all the religious razzmatazz that followed it. It had virtually vanished into thin television air.

Moments later, that unlikely trinity, Digby, Howie, and Kathy, came strolling triumphantly toward the car with their arms around each other's waists. From the sweat on their brows and the smiles on their faces, you'd think they were headliners at the New Frontier Hotel coming offstage after their fifth encore. Hey, who knew these days? Maybe a drug-addled preacher, an insult comedian, and a prostitute with a college vocabulary all doing their rendition of a gospel service would turn out to be the latest thing in the world of entertainment. Next thing you know, they'd be on the *Ed Sullivan Show*. Heaven knows, Sullivan needed a follow-up to the Beatles.

Elvis saw Timmy and his parents, all three of them teary-eyed, following behind Digby. Elvis sat up straight and signaled Timmy's father to come up to the car.

"I owe you, King," the man said as he approached Elvis.

"Glad to hear you say that, Joby," Elvis said. "I don't want to take advantage, but I'd like to cash in that debt right about now. My friend here, Howie, needs to do some business with that fella you know—the Owl. And I want you to make the introductions."

Joby's face flushed. "But . . . I'm, you know, done with all that stuff, Elvis. Born again, like. Anyways, you don't want to get involved with a man like that."

"I thought you said you owed me, son," Elvis said evenly.

Joby glanced back furtively at his family. "I'll see what I can do, King," he whispered.

"Good. But keep my name out of it for now, okay?" Elvis waved Pickles over. "Howie? Joby, here, is going to set you up with the Owl for that contract you want. Maybe you two ought to exchange phone numbers or something."

Pickles looked from Joby to little Timmy, then patted the boy on the head.

"Bless you, my son," Pickles intoned solemnly with a tragi-comic smile.

18

Sting Operation

"*I*'ve been meaning to ask, Miss Kathy, how's your husband doing?" Elvis said when they were back in the car.

"He's okay, I guess," Miss Kathy replied. "They've got his jaw wired up so he looks like a homemade bomb. He's happy enough though. Nobody hassles him at the hospital for watching TV all day."

"Reality check!" Ferguson suddenly cheered, pointing to his right as they cruised down the Strip. "Did we just drift into the twilight zone? Or have I been gobbling too many red devils?"

"Both," Pickles chimed back.

Elvis looked out. They were approaching the Hacienda Hotel. A white van was double parked in front and streaming out of it were five figures who looked like spacemen in their white coveralls with washing-machine-window helmets. Several of them were waving fine-mesh nets on long poles as if they were some kind of alien lacrosse players.

A siren wailed behind the car and Ferguson slowed down to let an ambulance swing past, then he hit the brakes as the ambulance screeched to a halt directly in front of them. Instantly, the rear door of the ambulance swung open and a pair of emergency orderlies popped out, dragging wheeled stretchers behind them.

"I'm gettin' out," Elvis said, opening the car door. He had just seen the entire bunch—spacemen and orderlies—racing toward the Little Chapel of the West on the Hacienda campus.

Not much of a crowd had gathered here and Elvis immediately saw why: there were bees everywhere. Whole swarming squadrons of them buzzing so loud that they literally drowned out the traffic. The few tourists around the chapel's entrance had buttoned up tight and turned up their collars, some with handkerchiefs tied across the lower half of their faces making them look like leisure-wear bandits. None of them seemed to notice Elvis's arrival.

"War! It's a bloody war!" Reverend Sweetser wailed as he limped up to Elvis.

Heaven knows, the reverend looked like a battle casualty. Flaming-red welts were rising from his neck, cheeks, and upper lip. And judging by his listing gait, at least one enterprising bee had pierced the clergyman's vestments and stung him in the crotch.

"Where'd they come from?" Elvis said.

"Where do you think, cowboy? The Good Samaritans. They sent some clown over here with a whole hive of Mexican bees. They get real hungry down there, you know. This guy strolls right up to the altar while I'm in the middle of a holy sacrament, for crissake—pronouncing a couple man and wife—and he sets them loose. Buzz bombers! They go right for the groom's face. The bride is wearing a veil, so they go right for her décolletage. And then it's my turn."

As Sweetser spoke, Elvis watched the orderlies returning with their cargo. The stretchers rolled side by side, one bearing the groom in his rented-by-the-minute tux and his grotesquely swollen face, the other bearing the bride, her face still covered by her veil, but the exposed part of her bosom as lumpy as a sow's belly. Riding shotgun, flailing their nets to prevent the wedding couple from getting more bites, were three of the white-coveralled men.

"You recognized the guy? The guy who brought the bees?" Elvis asked.

"How could I? He was wearing one of those jobbies." Sweetser pointed at one of the bee-herders.

"So you actually don't know who he was or who sent him, do you?" Elvis said.

Reverend Sweetser scowled at Elvis—at least, it was probably meant to be a scowl, but working through the welts on his face it came out more ghoulish than scowly.

"I don't know why I even talk to you, Elvis," Sweetser said. "For some reason I got it into my head that even a rock and roll singer could be more effective than our sorry excuse for law enforcement around here, but I'm starting to wonder. Let me spell it out to you, okay? I'll talk real slowly."

"Just get to the point, Sweetser," Elvis said.

"Okay, the point is that little steeple incident. Right after that, the Good Samaritans lost about seventy-five percent of their business. To sentimental types, it just doesn't seem like a promising start to get married at the scene of a recent murder. And seventy-five percent is more than enough to put you out of business—especially considering there is an alternative chapel to get married in, namely, my humble establishment. At this point, my place is looking pretty good by comparison—I mean, I only had that billboard business out on the highway. So that calls for the Samaritans to come up with a counter-marketing strategy."

"Payback," Elvis said.

The welts on Sweetser's face rearranged themselves into what was probably intended as a cynical smile.

"You said it!" Sweetser said. "Obviously, their little sting operation was calculated to put us out of business. I mean, getting married is always risky, but if you add in a few hundred killer bees—especially on top of our unfortunate billboard display—we'll go bust faster than the Edsel. For starters, do you have any idea how much rent we have to pay to the Hacienda? It's run by Jews, you know."

"Not good Christians like yourself," Elvis said.

Sweetser eyed him suspiciously, apparently unsure if there was any sarcasm in Elvis's remark.

"So tell me, Reverend," Elvis went on. "Did you have anything to do with that 'little steeple incident'?"

"What kind of man do you take me for?" Sweetser snapped back.

Elvis decided not to answer that question.

"And what about now?" Elvis said. "Do you have plans for any counter-marketing of your own?"

The good reverend paused a moment. "I'm just going to pray for peace, Elvis," he said finally.

"Sounds like the Christian thing to do," Elvis said.

"And then I'm going to make those sons-of-bitches wish they'd never been born!" Sweetser snarled.

"Please, Reverend, this payback stuff has got to stop soon or—" But before Elvis could finish, a lone Mexican bee doubled back from the stretchers and made for one of Sweetser's eyes. Sweetser skillfully flicked it with the back of his hand, sending it directly to what had been Elvis's good eye. The insect selected a fleshy little spot between Elvis's brow and lid, then drilled down and injected its venom to complete its suicide mission.

Elvis yelped so loud that the tourists now spotted him and came swarming toward the king of rock and roll. He spun around and jogged in what he hoped was the direction of Digby's Olds. But, darn, it was hard to tell. The swelling of his left eye had already overtaken the swelling of his right, and gazing through the narrow slit that remained open was like looking at the world from inside a mailbox. He bounced off one tourist only to slam head-on into another, then spun around to collide with a fire hydrant. Suddenly, a hand gripped his right arm and began to guide him. He felt like an old lady being led across the street by a Boy Scout.

"Mr. Presley, I am beginning to think you are accident-prone," his guide said. It was Kathy Lemon.

Man, did Miss Kathy think that shiner her husband gave him was an accident too? For an instant, Elvis felt like shaking loose of the woman, but he was stumbling as it was, so he hung on until she deposited him in the front seat of Ferguson's car. The sting was really digging in deep now, his entire head throbbing. Digby slipped the car into gear and, pulling away, he suddenly began improvising a hymn called, "Jesus Is My Ventriloquist."

Looking out through the narrow slit of his right eye, Elvis saw Sweetser peering back at him. The good Christian minister was laughing so hard that tears tumbled down his swollen red face. It wasn't difficult to believe that he'd flicked that bee directly at Elvis's eye on purpose. In fact, it was difficult to believe otherwise.

At that moment, if Elvis's finger had been a pistol, a bullet would have shattered Sweetser's skull. Yes, at that moment, Elvis fully understood the lust for payback—how easily the craving of an eye for an eye slipped inside your soul.

19

Elvis Interruptus

$\mathscr{T}$he thing is, Miss Shiva, if all this payback don't stop, it'll just get worse. More folks dead or stung or burnt or whatever. On and on, like that war over there in Asia—it'll just keep escalating."

Elvis paced back and forth in front of his bed where Shiva Ree sat cloaked in a sheet. She had been waiting for Elvis when he returned, curled up on the bed as if she had never left early that morning.

"But how? How do you stop it, Elvis?" she asked softly.

Elvis paused a moment to switch the poultice Shiva had fashioned for him from his left eye to his right. The truth was, he didn't have an inkling of a plan for halting this cycle of madness. But with all this payback spinning out of control, he was absolutely certain that halting any future crimes before they started was far more important than figuring out how the whole business got started in the first place.

"I've got this vision that keeps coming back to me, Miss Shiva," Elvis went on, starting to pace again. "It's the first time I saw you doing your dance downstairs in the nightclub. At the very end, with you on all fours, eye to eye with Abu, all still and silent like. What I thought was, 'Now that's the peaceable kingdom. That's what all of mankind should be aiming for.' "

"You understood!" Shiva cried. "That makes me so happy."

"And I've got to say, when I visited you up there at your place, the Center of the Light, I thought the very same thing again," Elvis said. "Everybody being so natural and happy and gentle with each other. None of that friction you get everywhere else, especially around here. You know the kind I'm talking about—Who's winning? Who's making more money? Who's going to do in the other guy first?"

Shiva jumped up from the bed, the sheet falling away. She was naked. She ran up to Elvis and threw her arms around him.

"God love you, Elvis," she said. "You understand everything!"

Elvis could have stopped his thinking right then and there, and just tumbled back into the bed with this wise and delicious woman. But he needed to work this thing through.

"I understand everything but that godawful food you eat up there," he laughed. He kissed Shiva and she returned to the bed.

"So how do you get these people to go from here to there— from killing each other to acting peaceable with each other?" Elvis went on. He paused again, shaking his head back and forth. "Heck, I bet wiser heads than mine have been wondering about that question since the beginning of time."

"Somebody just has to teach them," Shiva said softly. "Teach them that they will all be happier loving than killing. Happier and more fulfilled in every way. It's a simple lesson, really."

"Maybe it's simple, but most folks don't get it," Elvis said.

"Of course not. That's because they need to hear it from the right person," Shiva said. "Somebody who puts it in a way that reaches way down inside them so they can *feel* its truth. It's all wrapped up together, the lesson and the teacher. Just like the dancer and the dance, and the singer and the song. One person can sing a song and folks just don't get it. But then along comes somebody new with the very same song and the song just clicks. It gets people thinking and feeling in a whole different way. You know, like 'Mystery Train.' "

There was truth in that. When Sam Phillips had given Elvis "Mystery Train" back in Sun Studios, it had already been recorded by Little Junior Parker and the Blue Flames, but nothing had come of it. Junior had a great voice, but he just hadn't gotten inside that song the way Elvis and Scotty and Bill had.

Elvis looked over at Shiva. She was sitting cross-legged with her hands pressed together in front of her in that prayerful way. Her dark eyes sparkled out at him; she was smiling like an angel. Good Lord, she was a beautiful thing to behold.

Suddenly a shiver shot up Elvis's spine.

"Not me!" he blurted out. "No way, not me, Miss Shiva! I'm no teacher! Just a rock and roll singer, that's all!"

Shiva Ree kept smiling at him angelically.

"Listen, woman," Elvis went on, talking fast and loud, "I've got enough problem with these born-again types who think I've got healing hands. That's one blasphemy too many for me. I can't go running around preaching peace like I'm some kind of righteous mouthpiece. Because that's *not* who I am! And it would be a sin to act like I was!"

"A sin?" Shiva said softly. "A sin to get people to stop killing each other?"

"I'm just not the right man for the job!" Elvis roared.

Man, why was he getting so riled up at Shiva? She had barely said a word. Even now, she just sat there silently looking up at him with those innocent eyes of hers.

Elvis stepped to her, leaned down, and kissed the top of her head. "I'm . . . I'm sorry, darlin'. It just gets to me, all this stuff. Makes me sad and frustrated at the same time."

"I understand," Shiva whispered. "You shouldn't do anything you don't feel right about."

Elvis nodded. She was surely right about that. He should just put the whole thing out of his mind. And probably the best way to do that would be to get out of these darned clothes and dive right onto that bed with her.

"Anyhow, I'm no preacher man or anything like that," he murmured.

"No," Shiva said softly. "You're just a singer with a special gift. A God-given gift to send a song directly into people's hearts."

Elvis eyed her a moment, then started pacing again. "How the heck do you sing folks into stopping hurting each other anyhow?"

"I don't know," Shiva said. "Maybe you start by just getting them all together in the same place. And then getting them into a mood of gladness. Maybe even get them dancing together. You'd be surprised how much peace would come of that, Elvis."

"You'll pardon my saying so, Miss Shiva, but that sounds like a dream. A fetching dream, but a dream just the same."

"Could be," Shiva said. "But that folk singer, Joan Baez, seems to think it's real enough. She's been giving one peace concert after another."

A PR man over at RCA had told Elvis about Baez and her folksinging boyfriend, Bobby-something. But the PR guy had said they were a flash in the pan, that folksinging didn't stand a chance against rock 'n' roll. Of course, that was the same PR guy who had scoffed at the idea of a British pop group making it in the U.S.A.

Elvis kept pacing. "I already bombed in this town once, you know," he said.

"That was then, this is now," Shiva said. "Back then, at the New Frontier, you were singing for Colonel Parker, not for yourself. Not for peace. That's all the difference in the world."

Elvis had to smile. For somebody who didn't listen to radio or watch TV, Shiva knew a lot more about his career than he would have expected.

"So I do a special gig for all these angry people? Sing a few songs and see if I can get them talking to each other," Elvis mused out loud.

"All you can do is try," Shiva murmured. "With all this awfulness going on, just about anything's worth a try, isn't it?"

Elvis stiffened. The last time somebody said, "It's worth a try," he'd ended up laying hands on little Timmy. That was one dangerous path to go down.

"I, for one, would be very thankful and proud of you, Elvis," Shiva said.

Elvis stood still for a long moment. Then he burst out laughing. "What in the world are we talking about, woman? I couldn't put together a birthday party on my own, let alone something like this. And I'm sure as heck not going to ask the Colonel to do it for me."

"We could help," Shiva said.

"*We?*"

"You know, my friends at the Center. We could set it up for you. All you'd have to do is sing and maybe talk some sense to these people."

Elvis smiled. "That's mighty nice of you to offer, Miss Shiva. And no offense, but I think there's a lot more to organizing something like this than you think."

"You mean, it's not something a bunch of dropouts could do," Shiva said, laughing.

"Well, it's not exactly the same as growing blue corn in the desert," Elvis said, laughing with her.

"I know that, Elvis," Shiva said, abruptly earnest again. "But you see, before we came to the Center, some of us had experience putting on shows and things like that. Like Manovah—you know, the girl with the stew? She was a producer for the Sahara. That's how I got my job in the floorshow—she hired me. Then later, I brought her out to the Center and she just stayed."

"You're kidding." Elvis had been convinced that Manovah was nothing more than a teenage runaway. What made a person go from producing floorshows at the Sahara Hotel to cooking porridge on a commune?

"And Mufah, the man who led you into the Center?" Shiva went on. "He was head roadie for the Everly Brothers. A whole bunch of them were roadies and musicians and producers. Like Glomarah was a producer at MGM."

"Really? I've done a few pictures over there and I never heard about any Glomarah," Elvis said skeptically.

"That wasn't his name then." Shiva laughed. "Glomarah was called Phil Goldwyn in his former life. Nephew of Samuel Goldwyn. You know, the movie guy?"

"Yeh, the movie guy." Elvis looked critically into Shiva's eyes. "And how about *you*, Shiva? What did you do in your former life?"

Shiva looked down shyly. "Nothing much. I was just a kindergarten teacher. I was a dance major in college, but when my husband died—well, I needed to get a steady job to support Kali, our daughter. My name back then was Shirley—Shirley Lee."

This piece of news—including Shiva's ordinary, hometown name—made Elvis feel happier than he would have guessed it would. To be honest with himself, he'd pegged all those commune kids as losers in the outside world. Losers who had dropped out because they were unfit to do anything else, *not* because they wanted to do something more meaningful with their lives. And somewhere in the back of his mind he'd even supposed that Miss Shiva was some wild young thing who didn't even know who the father of her child was. Elvis felt real ashamed of himself.

"You really think they'd want to help?" he asked.

"I don't know, but I hope so," Shiva said. "It's easy to never want to leave our little paradise. But I think they'll see how important this is. They all believe in the same thing we do—about getting people to stop all their fighting and just come together peacefully." She held her arms out toward Elvis. "You know, to make love, not war."

Elvis dropped right down on his knees in front of Shiva and let her long arms fold around him, drawing his face against her naked young bosom. Oh Lord, *this* was paradise. What man in his right mind would trade even a moment of this to spite another?

"You are a wonderful, generous man, my friend," Shiva whispered. "And I am so very proud of you."

Suddenly, the hotel room door swung open.

"Oopsy-doopsy!" Kathy Lemon laughed, stepping inside. "Looks like we've switched places, Elvis. Last time you caught *me* in mid-tumble!"

"Elvis interruptus," Pickles piped up, just behind her.

Elvis pulled back his head, yanking up the sheet to cover Shiva, but not before Kathy Lemon could give Shiva's body an envious glance.

"Damnation!" Elvis hollered. "Couldn't you knock?"

"That's just what my trick said too," Miss Kathy said blithely.

Elvis felt like slapping the motor-mouthed whore right across her smirking face. Man, this turning-the-other-cheek business had to be one of the toughest lessons in the world. It went against every natural impulse in your being.

"It's all set, boss," Howie Pickles said, putting an arm around Miss Kathy. For some reason, the comic was doing a vocal imitation of Jimmy Cagney. "I'm meeting the Owl in an hour. Just came by for last-minute instructions."

Still on his knees, Elvis stared blankly back at Pickles. He'd almost forgotten about the Owl.

"The Owl?" Shiva asked softly. "Isn't that the man you chased after? The man who shot that dummy?"

Elvis nodded. He stood up.

"But that part's over, isn't it?" Shiva said. "I mean, you've got more important things to do now, don't you, Elvis?"

Elvis nodded again, but he couldn't help asking Howie, "Where are you going to meet him?"

"Out in the desert," Pickles replied. "Exactly seven-point-six miles east of the intersection on Route Five-fifteen."

"You going alone?" Elvis asked. He was trying hard to ignore Shiva's disapproving eyes just below him.

"Only Joby," Pickles said, dropping the Cagney impression. "You know, to make the introductions. To vouch for me."

"That's the part that worries me," Kathy said, clutching Howie's arm. "It doesn't sound safe, does it?"

"Of course, it's not safe!" Shiva cried. She jumped off the bed, letting the sheet drop away, and stood in the middle of the hotel room stark naked. If Shiva was trying to get everybody's attention, she had certainly hit on an apt technique.

Elvis blushed, embarrassed and angry in equal parts. It was one thing to walk around in your birthday suit up there at the Center of the Light, but it was altogether something else to bare it all to a bunch of strangers in a Las Vegas hotel room. Especially just after the two of them had been so intimate. Elvis picked up the sheet, held it wide, and started for Shiva like somebody's mamma holding out a beach towel at the seashore. But as soon as he got close, Shiva stepped back from him. Both Elvis's embarrassment and his anger racheted up about a hundred notches.

"Don't you see, friends?" Shiva pleaded. "You don't want to do business with some hit man. It'll just end in more murder. We've got to break this cycle of blame and recrimination." She looked beseechingly at Elvis. "Isn't that so, Elvis?"

All eyes were on Elvis now—that is, all except Ferguson's; he couldn't stop marveling at Shiva's perfect young body. That alone was enough to put Elvis's exasperation right over the top.

"You'd best stay out of this, Miss Shiva!" Elvis said. "There are some things you don't understand. We need to ask this Owl fella some important questions."

Shiva stared back at Elvis, tears filling her almond eyes, and then she spun around, raced into the bathroom, and slammed the door shut behind her.

Elvis felt his heart shrivel up in his chest until it was no bigger than a bee.

20

A Contract Suicide

Elvis rode in the back of Digby's car, Digby driving, Kathy Lemon beside him. A hundred yards ahead of them was a Plymouth station wagon, the model that sported genuine oak on its sides. Joby was at the wheel of that car with Howie Pickles in the passenger seat. The station wagon was the Lemon family car, usually employed to ferry Cindy Lemon back and forth to kindergarten, to shop for groceries, and to take Cindy's mom to her night job—that is, before the company plant had burned down.

Elvis had cashed a personal check for five thousand dollars at the Sahara casino. A piddling transaction by casino standards but, according to Joby, five thousand was the Owl's going rate for a contract murder. That meant that the value of a man's life in Las Vegas was roughly equivalent to a couple hours of a high roller's wagers at the roulette table. Joby had also said that he figured five thousand should be more than enough to buy the names of the Owl's most recent clients. The cash was now in Pickles's pocket.

The plan was for Elvis's group to park on the highway a quarter of a mile before the designated meeting point of the Owl with

Howie and Joby. It was dusk and their lights were off. Elvis figured they could then get close enough by foot to keep an eye on the Owl without being spotted themselves. It didn't give them much of an advantage if anything went wrong, but it was the only option Elvis could come up with. Kathy was particularly apprehensive. She kept saying that a hit man was more likely to kill Howie and steal the five thousand dollars than risk bartering his clients' names for the money. But Elvis figured that if the Owl didn't want to deal, he'd just walk away. That Kathy Lemon was a real worrier. Heaven knows, Howie Pickles brought out her maternal instincts.

Elvis had to strain to stay focussed on the venture. Looking out the car window at the evening sun-streaked desert, he kept flashing on Shiva's eyes as they burst into tears when he'd rebuked her. It was heartbreaking. He knew in his heart that it was just pride and prudery that had made him snap at her like that. Still, it wouldn't make sense to pass up an opportunity to question the Owl. It could get right to the core of this case—wrap it up in one five-thousand-dollar conversation. And that "peace concert"— well, maybe that was just one of those ideas that sounded more promising inside a bedroom with a beautiful woman than out in the open air.

"Seven-point-two miles. That's us," Ferguson said, pulling the Olds onto the side of the road. For a man with a drug-soaked brain, he certainly was precise with numbers.

The road ahead of them was perfectly flat and straight, so they could just make out the station wagon's brake lights as it, too, came to a halt a quarter of a mile ahead of them. No other car in sight. Now, they couldn't see anything. Too far, too dark.

Elvis and Kathy immediately hopped out of the Olds. They had taken a couple of sand-sinking steps before Elvis realized that Ferguson was lingering behind them. Turning around, Elvis saw him rummaging through his kit bag and spreading the contents on the hood of his car as if he were setting up a roadside tag sale. He selected a notebook, a pen, his camera, and a pair of binoculars, then stuffed the rest back into his bag and came trotting up beside Elvis.

"I'm calling this chapter, 'The Owl and the Pussycat.' " Ferguson laughed as he handed Elvis the binoculars.

That was when all three of them saw the headlights of an oncoming car in the distance. The lights shone on the station wagon, then pulled up to it, nose-to-nose, and stopped. Elvis put the binoculars to his eyes. Just as the headlights flickered out, he saw a man jump out on the passenger side. He was heavyset, wore a night watch cap, and had something covering the lower part of his face—definitely not the Owl. The man was carrying something long and metallic in both hands. A rifle.

"My Howie!" Kathy whimpered.

Elvis darted back onto the road and started to run straight ahead. *God spare him*, Elvis prayed inside his head. *He's just a crazy comedian trying to do something decent for the first time in his life. Spare him, Lord, please!*

Elvis heard a yell. Then he saw the rifle fire, saw it flash a full second before he heard the report of the explosion. Then a second shot. Both shots echoed over and over again, bouncing from distant hill to distant hill. Seconds later, Elvis heard car doors slamming, an engine gunning, and then he saw those headlights again, shining on the station wagon, then swinging away and disappearing as the car sped back to where it came from.

Elvis was sprinting as fast as he could. When he got close to the Plymouth, he cut back onto the sand where he immediately skidded, falling to one knee. One second and he was up again, tossing off the binoculars, loping like a wildcat.

Barely any light now. With both his eyes still swollen, Elvis was virtually running blind in the empty desert landscape, his arms flailing in the warm night air to help him keep his balance. No sight, no sound, not even the scent of anything out here—just pure weightless motion. For one dazzling moment, Elvis saw himself in his mind's eye—a swirling white tornado, the runner and the running indivisible.

No more than ten feet ahead of him, he saw them—two shadowy figures on their knees, utterly motionless. Elvis's heart thumped, breaking his trance. He had seen photographs in newspapers exactly like this: men on their knees, begging for mercy, a bullet through their temples. Gangland executions.

Then he heard voices: "Oh Lord, we are but humble men who come before you asking your forgiveness . . ."

Elvis skidded to a stop. He stood still a moment, catching his breath, then slowly circled around to the front of the kneeling men. It was Howie and Joby, both very much alive. They were praying together.

Staring at them, Elvis let loose with a great booming laugh of relief. Both men kept praying for several seconds, then Pickles began to laugh too, leaving Joby to worship on alone. Elvis reached out to help Howie onto his feet. The comedian's hands were cold and clammy.

"Geez, and I'd just gotten the bastard down to four thousand," Pickles cracked, gesturing to his left.

There, lying on his back with his legs splayed and his arms spread wide like a child making a sand angel, was the Owl. Even in this dim light, Elvis could see where the bullet had entered his right cheek and exited through the top of his head. But that was it. What blood had escaped the wound must have already seeped into the sand.

Elvis stepped over to the corpse. The Owl's outsized glasses lay completely unscathed a couple of feet away from his head, looking like a starlet's sunglasses left on the beach while she took a swim. And bundled up in the Owl's outstretched right hand was a wad of bills—fresh, crisp one-hundred-dollar bills straight from the Sahara's till.

"We'd just shaken on it," Howie said behind Elvis. "Four thousand for the name of his client on the fat-lady job. He insisted on counting the money first. Had to bring the bills right up next to those nasty glasses of his. And then—bang! bang!—he's flat on his back."

"I thought maybe you shot him, Elvis," Joby said. He had apparently finished his prayers and was now on his feet. "Not that I'd ever question anything you did, King. You know things I can't begin to understand."

"Did you see him? The man who shot the Owl?" Elvis asked.

"Just for a second," Howie said. "The Owl looked at him like he knew him. He even shouted to him. Said something about picking him up too early. Then the guy fired off two shots—he missed with the first. And then he ran back to the car."

"He ran kind of clumsy," Joby said. "Like a girl."

"Anybody with him?" Elvis asked.

"Not that I saw," Joby said.

"Me neither," Howie said. "But I saw his car. Big old Hudson like my Uncle Izzy used to drive."

"So he never got it out of his mouth," Elvis said. "The name. His client's name."

"No," Pickles said. "That means we can take our money back, right?"

"That's probably what they wanted—whoever shot him. To keep him from revealing that name," Elvis said.

"Serendipity-doo!" Ferguson sang as he and Miss Kathy ambled up behind them. Digby was holding a spent gun shell between his thumb and forefinger. "Twenty-two gauge," he said. "Looks like a contract suicide to me, boss." He snapped a Polaroid of the dead man.

When Howie Pickles counted out the fifty hundred-dollar bills and held them out to Elvis, Elvis shrugged. He couldn't take the money back. It felt dirty. The whole deal felt dirty. Because Shiva had been right—dead right. Trying to deal with the hit man had just brought on one more murder. It had just kept the war cycle spinning.

"Keep it," Elvis mumbled to Pickles. "You're out of work."

"But—"

"Take Miss Kathy out to dinner," Elvis said.

"For five thousand dollars?"

"Leave a big tip," Elvis said.

Elvis left Howie, Kathy, and Joby at the station wagon, then walked back to the Olds with Ferguson.

"Where to, Kimosabe?" Ferguson said, getting behind the wheel.

"The Sahara," Elvis said. It was just a few minutes past nine. Shiva would be arriving soon for the ten o'clock show. He needed to see her, to beg her forgiveness. That is, if she hadn't given up on him already.

"Ain't love grand?" Ferguson said, as they sped off.

Elvis looked over at him with his new bee-built squint. What the heck did Digby know about love and its complications? The man lived in a solo world.

"I'm calling this chapter, 'The Comedian and the Whore, a Love Story,' " Ferguson went on. "I tell you, Elvis, this book is writing itself."

"That so?" Elvis said, relieved that at least Ferguson wasn't talking about his and Miss Shiva's love story. "What made you decide to become a writer anyway, Digby? I thought you were on a spiritual search."

"Not when I can help it," Ferguson replied. "Turns out the spiritual search is even worse for your health than religion itself. Gives you indigestion. So I'm weaning myself from it with facts. *Worldly* facts. Exact opposite of chasing spiritual rainbows. And what could be better for keeping my nose to the ground than a true crime story?"

"If you've got indigestion, I bet it's those drugs you take, Digby," Elvis said.

"But the drugs *are* the search!" Digby said, wagging his head. "I don't think you've been paying attention, Elvis."

"I'm paying attention, all right, Digby," Elvis said. "But those drugs sound more like hiding than searching."

They were still a good three blocks away when they saw crowds thronging toward the Sahara. Good news for de Luca, Elvis figured. His little shoot-up at the Sands was already paying off in return customers, even if only a ventriloquist's dummy had caught a bullet. From payback to paying customers—that was still the name of the game.

But as they cruised closer, Elvis saw sawhorses cordoning off the hotel's entrance. And none other than Sheriff Turtleff was standing with a bullhorn just behind them. Ferguson pulled to a halt across the street from the Sahara, leaving his car double parked at a cab stand. Both men got out.

"Stand clear, please, ladies and gentlemen," Turtleff was announcing through the bullhorn. "Give my men room. If there's a bomb, they'll sniff it out."

Turtleff's men were apparently the five figures in white coveralls, all gripping German shepherds on short leads, who were now filing toward the hotel. The bomb squad looked remarkably like the bee-patrol—in fact, their white spaceman outfits were virtually identical. Probably because they *were* identical, Elvis thought.

Digby was already plucking the story from people in the crowd, and Elvis, following behind him with his head hunched low to avoid recognition, was able to piece it together pretty fast. Indeed, business *had* been picking up again at the Sahara; the casino was three-quarters full by nine. But then a phone call had come in declaring that a bomb was set to go off in the casino in ten minutes. Apparently, Luke de Luca had frittered away five of those ten minutes calculating the cost-effectiveness of going public with the news: on the one hand, if there was no bomb, he'd be losing a heck of a lot of customers for nothing; on the other hand, if there *was* a bomb, he'd be losing a heck of a lot of customers for eternity. Only in Las Vegas would a decision like that be a close call.

Elvis scanned the crowd looking for Shiva. To Turtleff's right, he saw the holy roller crew looking particularly self-righteous this evening. They were always where the action was, and sinful goings-on like a bomb threat seemed to really perk them up. Fronting this group, like Little Junior Parker with the Blue Flames towering behind him, was little Timmy, the born-again walker-and-talker. Once again, he seemed to be making up for his years of muteness by jabbering away, gesticulating animatedly, virtually dancing on his tiny feet.

On Turtleff's left, Elvis spotted some troupers from the floor-show—a couple of chorus girls, including the six-foot redhead he had passed up a couple of days ago, and the bony-faced crooner. But no Shiva. Elvis edged through the crowd until he was in front of them.

"Have you seen Shiva Ree?" he asked the skinny singer.

The young man shrugged.

"Lose your girlfriend again, Elvis?" the redhead chirped. She was once again wearing her feather headdress and gold pumps, but this time in between was a trench coat with enough buttons undone to leave no doubt that the coat was all that separated her pinkness from the night air.

Elvis nodded.

"She went back up to Camp Loads-o'-Fun," the chorus girl said. "I, on the other hand, am right *here*, Elvis."

"I noticed that right off, ma'am," Elvis said. "Thank you."

He doubled back through the crowd, grabbing Ferguson by the arm along the way. "I need a lift up to Indian Springs," Elvis said.

That's when the bomb went off and all the screaming and racing for cover began.

It wasn't a huge explosion, but it was enough to blow out all the windows at the far end of the Sahara—the night club. Elvis just stared at it, more sad than scared. He was probably the first to see Luke de Luca come running out of the building with his hair looking fried to a crisp.

"It's war!" de Luca was hollering. "All out war!"

Part 2
The Temptation

21

All God's Children

*N*either man talked much on the trip up to the Center of the Light. At one point, Ferguson abruptly began reciting the Sermon on the Mount in a singsong voice. Elvis had to wonder what it would be like to live inside Digby's head. His mind seemed to operate like a pinball machine, thoughts bouncing willy-nilly without sense or pattern. And yet that homily of his about the Lord sneaking up on you when you least expected had a certain poignancy to it. Maybe Digby had lost the melody of his calling, but he still knew the words.

Mufah, the Everly Brothers roadie-turned-communik, was standing guard alone at the Center's entrance as the Olds pulled up. "We've been expecting you, Elvis," he said.

"If you don't mind, I'll wait for you out here," Digby said to Elvis. "I don't mix well with young people."

Elvis smiled. In truth, he'd been debating how to keep Ferguson from coming along inside without hurting his feelings; maybe Digby was more sensitive than Elvis gave him credit for. Elvis took off his shoes, got out of the car, and headed for the gate. "I can find my own way," he said.

"You're a beautiful man, Elvis," Mufah murmured, unlocking the gate for him. "And you are doing the righteous thing."

Elvis didn't reply. He wasn't sure yet what he was doing, let alone if it was righteous or not.

Emerging onto the moonlit mountain clearing, Elvis felt like he had stepped into one of those old Italian paintings he'd seen in a book at Selma's apartment. It looked like a place that existed somewhere between heaven and Earth, between nature and eternity. An open fire blazed in front of the glacial pond, its flames reflected as star-like fragments on the pond's rippling surface. And in a semicircle around the fire, about fifty men, women, and children—undoubtedly the entire population of the Center of the Light—sat cross-legged. They were all wearing some kind of loose-fitting gowns that skirted out where they met the ground, one overlapping the other so that it looked as if they were all wearing a single silky garment.

A hum rose up from them—a haunting, minor-key sound, part wail, part hymn. It seemed to have words in a foreign language: *"Om/Shanti/Om/Shanti,"* over and over again. Elvis stood very still, watching, listening. The hum resonated deep inside him, echoing in his head, pulsing in his heart. It felt somehow connected to that *prana* feeling—a warm glow throbbing up his spine, white light showering his brain.

Then, as if an invisible signal had passed between them, the entire group rose to its feet and faced Elvis—still chanting, the whites of their wide-open eyes a luminous, otherworldly blue in the moonlight. One of them separated from the others and began to walk slowly toward Elvis. It was Shiva. Her eyes shone, her full lips separated in a smile that was a kiss itself. There was no question of asking her forgiveness. She walked to Elvis in total acceptance.

She took his arm, leading him back to the group in a slow processional as if they were bride and groom. Yes, that is exactly the way it felt and Elvis did not feel an ounce of resistance to it. This must be what the very first wedding ceremony had felt like, a coming together before God and the community—simple, silent, holy—in that long-ago time before organized religion and law had complicated the ceremony and numbed the participants to its original meaning.

Shiva brought them to the front, facing the fire, then spiraled down to the ground and sat cross-legged. Elvis followed as best he could, managing to cross one of his legs, but extending the other straight out for balance. The chanting had never stopped and now Elvis closed his eyes and joined in, *"Om/Shanti/Om/Shanti."* His own voice melded with the others, disappeared inside the haunting hum. At that moment, he felt freer than he could remember feeling in a very long time: he felt liberated from the loneliness of the solo. Still, just when his mind would be about to empty, the way that yogi said it should, stray thoughts bumped in. Like he found himself wondering how the Jordanaires would do this number. A little gospel harmony could lift this chant up to a whole new level.

Elvis had no idea how long they sat and chanted together. It felt like a few minutes. It felt like an entire night. When they finished, they all sat quietly for a moment. Then, one of the children, a shaggy-haired boy of ten or so, stood and smiled at everyone.

"I was wondering how we can help," the boy said. "You know, the kids?"

A ripple of sweet laughter passed through the group and then an older woman with frizzy gray hair and a narrow face stood up.

"I bet you kids could help putting up the posters, don't you think?" she said. "And then, at the celebration itself, I see the children getting the dancing started. I don't know about anybody else, but when I see kids dancing, I just *have* to join in. Can't stop myself, you know?"

Another wave of laughter swept through the group. Elvis saw Shiva's daughter, Kali, sitting with the other children. She waved at Elvis and he waved back.

A man near the rear of the assembly stood. It was Tzar, Shiva's accompanist. The laughter stopped completely. Utter silence but for the water lapping in the pond. Elvis looked up at Tzar: amazing eyes on that fella; they seemed to generate a light of their own.

"We need to find a good name for it, my friends," Tzar said softly. "At the beginning of everything is the Word."

More silence. Elvis thought some of the faces looked like they were starting to lose their tranquility, a bit of apprehension creeping in. Suddenly, a teenage girl with waist-length hair stood, smiled, and said, "I don't know, Tzar—How about, 'The Cool-It Conference'?"

The boy next to her giggled. "Come on, Chia! That sounds like a convention of refrigerator salesmen!"

This got a big laugh, including from Elvis.

But then Elvis stopped cold. *Man, how dumb could you get? They're talking about the peace concert!* His *peace concert! The one he and Shiva dreamed up in the privacy of his room just a couple hours ago. But, by golly, it was public knowledge now— at least out here. And that didn't sit right. No, sir, that didn't sit right at all.*

Suddenly, Shiva rose to her feet. The hurt in her face was plain to see, even in the moonlight. She seemed to struggle to get herself to speak.

"I feel really bad right now," Shiva said, finally. "We have treated a friend with disrespect and I am the worst offender. I betrayed a confidence." She looked down at Elvis ruefully. "I hope you can forgive me, Elvis," she said.

"It's my fault, Elvis!" The frizzy-haired woman called out as she got back to her feet. "My Lord, Shiva was so excited when she came back this evening. We just knew something was going on. So we pestered her and pestered her until we finally got it out of her."

"That's no excuse," Shiva said.

"I think it is," Elvis said. For heaven's sake, he'd come out here tonight to ask Shiva's forgiveness for a lot worse than this.

"Thank you, Elvis," Shiva said softly, still standing. "But from now on, every decision about this—even the little ones—have to be okay with you. And that includes whether you even still want to do this or not."

Elvis didn't have to think long. "I do," he said solemnly.

For some reason, the sound of those two little words made him grin. And then that grin turned into a chortle that immediately infected them all. They all laughed a while before another person stood up. It was Manovah, the pock-marked floorshow producer who had traded in her job for a life of simplicity and porridge.

"I had one idea for a name," she said. "How about 'The Don't Be Cruel Concert'?"

Murmurs of approval radiated out through the group. Another woman stood.

"I like it a lot," she said. "It's catchy. It says 'Elvis.' And at the same time, it's what we're all about. You know, laying down our hatreds and fears and just coming together as one big family."

"What do you think, Elvis?" Manovah asked.

"Sounds good to me," Elvis said. "But, you know, the thing I wonder about is how we are going to get the key people to come. Like Luke de Luca *and* Sol Epstein. Those two are at war with each other. A genuine war, complete with bombs. Same with Reverend Sweetser and the Good Samaritan folk. And that Bambi woman and what's-his-name from the Pink Palace. How the heck are you going to get them to come to the same place at the same time? If one comes, the other will stay away. Either that or he'll come to the peace concert at the head of an army."

A man about Elvis's age stood up. "I'll tell you how—you make it like a Hollywood dinner party," he announced, smiling. "You know, where everybody wants to get on the 'A' list. And if they don't, they just die of mortification."

A good round of laughter at this.

"So what we do is send out a personal invitation to de Luca," the man went on. "Special guest, front row seat—the whole 'A' list *schmooze*. Next thing you know, Epstein is miffed. Mighty miffed. 'Why didn't Elvis invite me?' We give Epstein a day to stew and then send out his personal invitation. He's thrilled. He's got to say yes. He's going to show the whole world what a fine gentleman and close personal friend of Elvis Presley he is."

"And maybe we could sweeten it by putting out the rumor that Elvis is thinking about doing more of these concerts," the frizzy-haired woman said. "You know, and that he might just choose to do the next one in one of their establishments. That is, if he takes a liking to them. They'll be climbing all over each other to be there."

"No!" Shiva exclaimed. "There is no way Elvis is even going to hint that he'll be doing any more shows. And certainly not in some heathen wedding chapel. Or in a *brothel*!"

Elvis smiled. That Shiva sure did have a passionate streak in her. He liked that—he liked it a lot. "Thank you, Miss Shiva," he said. "But you know, old Leadbelly used to sing in brothels and it didn't seem to hurt him none."

Elvis had no idea what made him say that. All he knew was that at this moment, sitting outdoors under the moon, he was feeling as buoyant and carefree as in the old days when he would sit with Scotty on his front porch, picking and strumming and dreaming out loud about singing their way across America.

"You are so generous, my friend," Shiva said for all to hear. "But you are much too good to perform for just anybody."

Elvis slowly stood. "I don't know, Miss Shiva," he said. "One thing you all got me thinking here is that maybe no one person is too good for anything. Or for any*body*. We're all God's children, for heaven's sake. And we've all got pretty much the same job to do, right? The job of keeping this world of ours spinning around as smoothly as possible. Smoothly and peacefully."

The entire assembly went completely silent as Elvis spoke and they remained that way for several minutes after he finished. They were all looking up at Elvis in a way that made him feel proud and uncomfortable at the same time. Something in their eyes was the uncomfortable part: it reminded him of the way those holy roller types gawked at him.

"Well, there's not much you can say after that," Tzar said finally. "Except—*Let's eat!*"

That night, Elvis and Shiva made love inside her tent. No back-walking this time. And no holding back either. Just pure, passionate lovemaking that went on until dawn. It was only then, when Elvis was finally drifting off to sleep, that he pictured Digby Ferguson waiting for him at the gate. Digby was probably reciting the entire gospel according to St. Mark to Mufah. Elvis smiled and fell asleep.

165

22

Soulful Solo Singer

"You sound different this morning, Mr. P.," Billy said, a smile in his voice. "Not like yesterday's troubled man."

" '*Yesterday's Troubled Man*,' " Elvis echoed, smiling himself. "How come everything that comes out of your mouth sounds like a gospel hymn?"

"It's my mamma's fault," Billy said. "When everybody else's mamma was reading them *Little Red Riding Hood*, mine was singing me to sleep with 'The Church in the Wildwood.' "

"Well, I *am* happy today, Doctor Billy," Elvis said into the phone. When Digby had dropped Elvis off at the Sahara that morning, there had been a note at the hotel desk saying that a Dr. William Jackson had phoned. Elvis called back the moment he got to his room. "You know how I always said I'd never meet a woman sweet as Selma ever again?"

"That I do, Mr. P."

"Well, I think I just did."

"Out there in Vegas?"

"Yes, but it's not what you might think," Elvis said. "She's not some honky-tonk showgirl. She's a woman with a solid-gold soul. And wisdom too, just like Selma."

"I am happy to hear that, brother," Billy said. "I hope it's not causing you any complications."

With Priscilla or Ann-Margret, Billy meant, and Elvis realized that he hadn't had a single thought about either of those two women in days. He also realized that he wanted to leave it that way.

"Nope, no complications," Elvis said quickly. "And there's something else I'm feeling real good about too, Billy. Real good and excited."

Elvis hesitated. Billy would be the first person outside of the Center to hear about the Don't Be Cruel Concert and Elvis was eager to see what his friend thought of the idea. *Anxious*, actually; Billy's opinion counted for a whole lot. In order not to complicate Billy's reaction, Elvis had decided not to say anything about what kind of faith healer he'd turned out to be. That Timmy thing was just a fluke anyhow, right?

"I'm throwing a peace concert out here, Billy," Elvis began. "Now that sounds crazy, I know, but listen. . . ."

After Elvis finished, there was a long pause before Billy said anything. "You sure are one of a kind, Mr. P.," Billy said finally.

"You think it sounds foolish, don't you?" Elvis said.

"New ideas always sound foolish," Billy said. "That's how you can tell they're new. And God knows any idea about peace and love sounds foolish in today's world. Now that's a sad commentary, isn't it?"

"So you think I should go through with it?"

"I don't see how it could hurt," Billy said, but Elvis could hear the hesitancy in his friend's voice.

"What does your gut tell you, Billy?" Elvis said. "You can tell me."

"I'm getting old, Mr. P.," Billy said. "And an old man's got an old man's gut. All twisted up and a little weak in the center."

"What does it say, Billy?"

"It says a great deal of good can come of this, Mr. P. It surely says that. But it also says to keep your eyes open, friend." Billy paused a moment. "You know those hooded robes the Ku Klux Klan wears down here?"

"Yes, sir."

"Well, those are the very same robes that Christian monks in Spain wear. Yup, genuine Christian holy men over there in Spain."

"I see," Elvis said, although he had to admit that he didn't.

"Now, listen, Mr. P.," Billy went on quickly. "I've got that info you asked for."

For a moment, Elvis could not remember exactly what he had asked Billy to find out for him. "Go ahead," Elvis said.

"Well, one part turned out to be pretty easy," Billy said. "Not that many Hudsons registered in the state of Georgia, pale blue or otherwise. Too wide for the country roads down there. And there's only one of them whose license starts with the numbers one-three-six. Registered to a man named Timothy Riley, Jr., in Macon. Riley's a savings-and-loan officer out there. But he doesn't drive it because he gave it to his daughter, Melissa, when she graduated from college. And Melissa left the state several years back."

"Know where she left for?"

"Not exactly," Billy said. "Out West somewhere to seek her fortune. Seems she cut off contact with her folks about a year ago and they can't find hide nor hair of her. A lot of kids doing that these days. Breaks their parents' hearts."

"I bet it does," Elvis said.

"The late police detective J. P. Whaley and his dealings with Atlanta Internal Affairs is another story," Billy went on. "Seems some of Whaley's colleagues were getting paid off by the head of the local numbers racket and Whaley had been subpoenaed to testify against his pals. That was supposed to happen a few days ago, but Whaley didn't make it. He was kinda tied up with his own funeral."

"Sounds like he was killed to keep him quiet," Elvis said. "And it had nothing at all to do with anything out here."

"Maybe. Except you've got to wonder why they went to the trouble of hoisting him up on that church steeple I read about," Billy said.

"You're right about that," Elvis said. "But tell me something, Billy, how the heck did you find out so much so fast?"

"My friend at the *Atlanta Daily World*," Billy said, laughing. "Colored reporters make it their business to know all about white folks' lives. Never know when it might come in handy. He put together a little packet of articles and stuff about Whaley. Riley too. I put it in the mail for you, Special Delivery."

"Thanks, Billy." Elvis sensed that Billy had to get back to work, but he wanted to hold his friend just a bit longer. "Billy, what songs do you think I should sing at this peace concert?"

"Well, I'm sure they'll be expecting 'Don't Be Cruel,' " Billy said. "But some gospel might catch the right spirit, you think?"

"Just what I'm thinking, Billy," Elvis said. " 'Peace in the Valley' for sure. But what else?"

"How about 'Somebody Bigger Than You and I'?" Billy said. "Sounds like a little dose of humility could go a long way out there."

"I hear you," Elvis said.

"And maybe 'Some Sweet Day, By and By'? That one's got a vision of peace as large as all outdoors."

"How does it go again, Billy?" Elvis knew the hymn, of course, but he yearned to hear his friend sing a few lines.

"You know, Mr. P.," Billy said, and he began to sing in his clear tenor:

> *"Oh, these parting scenes will end,*
> *Some sweet day, by and by."*

Elvis sang the last line along with Billy in a sonorous descant and then, spontaneously, the two took it from the top again and sang the hymn straight through in sweet gospel harmony. At the end, both men said, "Amen." It was the way they said good-bye.

Elvis set down the phone. He jotted down Riley's and his daughter's names on a piece of Sahara stationery, then waslked slowly into the bathroom. Man, he felt good. If he could sing like that at the concert—the way he and Billy just did on the telephone—they'd be halfway to Eden. Even Luke de Luca's hardened heart would have to creak open when he heard "Some Sweet Day."

Elvis looked in the mirror. The swelling in his eyes was virtually gone, but both remained circled in the deep purple of ruptured blood vessels, looking like heavy eye shadow. It gave his eyes a hooded, haunted look. And combined with the fact that he hadn't gotten around to shaving in the past couple of days, his whole face looked different to him—less boyish, less smooth and, well, *less pretty*. Good. He was getting too old and, darn it, too *conscious* to remain looking like some wide-eyed farm boy. Leave that to those Liverpool mop-tops. Elvis tilted his head to one side and peered closely at his reflection. There was something familiar about this dignified new look of his. It reminded him of a photograph of one of his Mississippi ancestors in Gladys's family album, one of those gaunt and bearded Pontotoc County uncles who obliged his family to say grace for a full half-hour while their dinners grew cold. Heck, maybe he'd skip shaving for another day or two.

The phone started to ring. Elvis sauntered back into the bedroom and picked it up. "Elvis here."

"You're in breach of contract, son!" It was the unmistakable shriek of Colonel Tom Parker.

"I'm just fine. And how are you today, Colonel?" Elvis replied coolly.

"Don't play me for a fool, Elvis!"

"Wouldn't think of it, Tom. So why don't we start all over again and talk like civilized folks?" Elvis felt a kind of calm control in his voice, rare for him when dealing with a revved-up Colonel Parker. Maybe it came with his new face.

"Let me spell it out for you, son," Parker said. "Amateurs and folksingers give free concerts. Not professionals. And last time I looked, you were neither an amateur nor a folksinger."

How the heck had Parker heard about the Don't Be Cruel Concert already? He was all the way out in Hollywood!

"I've done benefits before," Elvis said as steadily as he could, but he felt that cool control already slipping away. "Like for the *USS Arizona*. And I do believe that was your idea, Colonel."

"That's because I'm a patriot, not a patsy!" Parker barked back. "A *peace* concert, for Christ's sake! Have they been putting something in your food, son?"

"It's something I believe in, Colonel!" Elvis snapped back. Oh yes, the cool was gone, but it was being replaced real fast by hot anger. "It's not about dollars and cents. In other words, it's not something you'd understand."

"I'll tell you what I understand, boy. That you don't sing a note without me signing off on it. No-where, no-how! We've got a contract!"

Elvis sat down on the sofa. He sure could use a hit of that *prana* energy right about now, but he didn't have time to meditate. He took a long deep breath.

"Well, then, maybe it's time I thought about getting out of that contract, Tom," he said.

A long silence. Elvis heard a match strike at the other end, no doubt the Colonel relighting his cigar.

"You're right, Elvis," Parker said finally. "We should start this conversation all over and talk like the good friends that we are."

Elvis did not reply.

"First off," Parker went on in his most folksy voice. "I've been planning your Las Vegas comeback for a long time now. And after that New Frontier fiasco, we've got to be very careful, son. Very strategic. Two strikes and you're out in this business. Am I right or am I right?"

Parker paused, but Elvis remained silent.

"I mean, I've already got feelers out to the Sands and the Sahara," Parker said, the gusto of the old carny operator creeping back into his voice. "Got the bait dangling and the big fish snapping. Blood in the water already, you follow me?"

Oh yes, Elvis followed him, all right. Parker was aiding and abetting the very war that Elvis was trying to end. It couldn't be clearer.

"Pull in the bait, Colonel!" Elvis snapped. "Pull it in right now, you hear? I'm not performing in either one of them. The last thing I want is getting those two hotels bombing each other to smithereens over me."

"But they—"

"Now!" Elvis barked.

A deep, cigar-smoke sigh at the other end. Elvis was glad he wasn't there to smell it.

"Okay, okay," Parker murmured. "You're the boss, Elvis. And I'm just here to help you, right?"

"That's right, Colonel," Elvis said evenly.

"So let's talk about how I can help make this peace concert of yours into something . . . uh . . . something . . ." Parker paused, rattling through his internal thesaurus of promotional adjectives. "Something *exalted*."

"I can handle that myself, Tom," Elvis said.

"Of course you can, son," Parker replied. "But if you've got an important message, you want to reach as many people as possible, right?"

Elvis murmured something vaguely affirmative.

"Well, that's exactly where my TV contacts come in," Parker said.

"No!" Elvis blurted back. "You are not going to turn this into some TV extravaganza!"

"Why not? It's not like you'll be doing anything you're ashamed of, is it?"

Elvis gritted his teeth. Somehow the Colonel always turned things around so it seemed like Elvis was contradicting himself.

"Tell you what, son," Parker went on. "Take your time on this. Why don't you talk it over with those hippie friends of yours? See what they think?"

How the devil did Parker know about them?

"Who told you about this concert anyhow?" Elvis said, working hard to keep the anxiety out of his voice.

"Who *didn't* tell me is more like it," Parker replied. "It's been on the news since early this morning. I was still sleeping when the phone started ringing. Shole, from RCA in New York City. He wanted to know what the hell was going on and why I hadn't told him about it. It was an embarrassment, son, an awful embarrassment for me."

Incredible! It had already been on the news while Elvis was still sleeping in Shiva's arms. Word out coast to coast. How the heck did that happen? They didn't even have telephones out at the commune.

"I'll let you know about the TV thing," Elvis said. He wanted to get off the line as quickly as possible.

"Good," Parker replied. "Who knows? This peace business may turn out to be a blessing in disguise."

Elvis cringed. Only the Colonel would use the word "blessing" to describe a business windfall. Elvis mumbled good-bye and hung up. He walked over to the balcony's glass door, opened it, and stepped out. The mid-morning desert heat was already rising. The Strip was relatively bare, mainly night-shift croupiers and cocktail waitresses heading home, plus a scattering of all-night gamblers in sport coats and evening gowns strolling unsteadily back to their hotels and motels. Everything looked the same as it had yesterday and the day before. For some reason, that was a big relief.

Elvis came back inside and, still standing, flipped on the TV. The weatherman was saying that it was clear and sunny, with temperatures expected in the mid-eighties. It was the same thing he said every hour of every day. Now the news anchor, Herb Alan, came on in a solemn voice and announced that Vegas was in a state of high alert due to the recent bombing and the constant threats of reprisal. He said local folks were staying close to home out of fear for their lives.

"There's one bright light on the horizon though," Alan said as he faced another camera. "One hope that all of this craziness in our town will finally stop. And that's Elvis Presley's upcoming Don't Be Cruel Concert. The King's free outdoor event, scheduled for this Friday evening in Heritage Park and sponsored by a coalition of local religious groups, is dedicated to peace and under-standing in our little village." *This Friday?* Elvis dropped down on the sofa, his heart pounding as the newsman went on, "The spokesman for the coalition, a young man named Tzar, from the Center of the Light up in Indian Springs, is here to tell us more."

Elvis stared dumbfounded at the television screen. Tzar beamed back at him with those high-wattage eyes of his. No flowing robes today. The young man was wearing a colorful T-shirt emblazoned with the words, DON'T BE CRUEL CONCERT—A LOVE-IN. Incredi-ble, how fast these people worked.

"Hi," Tzar said into the camera. "Our whole idea, really, is just to have fun. You know, kick off our shoes and have a good time. Nothing fancy. Just a big picnic, really."

"And where does Mr. Presley figure in all of this?" Herb Alan asked.

"Elvis just wants to have a good time too," Tzar said, smiling. "Like a lot of us, he's very upset with the problems we've been having around here lately. These awful battles some of our citizens are getting into with each other. So he wants to see if he can help smooth things out. Like he said to us just last night, 'We've all got pretty much the same job to do—the job of keeping this world of ours spinning around as smoothly as possible. Smoothly and peacefully.' I can't put it any better than that."

"That's quite a catch for you people, isn't it? Elvis Presley?" Alan said. "I mean, there are a lot of people in this town who'd give their right arm to have Elvis as the entertainment at their little picnic."

Tzar laughed. "Oh, I'm grateful, all right, Herb. But, you know, the whole thing was Elvis's idea and we're just trying to help out the best we can." Now Tzar looked intensely into the camera and the cameraman obliged by moving in for a close-up. "You know, Herb, Elvis is an extremely spiritual person. Much more than most people realize. That makes following his lead a natural thing for all of us."

"Spiritual, eh?" Herb Alan laughed. "I admit, he's the king of rock 'n' roll, but let's get real—"

"All kinds of people can be spiritual, Mr. Alan," Tzar interrupted. "In fact, I believe that everybody in the world has the potential to be spiritual."

The way Tzar said that—polite and passionate at the same time—caught the newsman off guard. For the first time Elvis could remember, Herb Alan seemed at a loss for words.

"Who, uh, who else is in this religious coalition that's sponsoring the event?" the newsman said finally.

"Well, so far we've got Rabbi Kurtzman from Temple Beth Shalom—that means, 'House of Peace,' you know. And we've got the Church of the Second Coming on board too. They're a great bunch of people."

Here, Tzar made a summoning motion to someone off camera and suddenly Little Timmy scooted up beside him and looked into the camera with a big smile. The boy was wearing a white linen suit and red bow tie, looking like Eddie Foy, Jr., about to break into song.

Good Heavens! Elvis grabbed his forehead in his hand and began to clamp down hard, as if he were trying to squeeze a hallucination out of his brain.

"Little Timmy's a member of that congregation and he's hoping to sing a couple of songs at the concert himself," Tzar was saying as he threw an arm around the youngster's shoulders.

Elvis sucked in his breath. *How the heck did those two get together? Was Timmy now going to announce his miraculous healing on TV?*

"Only if Mr. Presley wants me to sing," Little Timmy piped up cheerfully. "He's the man, you know."

Elvis let his breath out, thankful that that was all the boy said.

"One last thing, Herb," Tzar said. "We want everyone to have a good time, but please, no drugs or alcohol, okay? You don't need them, folks. Peace." He flashed the two-finger peace sign.

Elvis snapped off the TV and sat down on the sofa again. His mind was hopping like dried corn in a hot skillet. Talk about your life racing along without you—right now his life felt like a runaway train. What he needed to do was settle down and take stock of this whole thing before that train jumped its tracks.

Elvis sat back and closed his eyes, then opened them, took the phone off the hook, and closed them again. His brain was still popping. Over here, the Colonel was blowing cigar smoke in his face, and over there, Tzar was doing cartwheels in the desert sand. And far off, there was Billy wrestling with a Ku Klux Klanner. Now, the blazing, brilliant light of the sun eclipsed everything. White light. Perfect stillness. Elvis was barely breathing at all. He could feel the *prana* begin to pulse up his spine.

Then, soft as a whisper, he heard the music. A hymn. A whole choir of achingly sweet voices singing in celestial harmony. Slow, yet urgent. Familiar, yet brand new at the same time. A single voice rose above the others, a voice resonant with soulfulness, a voice that reached down into the heart and made it glow: "You know I can be found sitting home all alone." The song was "Don't Be Cruel" transformed into a gentle hymn about man's desperate desire to overcome his loneliness, to reach out to God and to his fellow man. And that soulful solo singer was Elvis himself.

Elvis listened to his own voice as if he was hearing it for the first time. He could hear his entire life in it, every person he had ever met, every hurt he had ever endured. The voice was neither good nor bad; it was, quite simply, the song itself—naked, pulsing, yearning.

An angelic face suddenly appeared smack in the center of the white light. It was Gladys, Elvis's mamma, and she was smiling.

23

The Lump

The ideas were coming so fast Elvis could barely keep up with them. Pieces of Sahara stationery covered the coffee table, the sofa, and parts of the floor.

He'd divided the concert into three parts: First, the "Get Loose" part—Upbeat. Pure Fun. Get them kicking off their shoes, just like Tzar said on the TV. Elvis already had three definites for "Get Loose": "All Shook Up," "Good Rockin' Tonight," and "Shake, Rattle and Roll." Folks couldn't keep themselves from dancing to those if they wanted to.

Part Two would be the "Settle In" part. Slow things down. Not too sudden-like, just very gradually turn them inward. Get the people in touch with their deeper feelings, their tender feelings. "Love Me Tender," for sure. Then maybe slip in some gospel. Little Timmy could join in on those. Heck, the whole Second Coming chorus could join in. Maybe that rabbi had a choir in his synagogue. As long as it was Old Testament gospel, they could sing along too, right? That would be perfect—Christians and Jews standing together behind him, singing from their hearts. That was what the whole concert was about, right there.

It was Part Three that was confounding Elvis. He'd tentatively called it, "The Awakening." It was the part when people would finally start understanding that it just made more sense—more *heart* sense—to try to get along with each other than to do each other in. Sure, he'd sing the songs that he and Billy had talked about, plus that hymn version of "Don't Be Cruel" that had revealed itself to him in his meditation—he'd already jotted down some new lyrics for that song that made it more about life itself, instead of just about romance. But were songs enough to take people the whole route? To take them home to Eden? The concert should be like a meditation itself—it should gradually take you inward to that still place at your very center. *But how did you get to absolute stillness through music?*

That was the basic question in a nutshell, all right. Elvis searched around for a piece of stationery to write it down in exactly those words so he wouldn't forget it, but he found that he'd gone through all the paper in his room. He called down to the front desk.

"Yes, Mr. Presley."

"Morning," Elvis said. "Listen, could you send me up a whole bunch of paper? Stationery, scrap, it don't matter."

"Of course, Mr. Presley."

"Thank you very much."

"Mr. Presley? I hope you don't mind my saying so, but I think this concert you are giving is a wonderful thing. My whole family thinks so too. It's just what this town needs. Why, it's what the whole world needs."

"Thank you, I appreciate that," Elvis said. "Say, listen, while I've got you on the line, could you send me up a little something to eat?

"Sure thing, Mr. Presley. How about the 'Oasis Omelette'?"

"Sounds just fine," Elvis said. He hung up and walked out onto the balcony again. Since his meditation, even the view looked different—somehow gentler and full of promise. In his book, that yogi had written that objects actually change when the way you look at them changes. It hadn't made much sense to Elvis when he read it—after all, things are just what they are, no matter who is looking at them. But right now, Elvis understood exactly what the yogi was getting at: the *significance* of things changes when the attitude you view them with changes. Like that portly couple down there waddling up the Strip. You could look at them as just another pair of what Howie called, "Las Vegas losers"—overfed, dopey Midwesterners with nothing more on their minds than their next meal. Or you could look at that same couple and see two entire lives with unique biographies, people with their very own hurts and hopes and dreams—people who probably yearned for the very same things that Elvis and Shiva did, even if they couldn't put a name on those yearnings. Elvis smiled down on everybody he could see, just as he could feel Gladys smiling down on him, full of gladness for her son's awakening.

"Breakfast, Mr. Presley."

"Come on in."

The door opened and a room steward walked in carrying a silver breakfast tray. He set it down on Elvis's bed.

"This came for you just as I was getting in the elevator," the steward said, producing an envelope from his back pocket and handing it to Elvis.

After the man left, Elvis stretched out on his bed and lifted the cover off of the "Oasis Omelette." It was about the same as a western omelette back home, except for maybe the cheese—that did smell like it had been sitting out in the desert too long. While he ate, Elvis opened the envelope and emptied the contents onto the bed. It was the information packet that Billy's friend at the Atlanta newspaper had put together: half a dozen articles about an investigation of the city's vice squad, one featuring a photograph of the late J. P. Whaley with his arms around the shoulders of the two fellow officers—Elvis recognized the pair who had thrown J. P.'s Las Vegas birthday surprise party; a photostat of Timothy Riley, Jr.'s DMV registration of a blue, 1958 Hudson; and a splotchy photostat of his daughter, Melissa Riley, in the 1957 "Tattler," the yearbook for Macon's A. E. Miller High School. From what Elvis could see, Melissa looked like half the girls in his own class at Humes High—ponytail and bangs, eyebrows plucked down to a sliver, skinny lips, no chin to speak of, and either a case of acne or those photostat splotches were unfortunately arranged on the poor girl's chubby cheeks. Melissa's name was under the photograph and beneath that, one word: "Wanderlust." No doubt that was the only kind of lust a nice Macon girl could allow herself to feel.

A knock at the door.

"Who's there?"

"Candy." A woman's voice. Or was it Pickles doing one of his vocal imitations as a setup for another knock-knock joke? If it was, Elvis wasn't going to bite.

"I don't know any Candy," Elvis called back.

"Well, maybe it's time you did, Elvis," the voice crooned. If it was Pickles, he sure sounded sexier as a woman than he did as himself.

Reluctantly, Elvis swung off the bed, walked to the door, and opened it. Standing on the other side, with a lecherous smile on her ample lips, was the six-foot redhead whom Elvis had privately dubbed, "Red Tips." Fortunately, Miss Red Tips was currently fully clothed, although in a sweater that was stretched so tight across her bosom it looked like cheesecloth. She extended her hand to Elvis and announced herself, "Miss Candy Kane, at your service, Mr. Presley."

Elvis stared at her for one beat and then burst out laughing. Man, the woman ought to have a sign hanging around her neck that said TEMPTATION in big red letters. Because that was surely what she was. Even a pope would be sorely tempted by Miss Candy Kane.

"What's so funny, Elvis?" Miss Candy looked seriously peeved. No doubt it was rare that her appearance elicited a laugh from any red-blooded man.

"I'm sorry, ma'am," Elvis said, then improvised, "It's just your name, you know. That the one your momma gave you?"

"Nope," Candy said striding past Elvis into the room. "My real name is Meryl Rubeleski. De Luca made me change it. You know how it is in Vegas—'It don't mean a thing if it ain't got that swing.' " She punctuated the word "swing" with a double hip-twitch that had been personally choreographed by Satan.

Elvis self-consciously closed the door.

"As you can see, Miss Candy, I'm kind of busy at the moment," Elvis said, gesturing to the pieces of paper all around him. "I'm putting together the program for this concert that I'm—"

"But that's the reason I'm here, Elvis," she said, then added coquettishly, "Especially seeing as you're obviously not giving me any other reason to be here."

"About the concert?"

"Yes. I want to be part of it. To be *in* it."

Elvis scratched at the stubble on his chin. "It's, uh, it's not exactly a floorshow I'm putting on, ma'am. I mean, I'm sure you are very good at, uh, whatever you—"

"I'll have you know that I am a trained dancer, Elvis," Miss Candy said archly. "Just like your girlfriend. I know ballet and tap and even some polka."

"Polka?"

"I grew up with it," the former Miss Rubeleski said proudly.

"I see," Elvis said. Of course, what he could *not* see was this woman doing any kind of dance—even a polka—at a concert whose main purpose was to get people to turn inward to their quiet center. But Elvis was still feeling guilty for laughing in Candy's face; after all, she was another human being with her own story too, a Polish Catholic girl from someplace like Milwaukee who'd come to Las Vegas to become a dancer. "The thing is, Miss Candy," Elvis improvised, "I'm not in charge of that part of the show."

"So who is?" Candy snapped. "Little Miss Margaret? Margaret Reardon?"

"Beg pardon?"

"Or do you call her Manovah like the rest of those twits?"

Elvis had nearly forgotten that Manovah had been the producer of the Sahara floorshow before she joined the commune. "Your former boss, right?"

"Boss is the word, all right," Candy said, flouncing down on Elvis's bed. "Although 'bitch' would be a better one. Well, if Miss Margaret's your casting director, I can forget all about being in the show. Unless you put in a good word for me. I really want to be in it, Elvis. I'm a devout Christian, you know."

"You and Miss Manovah didn't get along?"

Candy belted out a hoarse laugh, then stretched out on the bed, elbows down, her head supported in both her hands. "She hated me," Candy said. "But I didn't take it personally, because she hated all of us, all the showgirls. She hated our bodies, basically. Our sexiness. Miss Margaret is not particularly gifted in the body department, in case you hadn't noticed. Of course, it didn't help that Howie Pickles ragged on her nonstop. He called her 'The Lump.' "

"Funny line of work to go into if you can't stand the sight of showgirls," Elvis said. He really ought to be thinking about how to get rid of this woman; he had work to do.

"Strange thing is, she was damned good at it," Candy said. "Fantastic choreographer, full of ideas, real original. She's the one who put the panther in Shirley's act—stroke of genius, that. Margaret trained for the biz right in town here, over at U.N.L.V. But it was one of those deals where the thing you're best at is the thing that makes you most miserable. Is there a word for that? Anyway, she was ripe pickings for what's-his-name . . . Tzar. You got to believe he was the Lump's first lay. That's all it took to make a convert out of her."

Yup, definitely time to get Miss Candy Kane out of here. Elvis had a load of business to take care of before the concert. Candy had picked a scrap of paper off of his bed—something from Billy's packet—and took a flustered look at it. Okay, just one last question. "I thought it was Miss Shiva who brought Manovah up to the Center of the Light," Elvis said.

"Shirley?" Candy let loose with another throaty laugh. "You gotta be kidding, Elvis. Why would she want another one of Tzar's slave girls up there? Especially in front of the kid and all?"

Elvis glared at Candy, his heart suddenly pounding like crazy. *Take a deep breath, my inner friend. Get that prana pulsing again.* He closed his eyes.

"Hello, love!"

Elvis popped open his eyes and spun around. Shiva was strolling through the door with her long arms extended in front of her, coming straight to him. But when she saw Miss Candy Kane lounging on his bed with a haughty smile, she came to a halt.

"I'm sorry. Am I interrupting you, Elvis?" Shiva said in an amazingly calm voice. "I can come back later."

"No!" Elvis bellowed. "We're done!"

"Done?" Candy Kane laughed. "We're only getting started, Sweet Lips."

"Truly, Elvis," Shiva went on, already backing toward the door, "I have some things to do downstairs anyway."

Elvis stared at Shiva incredulously. There was not an ounce of jealousy or anger in her voice, not even a hint of sarcasm. And heaven knows, it was not as if she didn't care. All Elvis had to do was look into her adoring eyes to know how much she cared for him. No, Miss Shiva actually *lived* in that inner place—a place of unconditional love, a place without suspicions and fears. A place of peace.

"Hey, I was only making a pitch to your boyfriend to get a gig in your concert," Candy said, crumpling up the scrap of paper and dropping it on the floor before getting to her feet. "And I got to tell you, Shirley, you've got yourself one loyal loverboy here. I didn't know they made them that way anymore."

Candy was striding toward the door when Shiva reached out and touched her arm.

"I'm sure there's a part in the show for you, Candy," Shiva said. "You've got a terrific voice. Maybe you and me and some of the girls can put together a little backup chorus thing. Okay?"

"Are you serious, Shirl?"

"You bet I am."

Miss Candy Kane smiled so genuinely and appreciatively that her entire face transformed before Elvis's eyes. There she was, plain as day: Miss Meryl Rubeleski, that tall and pretty girl from Milwaukee who went down to Las Vegas to become a dancer. Amazing!

The moment Candy walked out the door, Elvis threw his arms around Shiva and hugged her to him.

"I hope I wasn't out of line, Elvis," Shiva whispered in his ear. "You know, offering Candy a part in the concert?"

Elvis suddenly held Shiva out at arm's length. "You are a marvel, woman," he said ardently. "I've never known anybody like you."

Shiva shrugged shyly.

"No, I mean it, darlin'," Elvis went on rapidly. "Like what you did just now. You acted with trust in your heart and look what you got in return? You turned a bitter woman into a happy girl! Just like that. Truly amazing, that's what it is."

"It just makes sense to act that way, doesn't it?" Shiva said softly.

"Indeed it does," Elvis said.

24

Colonel Pussycat

Elvis felt such a surge of pure love for Shiva that he swept all the papers under his bed, picked her up in his arms, and lay her down on top of the bedspread. And then they made tender love for the second time that day.

Afterward, lying side-by-side, Elvis told Shiva about the problem he was having with the final part of the concert, the part he called, "The Awakening." How did you get from music to that silent, peaceful place inside?

"Well, you saw the way we do it up at the Center," Shiva said. "We chant together, getting softer and softer until we're just chanting inside our heads."

"That Omaha Shanty business?"

Shiva laughed. *"Om Shanti,"* she said.

"I don't think that'll work for just ordinary folks," Elvis said.

"Of course, it will," Shiva said. "It's cosmic magic. 'Shanti' is Sanskrit for 'peace.' And Paramahansa Yogananda says that the word 'Om' is the cosmic vibrating power behind all atomic energies."

"Beg pardon?"

Shiva smiled. "The sound just turns you on!" she declared, then added, "You know, naturally. No drugs."

"Well, it sure did make me feel some loving kindness last night," Elvis said. "Although at the time, I thought it was sitting next to you that was doing that."

" 'Om' is where 'Amen' comes from," Shiva continued earnestly. "That's how far back it goes. To the beginning of time."

Elvis nodded. Heaven knows, repeating "Amen" had a powerful effect on church people, especially colored church people who chanted it over and over again until "Amen" echoed inside your brain and made you feel somewhere between crazy and exalted. And the word sure did have a heartrending effect on Elvis whenever he and Billy used it to say good-bye to each other.

"I think somebody else better do that part," Elvis said. "Getting the chanting going, I mean."

"Tzar usually does that for us," Shiva said.

Tzar. Elvis immediately felt something tighten right up inside his gut. He knew exactly why, too: that stuff Candy Kane had said about Tzar seducing Manovah and bringing her up to the Center of the Light. Something else, too, something about Shiva . . .

"Or I could do it myself, I suppose," Shiva went on. "Or maybe one of the children. That would be nice, wouldn't it, love? If one of the children led the chanting?"

"I guess."

"I'll ask Manovah what she thinks," Shiva said. "She's kind of put herself in charge of the program at our end. Which is all right with us. She's got more know-how on putting on a show than all the rest of us combined. Of course, her boyfriend is feeling a little neglected these days, but he'll come around."

"Her boyfriend?"

"You know, Mufah," Shiva said. "They've been together ever since she came up to the Center with me."

"But I thought Tzar was her boy—"

"*Tzar?* I don't think so." Shiva laughed. "Tzar took a vow of abstinence a few years back. Manovah is a soulful woman, but she still needs her loving at night."

"Hallelujah to that," Elvis said, a rueful smile tugging at his lips. So Miss Candy had just been making up stories, maybe thinking it would help her get in the show. By golly, Shiva had done it again—stripped away the scourge of suspicion with the openness of her heart. When the devil was Elvis ever going to learn to do that himself?

The next three days whipped by so fast that Elvis felt like he was living in one of those speeded-up films his cousin, Harold Lloyd, used to make. One minute he'd be holding a meeting in his room with Tzar and Manovah and Mufah (who did look kind of moony every time he glanced at Manovah), talking about props and outdoor toilets and crowd control. And the next minute he'd be on the phone, discussing bass players and drummers, sound systems and dressing rooms. In between, Elvis made a couple of appearances on local radio and TV, doing a spot on Herb Alan's morning news in which Elvis and Little Timmy sang a single chorus of "Somebody Bigger Than You and I." They only did it in simple thirds, but the contrast between both their voices and their size was so, well, *adorable*, that even that sarcastic Herb Alan just sat there afterward, looking dumbfounded into the camera for a couple seconds before he murmured, "Fabulous!" During a station break, Alan told Elvis that since his concert had been announced, something unusual was definitely happening in Las Vegas: there hadn't been a major crime committed in days, even though everybody was holding their breath, waiting for the Sahara's retaliation for the bombing.

Elvis decided to do only one full rehearsal—and pretty much just a tech rehearsal at that. They set it for five-thirty in the evening on the day before the concert. Elvis felt so pepped-up, he wanted to walk all the way up to Heritage Park. With Shiva on his arm, he stepped out of the Sahara feeling like he was sixteen years old, on the way to a prom. That is when a taxi screeched up under the Sahara awning and out popped Colonel Thomas Parker.

Elvis glared at him, his face blanching. If anybody could ruin all this wonderfulness in a blink of his pig eyes, it was the Colonel. The man had an instinct for taking control of every little thing he set his sights on—taking control and then turning it into his own personal money machine. Here Parker was, just when Elvis had been feeling so good and easy. And right now, all Elvis felt was anger and resentment.

Elvis took one step toward Parker, raising his forefinger threateningly. "No national TV! No TV at all, Colonel!" were the first words that came out of Elvis's mouth.

Parker laughed. "Well, I've had unfriendly greetings in my day, but that one is right up there with the best." He spread his arms wide and started toward Elvis like a childless uncle come to visit his favorite nephew. Elvis sure as heck did not feel like enduring one of the Colonel's show-biz bear hugs right now, but with Shiva watching, it just didn't seem right to dodge an expression of loving fellowship, even if it was somewhat less than sincere. They embraced.

"Sure looks like life is agreeing with you, son," Parker said, smiling widely. "Makes me glad."

"True enough," Elvis replied, still feeling guarded. Behind him, the rest of his group was coming out the door—Manovah, Tzar, and Timmy.

"It's like I always say," Parker went on, loud enough for them all to hear, "If you follow your heart, you'll never go wrong."

Elvis could not remember Parker ever saying anything remotely like that, but nonetheless he appreciated the fact that Parker wasn't coming on strong. In fact, judging by the smiles of Shiva and Tzar, Parker was hitting the perfect note for the spirit of the day.

"Hey there, Colonel," Tzar called. "We're just going up to the concert site for a little run-through. Wanna come along? I'll have my people take care of your bags and things."

"Only if you don't mind, Elvis," Parker said deferentially. Man, Parker had either been born again as a pussycat or he was an even better actor than Elvis thought. Either way, it didn't make Elvis feel any more trusting of him.

"Guess that's all right," Elvis said. He almost added a warning to Parker to keep his comments and suggestions to himself, but that turned out to be unnecessary. Colonel Pussycat just propped himself under a palm tree in Heritage Park and silently smiled while they ran through the program for blocking and sound cues. At dusk, when the whole chattering, laughing group started back to the hotel, Parker scurried up beside Elvis and said, "Who *are* these people? They do a better job than anybody *I've* ever worked with."

Who knows? Maybe this get-along spirit was as infectious as Shiva said it was.

There were a half-dozen telegrams slipped under the door when Elvis and Shiva returned to his room. They sat down on the couch and began opening them. The first was from Steve Sholes, his producer at RCA. It said, simply, "Elvis. Stop. Good luck. Stop Sholes." Friendly, but not exactly overflowing with enthusiasm.

Shiva opened the next one. It read, "Elvis. Stop. I am so proud of you. Stop. God bless you. Stop. All my love, Priscilla."

Elvis felt himself blushing. "She's, uh, she's—"

"I know who Priscilla is," Shiva laughed. "No reason for you to feel funny about her. *I* don't."

"At some point I'm going to have to tell her about you and—"

"I don't want you thinking about anything but the concert just now," Shiva said. She pecked him on the cheek. "Anyway, things like that have a way of taking care of themselves."

Elvis opened the next one. Word for word, it was almost the same as Priscilla's, except this one was signed, "Ann-Margret."

Shiva took one look at it and burst out laughing. "You sure have been busy, haven't you?" she said.

Elvis couldn't help but laugh along with her this time. The next one was from Sholes again and this time he'd written, "You make all of us at RCA proud to be associated with you." Some time between that first telegram and the second, Sholes had probably held a meeting with his "client affairs" department and they'd bit the bullet and voted for more enthusiasm.

Shiva opened up the next one. "This is beautiful!" she cried, showing it to Elvis. All it said was, "Peace!" and it was signed, "Joan Baez."

Elvis smiled, then opened the last one. "DON'T TAKE CREDIT FOR TIMMY G'S CURE OR YOU'LL PAY FOR IT, BIG TIME! *STOP* DR. JED BUTTERFIELD/ DEPARTMENT OF PEDIATRIC NEUROLOGY/ UNIVERSITY OF ARIZONA."

"What the devil is this about?" Elvis said, showing it to Shiva.

Shiva shook her head. "So many unhappy people out there," she murmured, crunching up the telegram into a little ball. "And no matter how hard we try, we can't reach them all."

Elvis knew what she meant, but that didn't exactly answer his question. This doctor was obviously talking about Little Timmy's recovery. Joby had mentioned something about a specialist they'd seen in Tucson who hadn't been able to help the boy. Clearly this doctor didn't want anybody thinking that Elvis's laying on of hands had succeeded where his medical treatment had failed. Well, neither did Elvis. And sometime soon he was going to set the record straight on that. But you had to wonder about a doctor who'd get so angry about a thing like that that he'd threaten you. It made you think the doctor was afraid faith healing really *did* work and that if word got out, he and all his doctor pals would be out of business.

Late that night, while they were making love—at first wildly, hungrily, then slowly, sensually—a flame ignited inside Elvis's brain. The flame swelled, gradually becoming a torch of white light that suffused body and soul. And when at last he exploded, Elvis felt that light burst out of him, beam like a beacon out of the top of his head and radiate throughout the entire world.

"That was wonderful," Shiva whispered.

"Yes, it was," Elvis whispered back.

Shiva reached up and touched Elvis's forehead. "Your face. It's changed, hasn't it? In the last few days. It's become so much more—I don't know—*pure*."

"It's just all that black and blue around my eyes," Elvis said, smiling. "That and my whiskers. Makes me look like one of my Bible Belt cousins."

"Yes, that's it," Shiva whispered. "From out of the Bible."

25

The Don't Be Cruel Concert

They had scheduled the concert at five-thirty for a couple of reasons. First, because folks with regular day jobs would be able to come and bring their children with them. And second, because that way the final part of the concert would begin right around dusk. Perfect time for setting down in the grass and getting comfortable.

Elvis slept past noon. Shiva was already up and dressed and had a thermos of coffee waiting for him. He drank his first cup out on the balcony, gazing down on the Strip. The midday heat was reaching its peak, making the view shimmer and quiver as if it were a reflection on the surface of a pond. *Everything changes. Everything is changing every minute of the day.* He strolled back into the room where Shiva was doing some kind of yoga exercise that made her body parts look like they had been rearranged so that her feet poked out where her arms should be and her head was stuck on backward. It was awkward trying to talk to someone in a position like that.

"I'm feeling a little agitated this morning," Elvis said, addressing the place where Shiva's face would be if she were sitting properly. "I can't tell where the excitement stops and the fright begins."

"Don't you always feel that way just before a concert?"

"Yes and no," Elvis said. "I get nervous, all right, but not in my head, just in my stomach. This one—this concert—is different, you know. I'm not just going out there to get folks popping their feet."

"I know," Shiva said, twisting her head around to look at Elvis. "But you don't have to worry about a thing. It's out of your hands now."

"Is that a fact?"

"It's true, Elvis," Shiva said. She untangled herself in one smooth motion, like a snake slithering down a rail fence. "The spirit of the concert already exists. So all you have to do is show up and watch it materialize."

For some reason, that made Elvis think of that hymn Digby had made up, "God Is My Ventriloquist." He smiled. "If you say so, darlin'."

Elvis took a long hot shower, vocalizing snatches of "Good Rockin' Tonight" just to make sure his voice was ready to materialize when the spirit called upon it. Then he took a short nap and started to dress for the show. Shiva had laid out a pair of black pegged pants, a blue cotton shirt, and a red silk kerchief to be tied around his neck. Looking at himself in the full-length mirror in the bathroom, he wondered if he shouldn't shave after all—maybe he was starting to look a little *too* biblical. But what the heck, all he had to do was show up, shaven or not; the spirit was going to take care of everything else, right?

No one had predicted a turnout anywhere near this big, especially on only a few days notice. By the time Elvis and Shiva rode up to the corner of Washington Street and Las Vegas Boulevard in the back of Digby's Olds—with Howie riding shotgun—Heritage Park was packed tight and there was enough overflow in the outlying streets and sidewalks to fill the park two times over again. Digby and Howie locked arms at their elbows and marched ahead of Elvis and Shiva like a cow-catcher on a locomotive plowing through the crowd. Some of the folks reached out and touched Elvis on the arms or shoulders and Elvis smiled back, saying, "Thank you for coming" and "It's good to see you." At one point, Reverend Sweetser popped up beside Elvis, threw his arm around Elvis's shoulder, and grinned while somebody snapped a photo of them.

Halfway to the bandstand, Sheriff Turtleff appeared with his staff—for today's event, they were wearing riot helmets to top off their white jumpsuits. They joined arms with Digby and Howie on either side, forming a phalanx that brought them right up to the bandstand steps. Then Digby took off, saying he had to pick up a special guest.

Since yesterday's tech rehearsal, the bandstand had been decked out with ceramic pots full of flowers and satin banners hanging from the rafters. One of the banners was lavender with a white cross hand sewn at its center. Another was sky-blue with a white Star of David on it. And a third displayed a circle, black on one half, white on the other, with a wavy line separating the halves. "The yin-yang," Shiva whispered in Elvis's ear as he looked at it. "Symbol of perfect harmony." Elvis nodded. It wasn't something you'd see at the Grand Ole Opry, that's for sure.

The backstage area—a curtained lean-to set up behind the bandstand—was bustling. Elvis spotted Miss Kathy in a choir robe combing Little Timmy's hair, while next to them a tall, white-haired man wearing one of those Jewish caps—must be that Rabbi Kurtzman—was chatting away with Miss Candy Kane whose own choir robe did little to conceal her voluptuousness. At half-past five, they all gathered in a cramped circle, joined hands, and gradually went silent while outside the din of the crowd rose to a crescendo of anticipation. Manovah was standing directly across from Elvis. She smiled at him and said, "Do you want to say anything before we start, Mr. Presley?"

Elvis considered a moment. "I just want to say how grateful I am to all of you," he said. "Grateful for your help in making this happen. Thank you. Thank you very much."

The rabbi said, "Amen." Elvis reached for his guitar and strode out onto the bandstand.

The crowd roared.

"Thank you," Elvis murmured into the microphone, holding out the palm of one hand to quiet them. "Thank you."

But the cheering went on and on, dipping for a few seconds, then rising up again even more loudly. After five full minutes of this, they finally quieted down.

"Thank you all for coming," Elvis said. "I want us all to have a real good time today. A happy time. But maybe we can have a kinda thoughtful time too, you know? A time for taking stock of who we are and who we want to be. And what all that means about how we want to be treating each other." Elvis paused. "But hey, I'm getting ahead of myself, folks. 'Cause right now, I'm feeling kinda—I don't know—kinda 'All Shook Up'!"

With that, Elvis slammed a B-flat chord on his old "Slim Jim" and barreled right in with,

> *"A-well-a bless my soul*
> *What's wrong with me?"*

By the time he reached the end of the first verse, Bill Polar and Skip Jorgensen from the Sahara house band had scooted out of the lean-to, taken their places behind him at the drums and standing bass, and fallen right in.

They were rocking. And so was every man, woman, and child in Heritage Park and beyond as far as the eye could see.

After "All Shook Up," Elvis stepped on the applause, going straight into "Good Rockin' Tonight." Without even thinking, he started dancing that boogie himself, throwing out his right leg and letting it jive on its own, shaking and rattling like it was running on rocket fuel. For a second, Elvis wondered if dancing like this was appropriate to the occasion, but then he thought, *Hey, this is supposed to be joyful!* Right then, out of the corner of his eye, Elvis saw another leg shaking and rattling. He turned to see the bare leg of Miss Manovah kicking out from her white satin choir robe. God love her, she looked a whole lot prettier than Elvis had thought she ever could. Next to her, Miss Candy Kane was kicking out too, a joyful smile on her fleshy lips, her arm slung around Manovah's waist. Not an ounce of bad feeling between those two far as he could see. Next in line was Miss Kathy, strutting her choir-robed stuff right alongside of Miss Shiva herself. Yes, indeed, it was Shiva's little backup chorus thing. Catching Shiva's eye, Elvis winked, and she responded with an airborne kiss, neither of them missing a boogie beat.

Out in the park, the crowd was starting to boogie too. Just a few feet away, Elvis saw a young father in a postman's uniform with a toddler on his shoulders doing the twist with his pretty young wife. Next to him, a bunch of the kids from the Center of the Light were dancing in a circle, pretty little Kali in the center doing cartwheels. Over there, near the sidewalk, Elvis saw a line of men and women, not one of them under fifty, doing their own version of a backup chorus, kicking up their old legs like they'd just drunk a whole jug of Geritol. And holy moley, who was that up front doing a modified Watusi with a long-skirted woman?

None other than Colonel Thomas Parker himself, grinning and kicking with a dead cigar in his mouth! Dancing alongside of him was Sol Epstein looking positively goofy with joy. Oh yeh, folks were getting loose, all right. Getting loose and opening up to the spirit right on schedule.

At the end of "Rockin'," Elvis segued straight into "Shake, Rattle and Roll." He was wailing now, throwing off heat like a tin roof in July. One verse into it and there was hardly a soul in sight who wasn't jumping. Then, just after Elvis took the two beats leading into the chorus, he heard a crystal-clear soprano slide in with, "Well I said shake, rattle and roll!" a full two octaves above him. Elvis didn't have to turn around to know that it was Little Timmy backing him up, but Elvis turned around anyway and smiled at the boy. Man, this kid had it all! A fine voice, the dance moves of little Eddie Foy, and a face on him that would melt the heart of an Eskimo. Incredible! It was as if all those years Little Timmy had been mute and spastic, he'd been singing and dancing in his head from sunup to sundown. Was it faith or gumption that made that singing and dancing burst out of him? Hey, maybe faith and gumption were the same thing. Of course, that doctor down in Tucson didn't have any faith in gumption either.

Miss Kathy had Brylcreemed the boy's hair into a perfect part and pompadour making him look like, well, a little like Elvis himself. Elvis noticed that the kid was wearing black pegged pants and a blue shirt with a red silk kerchief tied around his neck, just like his own outfit. Manovah must've planned that out. The crowd was going crazy. In his mind's eye, Elvis saw exactly what the crowd was seeing: Elvis singing alongside this miniature replica of himself. Like his tiny twin. Like looking through a time machine and seeing Elvis singing a duet with his boyhood self. Elvis leaned his head down to Little Timmy and Timmy responded by taking a step nearer and looking up at Elvis, virtually nose to nose.

"I said flip flop and fly I don't care if I die."

The crowd roared so loud that a swarm of birds suddenly lifted off from a tree, did a loop-de-loop high over the park, and returned to their perches just as Elvis and Little Timmy were harmonizing a final, "Don't ever say good-bye." It was magic. Pure magic.

Everybody was dancing so hard Elvis could feel the earth rumble underneath the bandstand. Time to start swooping into the "Settle In" part of the concert, but do it so gradual-like that folks' hearts got there before they did. Elvis moved smoothly into some hard rocking gospel, stringing together a medley of "Traveling Along on the Jericho Road," "When the Saints Go Marchin' In," and "Down by the Riverside." Folks were now clapping more than they were dancing.

"I ain't gonna study war no more . . ."

Looking out, Elvis saw the Turtleff's deputies swaying side-by-side, clapping together like a soul train. And up near the front, there was Howie Pickles snapping his fingers over his head—by golly, right alongside Joey Filbert! They were clowning it up, for sure, but they were doing it together like a seasoned comedy team. *How about that!* And over on Washington Street, Elvis suddenly caught sight of Digby Ferguson. He was standing right next to a man with a bunch of wire twisted around his jaw. By golly, Digby's special guest was Gus Lemon, out of the hospital for a day trip with the man who put him there. Forgiveness was in the air, all right.

201

Elvis finished up "Riverside" and paused, wiping his brow with the back of his sleeve, then smiled out at the crowd. Man, he felt fine. This time, he had to wait a good six or seven minutes for them to quiet enough for him to be heard.

"Back home, at the church I went to with my mom and dad, we used to take a minute in the middle of the service to greet the people around us," Elvis said into the microphone. "So how about we do that now? Just turn to the right of you and say hello and shake hands. Then turn to your left and do it again."

In every direction Elvis looked, people shook hands and hugged each other. It was that easy.

"You all know what I like so much about being a human being?" Elvis said, making it sound like both a joke and something serious at the same time.

A joyful chorus of "What, Elvis?" came back at him.

"It's that we got so much going on inside of us," Elvis said. "So many different parts that make us who we are."

Not a sound out there. Not a whisper. They were listening to every word he said.

"I mean, we all got our boogeying parts, that's the God's truth," Elvis said.

A big cheer of agreement.

"And we've all got our tender parts. That's inside us too, standing right next to the boogey part, same way Little Timmy and me are standing next to each other right now." Elvis smiled out at the crowd. "And the sweet thing is, we've got songs for that part too." He took a deep breath and began to sing "Love Me Tender" a cappella, his voice coming out of him soft and clear, all soul and tenderness. When he came near the end, he turned and nodded to Little Timmy who instantly came in on "I'll be yours through all the years" in note-perfect harmony. There must have been half a minute of pure silence before the audience broke into applause.

The moment Elvis began the next song, "Bosom of Abraham," he felt like he was levitating a few inches off the bandstand floor, swooped up on the wings of the resonant harmonies of the choir which had suddenly materialized behind him. He turned his head. A good twenty men and women had joined Shiva's group, every one of them wearing white satin choir robes, every one of them with a voice as pure as a church organ pipe. Standing in front of the choir, with Little Timmy between them, were Joby and Rabbi Kurtzman, also in choir robes. Elvis recognized maybe half of this group as members of the Church of the Second Coming; the other half had to be from Kurtzman's flock at Beth Shalom. They sang half a dozen hymns one right after the other. At one point, Elvis spotted Reverend Sweetser out near the edge of the bandstand, all gussied up in his frock coat and black padre hat, linking arms with the man beside him. Manovah crept up beside Elvis, gestured toward the man next to Sweetser, and said in Elvis's ear, "That's Jones from the Good Samaritan Chapel." *Yes indeed, the magic was working.* They brought the hymn section to a close with the most stirring rendition of "Swing Low, Sweet Chariot" that Elvis had ever heard anywhere but in his own heart.

The sun was starting to set at the far end of Heritage Park, the last rays shining on the bandstand like a spotlight with a pink gel.

"You know, friends," Elvis said into the microphone. "It's no secret that we've been having some troubles around here lately. Awful troubles. Sad troubles. Some innocent people have lost their lives. We've had arsons and bombs and all manner of ugliness. And the thing is, we all know that it has to stop, but some of us are having a real problem doing just that. We keep thinking, 'Okay, I'll stop. . . . Right after I pay back the last son-of-a-gun who did me harm!' And of course, that way it never stops."

The crowd was perfectly quiet, hundreds of open faces looking up at Elvis as the dusk light singled him out, glowing in his hair and deepening the shadows around his eyes.

"A wise man once wrote that peace in the world begins with peace in our hearts," Elvis said.

Behind him, the rabbi said, "Amen."

"That's simple, but it's true," Elvis went on. "I mean, if each and every one of us could make peace with our own selves right in our own hearts—why, all our anger would just dry up and blow away!"

This time, several voices behind Elvis said, "Amen."

"And you know, friends," Elvis went on. "That's not as hard as it sounds. Because we all got that part inside us too. Right at the center of our heart, we *all* have that peaceful part."

"Amen" came from every direction now. The word rose up in Heritage Park like that flock of birds.

"So what we got to do is find that quiet place deep in our hearts," Elvis said.

"*Amen!*"

"Find that place that wants nothing more than to be alive. To breathe God's sweet air and walk on His green earth."

"*Amen!*"

"That wants nothing more than to love his family and friends."

"*Amen!*"

"And maybe make some new friends and love them too."

"*Amen!*"

He had not planned a word of this, but the words came out of Elvis's mouth without him thinking about them. Yup, the words were there already; he was just listening to them materialize. Who knows? Maybe God *was* his ventriloquist.

"It's a holy place that lives inside us."

"*Amen!*"

"A place that doesn't know hate!"

"Amen!"

"A place that doesn't know retribution!"

"Amen!"

From the corner of his eye, Elvis saw Reverend Sweetser put a hand to his eyes. By God, the man was weeping. But in the next moment, Elvis saw another man pushing through the crowd directly in front of him, a well-dressed man with bushy hair and a grim mouth. Luke de Luca. He was followed closely by three men in boxy suits that did little to hide their shoulder holsters. De Luca was heading straight for Sol Epstein with something glittering in his right hand. Elvis instantly took a step toward the bandstand stairs, raising his own right hand and stiffening it, ready to chop Lucky in his tracks. But just then Digby appeared from out of nowhere and linked his arm through de Luca's, urgently yammered some words into the man's ear, and then swung him off toward the edge of the crowd, Lucky's henchmen following behind them.

"No more jealousy!" Elvis said, stepping back to the microphone.

"Amen!"

"No more hate!"

"Amen!"

"No more payback!"

"Amen!"

Elvis paused. He could see Digby still talking a mile a minute into de Luca's ear, now patting him on the back and laughing.

"Amen is a wonderful word," Elvis said finally. "A word that goes way back to the beginning of time. A word that vibrates inside you and gives you the power to banish hatred from your heart."

"Amen!"

Elvis smiled out at the crowd. "I want to try a little experiment today, friends," he said. "Something a little different from what we're used to. But what the heck, if I'm not too old to try it, neither are you, right?"

A ripple of soft applause went through the crowd.

"And to lead us in this little experiment, I want to bring out a new friend of mine who's taught me a lot in these past few weeks. Come on out here, Tzar."

Tzar came trotting out of the lean-to in hiking shorts and his DON'T BE CRUEL CONCERT T-shirt. He came up beside Elvis, threw an arm around his shoulders, and said into the microphone, "We are so lucky to have this man with us, aren't we, folks?"

The crowd roared back, "Yes!"

"And I don't just mean lucky to have him here today at Heritage Park," Tzar continued. "I mean we're lucky to have him here on Planet Earth!"

Another roar of approval.

"What I'd like us to do now is take that word 'Amen' back to where it started. Back to when the way they said it was, 'Om.' " Tzar instructed the crowd to make themselves comfortable in the grass, sitting as close to one another as they could. As Tzar spoke, Manovah led the chorus off the bandstand and into the audience where they fanned out, sitting down here and there among the guests. Elvis saw Miss Kathy sit down with a middle-aged, bald-headed guy wearing a short-sleeved shirt with a clip-on bow tie. On her other side was a nice-looking blonde wearing a long skirt with a slit so high that sitting down in the grass presented no problem at all.

"That's Bambi Hummel and Harry Huff," Joby whispered to Elvis as he left the stage too.

Oh yes, the warring brothel entrepreneurs were sitting down together like the lion and the lamb. Now Elvis saw Candy Kane and the rabbi getting down in the grass with Colonel Tom, Sol

Epstein, and so help me, God, Luke de Luca. *Amazing!* It was a beautiful thing to behold.

Tzar had just told the audience to close their eyes for a moment, then slowly open them again. Kali clambered up the stairs to her mother's side. Beside Tzar, only Shiva, Kali, and Elvis remained on the bandstand and now Shiva sat down on one side of Elvis while Kali sat down on the other. Elvis lowered himself down too, letting his legs dangle off the edge. Once again, he glimpsed in his mind's eye just what the folks in Heritage Park saw before them: a virginal-looking young woman, a little girl with an angelic face, and a lightly-bearded man with hooded, soulful eyes. Like a holy family.

Tzar asked the audience to close their eyes again and to repeat softly after him.

"Om."

"Om."

"Shanti."

"Shanti."

"Om."

"Om."

"Shanti."

"Shanti."

Part 3
The Awakening

26

Patient as a Mother

Prana pulsed up Elvis's spine. It was there when he awakened that next morning, dazzling his brain, shining out of his eyes.

He sat up against the headboard. In the middle of the room, Shiva was doing her yoga exercises, standing with her feet wide, both arms slowly rising above her head. All she wore was a pair of shorts and a T-shirt. She looked like an angel. Elvis felt about as peaceful and contented as a man had any right to feel.

His entire life had changed yesterday. There was not one doubt in his mind about that. He was a new man with a new purpose: *to use his gifts to make the world a better place for everyone.* Simple as that. It was so obvious, he had to wonder why he'd never realized it before. But, of course, that was because the time had not been right yet. He was just like that Yogananda fella—he'd had to live this other life first, make those mistakes, be seduced by those temptations, before he could see what was missing. Before he could finally grasp what he should do with his life. Like the Bible said, everything comes in its own season.

Elvis's mamma had visited him more than once while he had

slept. Each time, all she did was hover in the corner of his dream, her long, big-jawed face smiling blissfully down on her son. *"Thank you, darlin','"* she whispered.

"Good morning, Elvis," Miss Shiva said, slowly lowering her arms. "I finally had to tell them to hold your calls. I figured you couldn't sleep through many more of them. And they just brought up a whole bagful of telegrams."

Elvis nodded. There would be time for all that later. Right now, all he felt like doing was breathing in and breathing out and watching this vision of a woman do her slow yoga dance.

"You won't believe the people who've called," Shiva went on, continuing with her yoga exercise. "Starting with Billy Graham himself. No secretary, nothing, just the Reverend Billy Graham calling personally to say how impressed he was with what you did yesterday. And how much he'd like you to join him in one of his crusades. I told him that you'd call back."

Elvis kept nodding.

"A raft of other preachers called too," Shiva said, finishing up her yoga with a corkscrew twist. "And a couple of rabbis. Then the young people started calling from all over, one from way up in Canada somewhere. Peace kids. They are so proud of you."

"How about that."

"And listen to this, Elvis," Shiva went on. "It's working already! Kathy Lemon called. She said to tell you that Bambi and Harry Huff kissed and made up. They had a meeting and they're going into business with each other."

"Really? They're in the brothel business, you know."

"I know that, love," Shiva said. "But the important thing is that they aren't fighting anymore, isn't it?"

"I guess so," Elvis said. "What else did Miss Kathy say?"

"Just that Bambi and Harry are putting together their fire insurance money to build a brand new house."

"You mean, the fire insurance money they got from burning down each other's places?" Elvis said. "That doesn't sound just, does it?

"I suppose not," Shiva said. "But I am just so happy that they won't be doing that kind of thing anymore."

"Me too," Elvis said. He thought a moment and said, "But what if that Bambi woman started this whole thing with the murder of that customer of Miss Kathy's? It sure doesn't seem right that she should be rewarded for that, now, does it?"

"But she didn't," Shiva blurted out.

"How do you know?"

Shiva shrugged. "Well, Kathy said that too," she said. "She was at their meeting and Bambi swore up and down that she had nothing to do with that man's murder."

Elvis nodded. There was no reason for Miss Bambi to lie to her new business partner at this point. Elvis had never really bought the theory that she was behind that murder anyhow.

"They all just wanted to thank you, Elvis," Shiva went on cheerfully. "And Kathy said to tell you that at the end of the meeting they all sang a chorus of 'Down by the Riverside.' "

"Well, at least I've got 'em singing," Elvis said.

"You've got them more than singing, Elvis," Shiva said, earnestly. "You've brought a big hunk of peace into their lives and you know it."

"I do hope so."

A sharp rap at the door.

"Who's there?"

"Your old friend, Tom." The Colonel's new pussycat voice.

"Tell him we're busy," Shiva whispered, touching Elvis's face.

"We need to talk, Elvis," the Colonel said through the door. "A problem's come up. Serious problem."

"Can't it wait, Tom?"

"Afraid not, son," Parker said.

Elvis got out of the bed and slipped into some trousers and a T-shirt before opening the door. Parker marched in looking more like a lion than a pussycat. He glared at Shiva.

"Alone," Parker growled. "We need to talk alone, Elvis."

"Then we won't be talking at all," Elvis replied. "I have no secrets from Miss Shiva."

"Is that a fact?" Parker growled. He paced up and down in front of them, apparently still hoping Shiva would leave, but when it was clear she was staying, Parker said, "You know, I think I've been a pretty damned good sport in all of this, Elvis. Patient as a mother. Going along and getting along."

Elvis said nothing.

"But I've just about had it! Had it up to here and then some!" Parker pointed at his fleshy neck.

"What's the problem?" Elvis said.

"Your friend Mr. Tzar is the problem," Parker said, staring at Elvis as if Shiva weren't there. "He's squeezing me out. And squeezing you dry in the process."

"What are you talking about?"

"The calls, the phone calls," Parker said. "Scores of them, I hear. From all over the place. And they all want the same thing—another Elvis peace concert. In their city. Free, of course."

"I thought that might happen," Elvis said. "Well, maybe that's my destiny. I've got a lot of thinking to do."

"*You* don't have any thinking to do," Parker said sarcastically. "All your thinking is being taken care of by Mr. Tzar. *He's* the one who's taking the calls. I don't know how many free concerts he's signed you up for already."

"Can't be," Elvis said. "Tzar doesn't even have a phone."

"Well, he's got one now, Elvis," Parker said. "Right here in town. Over at your miracle boy's house, Little Timmy's. Tzar worked it out with the Sahara operator. She relays all your business calls out there."

Elvis swallowed hard. "You sure about this?"

"Oh, I'm sure all right," Parker said. "When I tried to call you this morning, I got him. And he made things very clear to me. He's taking over. He's your manager now."

"I'm sure Tzar just wants to—" Shiva began, but Elvis cut her off with a wave of his hand.

"That can't be, Colonel," Elvis said.

"I am sure glad to hear that, son," Parker said. "Because that man is giving you away. He'll break your bankroll faster than a night of high roller roulette."

"This is not about money anymore, Mr. Parker," Shiva said quietly.

Parker put his hands on his hips and glared condescendingly at her. "Is that so, Miss Shirley? You don't really think this is all about God and love, do you now, girl?"

"Don't you dare talk to her like that!" Elvis suddenly hollered. Without realizing it, he had raised a fist under Parker's chin.

Parker just stood there, fuming.

"That's all right, Mr. Parker," Shiva said in a soothing voice. "Maybe you should cool down a little bit now. Go sit by the pool. Close your eyes."

The Colonel was breathing so hard you'd think he'd just been working out on his boxing bag.

"Close my eyes?" he shouted. *"I just opened them, woman!* And I know a flim-flam when I see one!"

"Go!" Elvis roared. "You leave right now, mister!"

The Colonel spun around and marched out, slamming the door behind him.

"Man, that felt good!" Elvis cheered as soon as Parker was gone. "I can't tell you how long I've been wanting to do that."

Shiva looped her fingers through the belt loops on Elvis's pants and tugged him toward her.

"It certainly is hard to hold onto a peaceful feeling around that man," she said.

"It surely is," Elvis said. He kissed her on the forehead. "That thing about Tzar is strange though, isn't it? I mean, he didn't say anything to me about—"

"He's just trying to help out, I bet," Shiva said. "You know, with all those calls coming in. Just giving you a chance to recuperate from yesterday and think things over."

"Yup, that must be it," Elvis said. "But I don't mind letting the Colonel think otherwise for a while. You know, maybe it *is* time for him and me to part ways."

27

Pope Elvis, the First

l-*vis*! El-*vis*! El-*vis*!" A chorus of voices came through the balcony window.

"What the devil is that?" Elvis asked.

"Oh, they've been doing that, off and on, all morning," Shiva said, smiling. She walked to the balcony and slid the glass open.

Louder: "El-*vis*! El-*vis*! El-*vis*!" Reflexively, Elvis shuddered. He'd heard those cries before—about a million times. People screaming out his name while waiting for him outside an auditorium or when they spotted him in the street. People who desperately wanted something from him, although whatever it was, he surely couldn't give it to them. *Could he now? Had that changed too?*

Shiva was beckoning him to the balcony. Reluctantly, Elvis stepped out onto it with Shiva at his side.

A good thirty people were gathered below on the sidewalk in front of the Sahara. When they saw Elvis, instead of screaming louder, they all went quiet. They were folks of all ages and all types too. In fact, that heavyset pair in Bermuda shorts gazing up at him from the front of the crowd looked to be the very same couple he'd seen strolling by a few days back, the couple he'd realized had their own hurts and hopes and dreams just like everybody else. Suddenly, one voice piped up from the group, full of feeling: "Thank you, Elvis."

Elvis waved down at them, smiling softly. Beside him, Shiva was waving too.

Suddenly, from the back of the crowd, a young Negro woman rolled herself forward in a wheelchair. "Please, Elvis!" she called out. *"Heal me!"*

The blood drained out of Elvis's head so fast he had to brace himself on the railing. *Please, God, no! Not this! This isn't part of the deal! It can't be!*

"Ma'am," Elvis called down to her. "I'm real sorry. Honest to God, I am. But I can't—"

Shiva took Elvis's arm, squeezed it hard. "Just leave it be, Elvis," she whispered to him. "No need to say anything."

"But—"

"By God, it's the pope! Pope Elvis the First!" Digby Ferguson shouted. He had just now stepped around the corner and was pointing up at Elvis with a smirk on his florid face. Just seeing that face made Elvis feel better—saner, somehow.

"Hey there, Digby!" Elvis called down to him. Only now did Elvis notice that standing next to him was Gus Lemon, still wired up like a human bear trap.

"We need to talk, cowboy!" Digby called back. "But security is tight. Tell the Sahara I'm one of your cardinals!"

"You bet!" Elvis rushed back into the room and called reception. He described the two men who he wanted ushered upstairs for a personal audience.

* * *

218

"I've got good news and I've got bad news, Big Guy," Digby Ferguson cracked as he entered the room, Gus beside him. "And the good news is I solved one of those murders. Signed, sealed, and *serendipitied!*"

"Is that a fact?" Elvis said wryly.

"Remember that story about the rabbi who says everybody's right, even when they contradict each other?"

"I remember," Elvis said.

"Well, the rabbi was right!" Digby said. Both he and Gus began laughing uproariously, a response that obviously caused considerable discomfort to the man in the wire mask.

Elvis began laughing it up too, although he wasn't sure why. He looked over at Shiva, feeling kind of embarrassed for behaving so childishly, but Shiva was studying that yogi's autobiography by the window and didn't pay him any mind.

"Hold on a minute, Digby," Elvis said finally. "How the heck did you two end up palling around together?"

"I went out to the hospital to apologize to Gus for cracking his jaw and putting his face in traction." Digby said. "The guilt just got to me. You know, 'You can take the boy out of the church, but you can't take the church out of the boy.' "

Gus made a complicated sound, a kind of articulated grunt.

"He says he accepted it," Digby said, apparently translating. "My apology, that is. So we got to know each other real well. Nothing like an apology to break down the psychic barriers. 'The truth shall set ye free,' and all that."

"I saw you brought him to the concert," Elvis said.

"Beautiful concert, by the way, Elvis," Digby said. "A little over-the-top, but beautiful nonetheless."

Elvis smiled. There sure was something consoling about Digby's company this morning.

"And after the concert," Digby continued, "I introduced Gus to the magical world of mushroom heaven. Although I must say, introducing it into his mouth was a little problematic. Anyhow, we had a splendid conversation out there under the moon. That's when he told me about that hanged man, the late Bruce Donaldsen."

"I . . . hear . . . Donaldsen . . . make . . . deal," Gus sputtered through his wires. At least that was what Elvis thought he said.

"What deal?" Elvis asked.

"With the Owl. His deal with the Owl," Digby said. He pulled out his spiral notebook and began rifling through the pages. "I've got it all right here, boss. I'll start at the beginning."

"Go ahead."

"So about ten days ago, Gus was up at Fanny's in North Vegas," Digby began, reading from his notes. "It's a bar for locals. A *real* bar, not one of those casino bars that looks like it's out of some Rock Hudson movie. Fanny's always has the TV on and the local news was doing their five millionth piece about wedding chapels. How cute they are, how quick they are, how cheap they are. They're showing this long line of couples waiting outside the Little Chapel of the West when an old cowboy at the far end of the bar yells, 'Lambs to slaughter!' "

"Lamb . . . slaughter," Gus grunted.

"This little witticism got a good laugh," Digby went on. "And then this other guy yells, 'Jesus! It's the Owl!' And sure enough, one of the guys in line outside the chapel is the Owl. Well, that got everyone laughing, because—listen to this, Elvis—because everybody at Fanny's knows that the Owl's been married six times already! And that what they're showing up there on the TV is already out of date, because the woman he married that day has already left him. The Owl, it seems, was not good husband material."

"What's this got to do with Donaldsen?" Elvis asked.

"He was at Fanny's too," Digby went on. "A couple guys down the bar from Gus. He'd already heard Donaldsen yakking about what a pain in the ass his wife was. How she'd been pestering him for years to take her to Vegas. How they'd been eating meatloaf every night so she could salt money away into their vacation savings account. And how ever since they got here, all she wanted to do was eat and go to shows. She wouldn't let him near the casinos."

"How the heck did he know it was Donaldsen?" Elvis said.

"He didn't at the time," Digby said. "But later, when he saw Donaldsen's picture in the newspaper, he put it together. You know, the one of him hanging like a dummy in his cell." Digby suddenly beamed. "I sold them that picture, you know. Twenty-five bucks, cash on the line. I held on to the book rights though."

Behind Digby, Elvis saw Shiva look up from her yogi book and roll her eyes, as if to say that Elvis must be getting seriously bored with this screwball.

"Gus is telling you all this while the two of you are soaring around in mushroomland, right?" Elvis said. "So how do you know it wasn't an hallucination?"

"Because it didn't *feel* like one, Elvis," Digby said, grinning.

Elvis shrugged. "A lot of people complain about their wives, especially on vacations. That doesn't prove anything."

"I haven't finished yet," Digby said.

"Finish."

"So when everybody starts laughing about the Owl getting married again, Donaldsen asks the guy next to him who the heck the Owl is. And the guy tells him. He tells him the Owl's specialty, that he kills people for money. And that's when Donaldsen says, 'Man, I wonder how much it would cost to kill my wife.'"

"You heard him say that," Elvis said, looking at Gus.

Gus nodded energetically in the affirmative.

"He wasn't the only one who heard him either, Elvis. The guy next to Donaldsen, being a helpful sort, not only tells him the going rate to have your wife offed, but how to get ahold of the Owl. He writes down the Owl's phone number on a beer coaster like he's giving him the number of his bookie."

"And Gus believes Donaldsen called him," Elvis said.

"He *knows* he called him," Digby said. "He called him right from Fanny's. From the booth in the back. Gus says it was funny the way Donaldsen was so eager to take care of business. A man of action. You wouldn't figure him for that because Donaldsen was one skinny bastard." Digby scrutinized his notebook. " 'Like he was stitched together out of prairie grass,' as Gus put it. Poetic, isn't he?"

"Very," Elvis said. "Can you speed it up any, Digby?"

"But I want to give you every nuance," Digby said. "That's what makes great literature."

"I'm looking for a fast read," Elvis said.

"Okay. So Gus followed Donaldsen to the phone booth where he heard him call the Owl, make the deal, tell them where they were staying, and when to come by."

"Did Gus tell the police?" Elvis said.

"You mean Turtleff? Surely, you jest, Mr. Presley," Digby said.

Shiva came up alongside Elvis and took his hand.

"But here's the pièce de résistance," Digby went on. "When Donaldsen came back to the bar, he ordered drinks all around and started in about what a pig his wife is. How she always orders two main courses in the restaurant. How she's so fat people always point at her and laugh. He was more than nasty—he sounded like a nut case. But get this: finally Donaldsen stands up—he's sloshed by now—and he says he's got to get ready to go out to dinner

222

and a show. He says his wife has been pestering him to go see Howie Pickles!"

"God almighty!" Elvis cried. His brain was suddenly clicking along like an express train. Of course, Bonnie Donaldsen's murder was commissioned by her husband. Like 99 percent of murders, it was all in the family. And the theory that Sol Epstein had commissioned the murder to put a hex on the Sahara was just as plain dumb as it had seemed to Elvis from the get-go. That was crystal clear now.

"Where have I been all this time?" Elvis said excitedly. "It's like that mountain thing, Digby. The mountains are mountains again. Things turn out to be just what you thought they were in the first place."

"You're a genius!" Digby laughed.

"What has gotten into you, Elvis?" Shiva said, squeezing his hand.

"So Turtleff was right after all," Elvis went on, ignoring her. "About Donaldsen's suicide too. A guilty man feels guilty—guilty enough to kill himself. It all adds up, pure and simple."

"It gets even better," Digby said. "Wait until you hear about the Reverend Sweetser connection."

"What is going on here?" Shiva suddenly blurted out. "You're not a policeman, Elvis. There's no reason for you to get involved in this business. Especially not now. Not after yesterday."

Elvis was taken aback. He looked at Shiva inquiringly, but then he smiled and clucked her under the chin.

"It's all right, little darlin'," he said. "It's like you once said, a man can do it all—sing rock 'n' roll, give a peace concert, and even see a little justice done along the way, right?"

" '*If you want peace, work for justice,*' " Digby intoned solemnly. Then he winked. "Pope Paul said that. You know, the *other* pope, the one in Rome."

"But . . . But what if you lose it, Elvis?" Shiva said softly.

"Lose what?"

"The peacefulness. The *prana*," Shiva said. A couple of tears were spilling from her eyes onto her cheeks.

"I do not believe I will, Miss Shiva," Elvis said, tenderly wiping away a tear with his fingertips. "If it's true peacefulness, it should be strong enough for anything, don't you think?"

"But it will distract you," Shiva murmured.

"I'll keep a watch on that, darlin'. Don't you worry now."

Shiva let go of Elvis's hand and slowly walked to the window, her back to him. Elvis could see that she was really weeping now. What the heck was she getting so upset about? He should just go and comfort her whatever it is. Elvis hesitated.

"The crucifixion of Mrs. Donaldsen," Elvis said to Digby. "How does that figure in this?"

"That's the sweet part, Elvis. The Sweetser part," Digby said. "And this one's straight from the horse's mouth—*my* mouth, that is. A few days ago when I was driving around with Howie and Kathy, they suddenly decided that she should get divorced. From Gus, here." Digby patted Gus on the shoulder. "I already told Gus all about this and he's at peace with it now, aren't you, Gus?"

Gus nodded somberly.

"Get to the point, Digby!" Elvis snapped. Watching Shiva sniffling alone there was just about breaking his heart.

"Up in Reno they specialize in no-contest divorces," Digby said hurriedly. "So we drove up there and stopped at the first divorce mill we came to. And while Kathy is talking business with one of their so-called lawyers, I inspected the diplomas and licenses on the wall. Now get this—who is the principal operator of this little outfit? None other than Tyrone B. Sweetser. Our friend, Reverend Sweetser."

"It's probably a common name," Elvis said.

"Tyrone Sweetser?" Digby laughed. "I don't think so, cowboy. Anyway, it's the same man, all right. I had a little talk with the receptionist. Loquacious woman. She said Mr. Tyrone got his law degree from the same mail-order university he got his divinity degree from. They probably gave him the two-fer special."

"The *point*, Digby!" Elvis snapped.

"Okay, this is it. The whole *serendipity-doo*. The receptionist says that Sweetser brags to her that he gets folks coming and going. That he can spot a marriage that isn't going to last the minute they walk into the Little Chapel. He can see it in their eyes, especially the women. So he keeps their addresses and a couple months later sends out a solicitation from his divorce office offering his other service. Of course, nobody in Vegas knows about his Reno business."

Elvis stood perfectly still. The pieces were clicking together in his mind like glacial plates in the Ice Age.

"We best go talk to Sweetser right about now, shouldn't we?" Elvis said.

"Yes indeedily-doo, partner!" Digby chirped.

They started for the door.

"Don't go," Shiva murmured, still whimpering. "I love you, Elvis."

Elvis turned and looked at her. He felt about as torn as a hound dog with two scents in the air. But he had to go.

"That's a sweet thing to hear," Elvis said softly. "But we have our whole lives, don't we, darlin'?"

He walked out the door.

28

The Bad News

hat's the bad news, Digby?" Elvis asked. "You said you had good news and bad news."

Elvis was sitting in the back seat of the open Olds with Digby, who was scribbling madly in his notebook. Up front, Gus was driving, tilting his head back and forth to improve his vision through his wire mask.

"Bad news?" Digby said, clicking his ballpoint shut. "I forget. But that's the way it should be, boss—forget the bad news and remember the good."

"Seems Gus is taking his bad news pretty well," Elvis said quietly enough so Gus wouldn't hear. "You know, about the divorce."

"We had a long talk about that too, last night," Digby said. "Gus realized he never had a peaceful moment with that woman. She brought out the devil in him. He wants a fresh start. Your concert helped."

"More likely it was your mushrooms that helped."

"That too, Elvis. Good combo, peace concert and magic mushrooms." Digby wagged his head thoughtfully. "Like I say, it all fits. I was feeling particularly guilty after driving Kathy up to Reno. Aiding and abetting in breaking up a marriage. So the very next day I went out to the hospital to see Gus, here, to ask his forgiveness. And *serendipity-doo*, that led to hearing the skinny about Donaldsen."

Elvis nodded. He was trying real hard not to think about Shiva whimpering back in his room.

"I was married once myself, you know," Digby said softly.

"Really?"

"Hard to believe, isn't it? Beautiful woman, too. Fellow divinity student. I barely knew her before we took that first mushroom trip together, but Bonnie and I made an incredible connection that night. A 'cosmic connection,' as Tim Leary likes to say. In one psychedelic flash we saw that we were soul mates. It wasn't more than a week afterward that Bonnie and I tied the knot in Cambridge City Hall."

"What happened, friend?" Elvis asked gently.

"Sex happened," Digby said. "Our spiritual guide, Professor Leary, went to great pains to teach us that the only route to transcendence was by killing the ego. *'Death to the ego!'* " Digby uttered a pained laugh. "So he had his way with her. He made it with my Bonnie as an object lesson in letting go of my ego. Unfortunately, my ego failed the test."

"My ego would've failed that test too," Elvis said. "Any man's would've."

"Maybe," Digby said. He abruptly slapped Elvis on the shoulder. "Hey, no matter, man! It made me the incredibly sensitive fellow that I am today."

Gus pulled up in front of the Little Chapel of the West. Business was booming; a line of customers ran all the way back to the

227

Hacienda Hotel's parking lot. Elvis found the sombrero under the front seat and put it on, this time turning the brim so far down it covered half his face. No one recognized him as he and Digby made their way to the chapel's entrance.

Elvis heard the music before he saw Sweetser's brand new sign. Wafting out of the chapel's doors was Elvis's voice singing, "Love Me Tender."

"At least it's not 'Dying in the Chapel,' " Digby quipped.

The freshly painted sign on the door read, BLESSED BY ELVIS. And beneath that in smaller letters, "Weddings in the Spirit of the Elvis Peace Concert." Tacked up on the other door was a huge blowup of a photograph of Sweetser with his arm around Elvis, the one taken yesterday just before the concert. It was all Elvis could do to keep himself from ripping down the whole shebang right then and there.

Elvis and Digby walked inside. No more than ten feet in front of them, the Reverend Tyrone Sweetser, sporting a white choir robe, was reciting the holy sacrament of marriage to a fresh-faced couple who looked barely out of their teens. Next to Sweetser, a 45-record player was coasting into the last verse of "Love Me Tender." Sweetser looked up.

"*Wait your turn*, damn it!" Sweetser snapped.

Elvis removed the sombrero.

"Hey! It's my pal, Elvis Presley!" Sweetser cried.

The wedding couple stared at Elvis, both blushing with excitement.

"I told you Elvis was my personal friend," Sweetser said to them.

"Goodness!" the bride exclaimed. "Can we get a picture with you?"

"Cost you twenty-five bucks," Sweetser said.

"I need to talk to you right now, Sweetser," Elvis said.

"Almost done here," Sweetser replied. He looked back at the couple and said, "I now pronounce you man and wife." Then he said, "Tell the next couple to wait a couple minutes."

It took a while to get the starstruck bridal party out the door.

"I need some honest answers, Sweetser," Elvis said. "And if I don't get them, I'm going to start by ripping down your new sign. And finish by telling everybody in that line out there about your double-duty divorce business up in Reno."

The good reverend blanched. "Okay," he said.

"First, do you have any idea who's responsible for the murders?"

"No," Sweetser said. "I know I had nothing to do with them. And neither did Jones from the Good Samaritan Chapel. We talked yesterday at the concert. He admitted to the bee-sting thing, but no murders. And he has no idea who tacked up the fat lady on my billboard. I don't think he's lying either."

"Neither do I," Elvis said. "Now tell me, did you ever do business with any of the Owl's ex-wives? Divorce business, I'm talking about."

Sweetser scratched furiously under his robe.

"Hurry up, Reverend."

"Okay, the truth is, I did business with every blessed one of them," Sweetser said. "In fact, the Owl died owing me a bundle in alimony. Payments came through me—I work on commission. He'd been putting me off, saying he had a big payment coming in for a job he'd already done, and next thing I know, he's a goner."

"You'd think a man like the Owl would find a less expensive way of dealing with his ex-wives."

"You mean by killing them?" Sweetser said. "Not the Owl. He was real sentimental when it came to his exes. Actually, he didn't have the heart to kill anybody he knew personally."

Elvis shook his head. Maybe he could see the mountains now, but he didn't think he'd ever be able to understand the convoluted moral principles of the Las Vegas underworld.

"That was probably a lucky thing for you, Reverend," Elvis said. "I can't imagine the Owl felt very sentimental about you."

"Oh, he hated my guts, Elvis," Sweetser said, unable to hide just how proud that made him feel. "And for good reason too. That man was caught in my revolving door."

"He surely was. That's all for now, Reverend."

Elvis and Digby snuck out the back of the chapel—undoubtedly the word had gotten out that he was in there with Sweetser. They found Gus idling in the Olds in the driveway behind the Hacienda.

"I'll bet you the farm that the billboard crucifixion was the Owl's own personal touch," Elvis said as soon they were back in the car.

"Absolutely!" Digby said. "The Owl got paid to kill Bonnie Donaldsen, but what he did with her body afterward was his own business. Dealer's choice. So he decided to use her corpse to make a statement about the Little Chapel. A major statement. Big as a billboard."

"Like you say, Digby, it all fits," Elvis said, grinning like a cat. He sat back in his seat. Man, did it feel good to finally be taking care of business. He felt like he'd awakened from a long sleep and when he'd opened his eyes, everything was transparent and simple. It had to be that super-consciousness the yogi wrote about—that white light shining out of your eyes made everything you looked at clear as rain. Elvis had Parmahansa Yogananda to thank for that. Tzar too. And most especially Miss Shiva—she'd shown him the way from the start, God love her.

"And J. C. Whaley's murder is just what it seems too," Digby said.

"Absolutely."

"Hey, Big Guy. We're finally on the same wavelength, aren't we?"

"Is that so?" Elvis said, grinning. "So where are we going next?"

"Sheriff Turtleff's."

"Bingo!" Elvis said. "Listen, Digby, there's a question I been meaning to ask you. Yesterday at the concert, what did you say to de Luca that made him cool down so fast?"

"I told him that God is love," Digby said. Then he laughed. "I also told him that if he caused any trouble, I knew exactly where his daughter and grandchildren lived and what would happen to them wouldn't be pretty."

"That's awful!" Elvis said.

"There's all kinds of ways to keep the peace," Digby said.

They rode in silence for a few minutes and then Digby said, "I just remembered the bad news, Elvis."

"What's that?"

"God is dead!" Digby Ferguson cackled.

29

Sergeant Digby Ferguson

*W*hat's a nine-letter word means hardening of tissue?" Turtleff asked, barely looking up from his newspaper as Elvis and Digby marched into his office.

"Sclerosis," Digby said in a heartbeat.

"How do you spell that?" Turtleff said.

"We got to talk, Sheriff," Elvis said. "Right now."

Turtleff put the newspaper down, but then put his feet up on his desk before replying. "Wonderful concert you gave yesterday," the sheriff said. "That peace business works like a charm. Haven't even had a jaywalker in the past twenty-four. You're going to put me out of business, Presley."

"I've got some business for you right now," Elvis said. "So listen up."

Digby had braced his notebook against the office wall and began furiously taking down every word.

"Okay," Elvis went on. "So you turned out to be right, Sheriff. Bruce Donaldsen *did* murder his wife. Or at least, he hired the man who did. So you put the right man in jail. One of them at least."

"Of course, I did," Turtleff said proudly. "I've been at this job for a while, Elvis. You learn a thing or two."

"Awful shame about Donaldsen hanging himself in his cell right here, but you can't blame yourself for that, right?" Elvis said, deadpan. "You can't keep an eye on lockup while you're out solving crimes, can you?"

Digby chortled, but kept writing.

"But we've got this other murder, don't we?" Elvis continued. "The murder of J. C Whaley, that policeman visiting from Atlanta. Up to now, that one's unsolved. But that's going to change right now."

"Is that so?" Turtleff said.

"It's clear as day who's responsible for that murder," Elvis said. "J. C. was just about to testify against two of his friends on the Atlanta force, so they came out here to keep J. C quiet the old-fashioned way. Of course, they didn't do it themselves, not when murder-for-hire is only a nickel away in the local community. So they hired the best in the business, the Owl. Now these cops know they're the natural suspects, so they ask the Owl if there's any way he can make it look like somebody else ordered up J. C.'s murder. And the Owl says, 'It'll cost you extra, but here's what I can do.' He tells them that he'll make sure that J. C attends Pickles's show at the Sahara just before he kills him. That probably wasn't too hard to arrange—send him free tickets or something. And then he says he'll put him up on that steeple after he's dead."

"I don't follow," Turtleff said.

"To make it look like a pattern! A series of murders!" Elvis said. "You know, the 'Insult Murders' or the 'Chapel Murders,' take your pick. Both those theories were all over town right after

Mrs. Donaldsen's murder. Now the Pickles connection to Mrs. Donaldsen was just an accident, but she had to be somewhere just before she was murdered, so why not Pickles's show? It was one of the biggest draws in town. So then you send J. C. to the same show before *his* murder and it looks like there's a direct connection. Nothing to do with Atlanta cops or Internal Affairs testimony. Same with the steeple—that connects to the so-called Chapel Murders the same way. The connection to the whorehouses was just a fluke, though the way people think in this town, not much of a fluke really. And as a little sideline, the Owl primes the pump for future business, like de Luca's contract on that ventriloquist over at the Sands. It's fine with the Owl that de Luca thinks those other murders were commissioned by the Sands management because it keeps the Owl in work. And he needs all the work he can get because he's thigh-deep in alimony payments."

Turtleff took his feet off of his desk. He was suddenly all ears.

"So basically, you're saying it's got nothing to do with the casino people, right?" Turtleff said.

"Except for the botched job on the ventriloquist and that bomb at the Sahara," Elvis said.

"Well, those don't really amount to much, do they?" Turtleff said. He was looking mighty relieved and Elvis surely knew why: the sheriff had compelling reasons for not enforcing the law against casino owners, reasons that undoubtedly involved payoffs, not to mention his own personal safety.

"Anyhow, the steeple was a special bonus for the Owl," Elvis said. "He was working his own little angle on that one."

"What angle are you talking about?" Turtleff asked.

"Long story," Elvis said. "And not that important just now. Because you know what you're going to do right now, Sheriff? You're going to pick up the phone and call the Atlanta Internal Affairs people. And you're going to tell them that you're just

about to file extradition papers for Sergeant William 'Bucky' Bucowitz. Because he's wanted for murder in Las Vegas, Nevada."

Turtleff's face dropped. "I don't think that's a good idea, Presley."

Elvis had expected that reaction. After all, Turtleff was a cop
himself, and heaven knows, he was the kind of cop who would
end up doing some serious hard time if the Internal Affairs people
in the state of Nevada ever took a close look at his dealings with
the local crime bosses. So Turtleff didn't want to stir any I.A.D.
pots around here. And extraditing some out-of-state cops could
amount to some heavy stirring.

"But you know what, Sheriff?" Elvis went on. "The Atlanta
I.A.D. isn't going to want to give up Bucowitz so easy. Makes
them look like they failed at their job, like they've been asleep at
the switch, and now some sheriff out in Nevada has to take over
for them. So there's probably a better way to bring those Atlanta
officers to justice. A way that makes the Atlanta cop-watchers
look more professional. And along the way, makes you look
more—you know, very congenial."

Turtleff looked up at Elvis expectantly, almost gratefully.
"How?"

"Just call them up, Sheriff," Elvis said. "Then put me on. Tell
them I'm your deputy."

"What are you going to say?" Turtleff said.

"Trust me, Sheriff," Elvis said.

Turtleff hesitated only a moment before calling the Atlanta operator and getting through to the Atlanta police's Internal Affairs
Department.

"Good morning, Captain," Turtleff said into the phone. "You
are speaking with Sheriff Reginald Turtleff in Las Vegas, Nevada.
And I'm investigating the recent murder out here of an Atlanta
police officer, one J. C. Whaley."

Turtleff nodded earnestly while he listened to the captain's reply.

"Yes, Captain Camerone," Turtleff said into the phone. "But let me turn you over to my man who's heading up that investigation. My deputy, uh, Sergeant—" Turtleff hesitated, looked questioningly at Elvis.

"Digby. Digby Ferguson," Elvis whispered to Turtleff.

"Sergeant Digby Ferguson," Turtleff said to the I.A.D. captain, then handed the phone to Elvis.

"Ferguson here," Elvis said evenly. "Good to speak with you, Captain Camerone."

"You know who you sound just like, Ferguson?" Camerone said, laughing.

"Yeh, Elvis Presley. A lot of people say that," Elvis said. "Now listen, Captain, I have a warrant for the arrest of Sergeant Bucky Bucowitz on a charge of first-degree murder, so I'm going to be filing extradition papers to bring him out here soon as possible."

Turtleff turned red. He grabbed for the phone, but Elvis blocked him with his free hand.

"Of course, Captain," Elvis went on, "if you could get a confession out of Bucowitz or his pal out there in Atlanta, you could probably try him out there too and save us all an airplane ticket."

A long pause at the other end. "How long do I have?" Captain Camerone said finally.

"Twenty-four hours, Captain."

"That doesn't give me very much time."

"Maybe you can play them off each other," Elvis said. "Bucowitz and his partner in crime."

"You mean, Sergeant Bulkley?"

Right, Bulkley. Elvis had forgotten the name of the other man in the newspaper photograph that Billy's friend had sent him. "Yes, that's exactly who I mean," Elvis said. "Offer one of them

236

some kind of deal to testify against the other. That shouldn't take more than twenty-four hours."

"We've already tried that, Ferguson," the captain said.

"Try again," Elvis said. "But this time tell them about our little extradition plans. And tell them that out here in Nevada we aren't too squeamish about making use of the death penalty."

"That might do it," Captain Camerone said.

Elvis read Turtleff's number out loud from off of the phone. "I look forward to hearing from you, Captain." With that, Elvis hung up the phone and started out the door, Digby following after him.

"Hey, where are you going now?" Turtleff called.

"To tie up the last loose end," Elvis said over his shoulder.

He and Digby were no sooner outside when Digby whooped like a rodeo rider. "Who was that masked man?"

Elvis was amazed himself. He was working out these murders as if he was reading lines off a teletype dispatch. Like a song singing itself, the crimes were solving themselves. All he'd had to do was open his eyes and see things for what they really were. He could feel that *prana* energy pulsing through him like a white tornado.

"How the hell did you figure all that out, Elvis?" Digby said when they were in the back seat of the car again.

"Instead of looking at it complicated, I looked at it simple," Elvis said.

"But how did you know those Atlanta cops hired the Owl?"

"J. C.'s widow said he was picked up out in the desert in a Hudson with Georgia plates. And that he must have known someone in the car—that's why he got in, no questions asked. Well, that had to be his birthday buddies in the car. Who else did he know out here? And that was the same Hudson car that snatched up the Owl over at the Sands when I chased him out back. So the

Hudson has got to belong to someone connected to the Owl. Probably his driver. I figure with his eyesight, the Owl needs a driver, right?"

Digby was scribbling in his notebook again. "But wasn't that the same car that the person who killed the Owl was driving?" he said.

"That's true too," Elvis said. "I'm sure it was the Owl's own driver who murdered him. Probably to keep him from talking to Howie Pickles about his recent clients. Although for the life of me, I don't know why she'd do that."

"She?"

"Yes, Melissa Riley is her name. From somewhere out near Atlanta too. She's the one who owns that car. Howie said the Owl's killer ran like a girl. Well, that's because it *was* a girl, a girl with a bandana across her face, wearing a night watch cap and a pair of men's trousers."

"Hot diggidy-doo!" Digby crowed. "That's my last chapter right there, 'The Girl in the Night Watch Cap.' Let's go get her now."

"I'd sure like to, Digby. Nothing I'd like better than to wrap this all up and get back to my new life. But the thing is, I don't know who the girl in the night watch cap is."

"I thought you said her name was Melissa something."

"It was. But Melissa is hiding from her parents for some reason. Doesn't want them to contact her. So I'm sure she changed her name when she relocated out here." Elvis paused. "I do have a picture of her, though. It's an old picture and a splotched-up photostat to boot."

"Where is it?"

"Back in my room."

"Let me have a look at it, Elvis," Digby said, rooting around in his kit bag. "I've got a pill in here that sharpens the senses.

Gives me X-ray vision, only deeper. Much deeper."

Elvis shook his head. "You really ought to think about kicking those drugs, Digby." But a moment later, he said. "Heck, it's worth a look, I guess."

"To the Sahara, Driver!" Digby called up front to Gus. "And be quick about it, would you, pal?"

30

Everything Reveals Itself

lvis had the whole speech worked out in his mind: he'd tell Shiva that starting this very night, they would sit down and start making plans for his new life—*their* new life. Because she was coming along on this ride, all right. She was his inspiration. She had shown him the way to the real purpose of his life. With her at his side, who knows how far this thing could go? More peace concerts. A whole new kind of motion picture too, something with a lesson of peace and good will. Maybe a Christmas movie. Heaven knows, he'd be canceling that *Roustabout* movie first thing. He was finally done with those idiotic movies.

What's more, Elvis would explain to Shiva that without even realizing it, she'd helped him solve these crimes by teaching him about meditation and *prana*—how everything just reveals itself when your mind is finally clear of clutter and nonsense. Yes, he would take her in his arms and tell her how she'd helped him see justice done. And that was part of bringing peace to the world too, little darlin'.

Elvis knocked on his hotel room door. "You decent, Miss Shiva?"

No answer.

Elvis knocked again. Next to him, Digby tilted his head back and dripped eye drops into one eye at a time. Digby had chewed down two bright blue pills in the car and his face was rapidly turning purple.

Still no answer. Elvis unlocked the door, opened it.

"Miss Shiva?"

The note was on the telephone table, jutting out from the pages of *The Autobiography of a Yogi*, where she usually left her messages. Elvis went right to it.

My Dear Elvis,

I went back to the Center to pick up Kali. I'll meet you here in an hour. And then I want us to go away, my love. Just the three of us. Go away and start fresh and clean. We will have a beautiful life together, I promise you.

I made an awful mistake, Elvis. But I really do love you now. Please believe me.

All my love,
Shiva

"So where's that photo, Big Guy?"

From the corner of his eye, Elvis saw Digby rifling through a stack of papers on the coffee table. Elvis suddenly wanted him gone. For Digby to get his purple face and bulbous belly button the heck out of here. The man *was* a distraction—a distraction from everything that was truly important in Elvis's life. That was clear as rain too.

"Don't tell me the cleaning lady tossed it!" Digby said, getting down on all fours.

"Forget it, Digby," Elvis muttered. He looked down at the note again. What did Shiva mean, "an awful mistake"? And what the devil did she mean that she really loved him *now*?

"Serendipity-dippity-doo!" Digby bellowed from under the bed. He crawled out with a sheet of photostat paper in his teeth, then turned over on his back and held the paper up straight-arm. "Take some fat from Melissa's ass and inject it in her lips! Puff 'em up, baby! Puff 'em up!"

"I need to be alone, man," Elvis said.

"Chisel down that chin, Doctor!" Digby hollered. "Yes in *doodle-deedy*, pull that skin tight as a kettledrum over her cheekbones! We're closing in on the Aristotelian Mean, Doctor! We're just a color and a rinse away!"

"Get out, Digby," Elvis said.

"Red!" Digby yodeled. "Color me red!"

"Out!"

"X-ray eyes don't lie, cowboy," Digby replied. "I'd recognize her anywhere."

"Now!" Elvis barked.

The phone rang. Elvis picked it up while it was still ringing. "That you, Miss Shiva?"

"No, it's Turtleff," the voice on the phone said. "That you, Elvis?"

"What do you want, Sheriff?"

"Thought I'd share the good news with you, pardner," Turtleff said. "I just now got off the phone with our friend, Captain Camerone, in Atlanta. Bucky Bucowitz copped a plea. Murder one for his partner, manslaughter two for him. Now that didn't take long, did it?"

Elvis just stood there. He suddenly felt empty—empty and very tired.

"I'm calling a press conference right away," Turtleff went on happily. "Thought you'd like to be there too. I couldn't have solved this case without your help, Presley. And I believe in giving credit where credit's due."

Elvis replaced the phone on its cradle without saying another word. Digby was skulking out the door.

"Wait a second, Digby. Who is she? Who's in the picture?"

"Candy. Miss Candy Kane."

"What?"

"Candy plus a hundred grand's worth of plastic surgery. And that's just her face. God knows how much of that treacherous body came with her genes. Like those headlights of hers—I always thought they came off the assembly line."

"You're crazy!" Elvis suddenly shouted at him. "Your whole darned life is an hallucination! You couldn't recognize your own face in the mirror!"

Digby slowly walked back from the door. He held the copy of the photograph of Miss Melissa Riley out in front of him.

"I didn't need X-ray eyes for this, Elvis," Digby said quietly. "I recognize her from when she first came to Vegas. She worked with my father in the kitchen here. Can't remember what she called herself then. Anyhow, she left after a year and I guess I didn't recognize her when she first came back. But I do now."

"I don't see Candy nowhere," Elvis said, grabbing the photostat. "Not a sign of her."

"See that?" Digby said, pointing at the girl's face. "That little pockmark on her left cheek, north-by-northwest of her left nostril? Tiny, but a strange shape. Like she got snagged by a fishhook when she was little. I'll bet you a million it's still there. That's one thing plastic surgery can't correct."

They took the stairs down and headed straight for the Sahara's nightclub. A pair of tourists in the casino spotted Elvis, called out his name, but Elvis shot them a glare and kept moving. Digby had to break into a trot to keep up with him. Elvis hopped up onto the stage and through the drop-curtain.

There was much more traffic backstage than the first time Elvis was here. Stagehands were moving out the ice cream cone flats of the "Scoopy-Doop" dance number and moving in flats depicting the palm trees and ragged shore of a deserted island. Dodging these flats were a half-dozen showgirls in various stages of dress or undress, depending on how you looked at it. The costumes for the new number were the tattered garments of a bevy of ship-wrecked wenches, their rips and tears artfully arranged to reveal a nipple here and a buttock there. The "Desert Island" number. Somebody at the Sahara had to come up with a new theme for flashing skin every week of the year.

"Miss Candy?"

One of the showgirls turned around.

"Elvis, hi! What are you doing here?" Miss Candy Kane said. Her outfit had so many rips and tears that it was a wonder it remained suspended on her voluptuous body. And if Digby was right, it was also a wonder that any kind of plastic surgery which could produce a body like that was legal.

"I'm looking for you, ma'am," Elvis said, scrutinizing Candy's face. Oh yes, underneath all that foundation there was definitely a double pockmark north of her left nostril.

"What are you looking at, Elvis?" Candy said, shrugging un-comfortably. All it took was that single shrug for one of the rips to reposition itself dead center on her right breast.

"What was your name before you went into show business, Miss Candy?" Elvis said, looking steadily into her eyes.

"I already told you. Meryl Rubeleski."

"Okay, then before that," Elvis said.

"There was no before," Candy said, starting to turn around. "Listen, I've got to change, okay?"

Elvis grabbed her arm, brought his face in close to hers.

"I mean your name when you graduated from high school in Macon. Macon, Georgia."

Candy froze. Her face went slack, every hot spark of sexuality suddenly gone cold. And in that instant, Elvis could make out the frightened pale eyes of Miss Melissa Riley.

"Don't do this to me, Elvis," Candy murmured. "Please don't do this to me."

"You brought it on yourself, Miss Melissa," Elvis said, tightening his grip on her arm.

"All I wanted was a new life. A new face, a new body, and a new life," she said, her voice trembling. "What's wrong with that?"

"Are you asking me what's wrong with murder?" Elvis said evenly.

"*Murder?* What are you talking about, Elvis?"

A couple of the other showgirls stopped, apparently hoping to get in a few words with Elvis too. Elvis looked hard into Candy's eyes. "Where's your dressing room?"

She gestured to the left with her head, just as Digby Ferguson came panting up beside Elvis.

"Wait here," Elvis said to Digby, still gripping Candy's arm as they started for her dressing room.

"Oh sure," Digby groaned. "I solve the mystery and you have all the fun."

Elvis closed the dressing room door behind them.

"How much did the Owl pay you?" Elvis said. "Speak up, woman. Did he pay you enough to pay off your surgery bills?"

"Honest to God, I don't know what you are talking about," Melissa/Candy whimpered. "The Owl never paid me anything."

"You telling me you drove him for free?"

"Drove him? *Where*?"

"You know where. In your Hudson. The baby blue Hudson your daddy gave you for graduation."

Melissa Riley stared at Elvis incredulously. And then she broke into a pure Candy Kane laugh.

"Why, I sold that car a year ago, Elvis!" she cried. "One of my admirers gave me a brand new Thunderbird, so I could finally get rid of that junk heap. Got rid of my last connection to Macon too. I can show you the bill of sale if you want. I've got it here somewhere."

"Who did you sell it to?"

"Margaret," she said. "You know, she needed a car once she moved up there to the funny farm."

Elvis could feel the blood drain out of his face.

"Manovah?" he said.

"Yes, that's right. Manovah."

31

Prophet and Loss

Shiva,

I've gone to the Center to get you. If you get here first, wait for me. Don't let anybody in. Shiva, whatever has happened, we can work it out.

Forever,
Elvis

Elvis slipped the note under his door, then took the stairs down. Digby was behind the wheel, Gus snoozing in the back seat, sealed like a sloth to the hot leather upholstery. Elvis got in beside Digby.

"Everything else is clear as rain, but this is pure mud," Elvis said, as they pulled out onto the Strip. "It don't make sense, any of it. Why would Manovah work for the Owl?"

"The usual reason, a paycheck," Digby said. "Man cannot live by blue corn alone. It's the same reason that Shiva and Tzar work that gig in the nightclub—to pay for T-shirts and tents and tofu."

"She's devoted to peace, for God's sake," Elvis said. "You don't take a job chauffeuring around a hit man if you're devoted to peace."

"Joan of Arc was devoted to peace," Digby said.

"But what the heck would Manovah murder him for?"

"Well, as I recall, Joan said she was doing God's will," Digby said.

"Maybe somebody else is using her car," Elvis said. "That's the only thing that makes sense."

They were entering the highway now and Elvis needed to keep his eyes pealed on the opposing traffic. If he spotted Shiva and Kali heading back to Vegas, he'd tell Digby to make a U-turn and catch up with them. But that didn't seem likely; he didn't even know what kind of car to look for. Digby turned onto Route 146 and gunned it. A few minutes later, they passed the sign that read, INDIAN SPRINGS, NEVADA, THE PLACE WHERE HEAVEN AND EARTH MEET.

"Slow down," Elvis said. "We're coming on it any second now."

At the crest of the next hill, Elvis saw the five-pointed redwood star announcing the Center of the Light on the dirt road to the right.

"Park here. We'll walk," Elvis said. No reason to broadcast their arrival; they had some exploring to do first.

"You've got to be kidding, Big Guy," Digby said "It's over a mile from here. Only mad dogs and Englishmen go out in the midday sun."

"Here. *Now*," Elvis said.

Digby hit the brakes, pulling onto the highway's sandy shoulder. Elvis got out and waited while Digby loaded up his pockets with notebooks and pens, took a couple steps toward Elvis, stopped, pivoted around, and returned to the car where he removed a handkerchief from his back pocket, tied the corners in little knots, and carefully spread it across Gus's jaw grillwork to shield it from the sun. It struck Elvis as about the most tender gesture he had seen anybody perform in a long time.

They had walked along the highway almost a hundred yards when Digby said, "Since we're playing Lewis and Clark, we might as well do this right," and he turned straight into the dense growth of scrub pine and steershead lilies that bordered the road.

"You know where you're going?" Elvis said.

"I was an Eagle Scout," Digby replied, not turning.

Elvis followed silently after him into the dark forest, fighting back a throb of foreboding. *I made an awful mistake, Elvis. But I really do love you . . . now.*

"Smell it?" Digby said, stopping.

Elvis sniffed. "Smell what?"

"Motor oil," Digby said. "Heavy-duty. I'd say a viscosity of twenty, if not twenty-five. It's got that heavy-duty stink."

"Where? What are you talking about?"

"To drive a big old Hudson in this heat, you need an oil of that grade," Digby said, turning his head this way and that while he flexed his nostrils. Suddenly, he extended his arm and pointed to his left at a stand of Christmas tree–sized blue spruce. *"Voila!"*

The fat backside of a pale blue Hudson jutted out from the stand of fir trees.

The two men walked up to it. Georgia plates, THE PEACH STATE, number 136798H. Four years out of date, not that the local authorities would notice. Elvis walked around to the driver's-side door and looked inside. Dangling by a ball-chain from the rear-view mirror was a small metal disk, black on one half, white on the other, with a wavy line separating the halves—that yoyo thing Shiva had pointed out to him on the bandstand. The symbol of perfect harmony.

The door was unlocked. Elvis opened it and slid inside. The

dashboard had as many knobs and levers as the control panel of a piper cub. A couple of Baby Ruth candy wrappers lay on the floor. Baby Ruths surely were not on the commune diet, but then again, there had been a lot of people with a lot of different eating habits coming and going in this car lately. Elvis leaned over and popped open the glove compartment. *The Happy Hudson Owner's Guide*; a City Service map of the Southwest; a little book called *Spanish Through Pictures*, and another little book with the unmistakable photograph of Parmahansa Yogananda on the cover.

Elvis took the book in both his hands. He stared down at the yogi's face, at his dark, deep-set eyes under woolly white brows. Such incredibly kind eyes, Elvis thought. Wise. Accepting. Peaceful. You could practically see the *prana* emanating from those eyes.

Or was that sunlight glinting off the book's slick cover?

Elvis flipped the book open randomly. Here and there words and phrases were underlined in red pencil: *Heaven on Earth . . . transforming power of Cosmic Consciousness . . . the beauty of the Spirit*. Elvis opened to another page: *We have it within us to create history* was underlined and so was *grappling with the Forces of Evil in their own province*. And on the next page, double-underlined was one word: *Utopia*. He flipped back to the first page. Written in the heavily slanted cursive of the Palmer Method was: "This book belongs to Margaret Reardon." But that name was crossed out and next to it, "MANOVAH" was written in block letters.

A sudden jolt! The car rocked to one side, then swung back. Elvis spun around in his seat, his heart pounding.

"Damn!" Digby hissed. The Hudson's rear window was set at such a deep slant that all Elvis could see was a hand—Digby's flushed hand, the one he had obviously just smacked against the trunk in a futile effort to open it. But that jolt was more than enough to dislodge a stapled sheaf of papers from the back of the glove compartment and onto the car's floor. Elvis saw it when he swung back in his seat.

The Utopian Manifesto, the hand-lettered cover said. Under that in smaller letters, "From Sodom to Paradise, a Program for Enlightenment." And in the bottom right-hand corner, "Conceptualized by Tzar, Prophet."

Elvis pushed open the car door, called to Digby. "Look at this!"

Digby walked up to Elvis, holding his bruised hand. Elvis showed him the homemade booklet.

"God help us, not another prophet," Digby grimly shook his head. "It's always the same, isn't it, Elvis? The temptation of personal divinity. Prophet and loss."

Elvis turned to the first page. This too, was hand-lettered in a fine-tipped pen, almost like calligraphy:

> "To show the world the transforming power of cosmic consciousness, we must deliver it straight to Sodom. We must grapple with the devil on his own turf. Thus will we set an indisputable example: if we can transform Sodom into Utopia, the entire world can attain peace and harmony. It is an awesome responsibility. It is *our* responsibility."

"Vegas," Digby said. "Vegas is his Sodom."

Elvis flipped to the next page. It was headlined, "The Program" and under that, "I. Out of the Clamoring of War, a Voice of Peace."

> "The ugly war is here already. But it is too small for the eyes of unenlightened consciousness to see. We must build it large—a billboard of sin. We must light a spark to it."

"The Casino Wars. The Chapel Wars," Elvis murmured. "It was Tzar who wanted them, not the Owl. That was *his* spark. He needed to whip things up in Vegas so he could charge in on his white horse to bring them peace and harmony."

"Exactly," Digby said. "But I'm afraid that you, my friend, are their voice of peace." He pointed to the next section, the one labeled. "A Little Child Shall Lead Us."

> "We must bring the people into one place and make a joyful Noise."

Next to this section, in script and red ink, was written: "Elvis" then a little arrow and "Shiva."

Elvis snapped his eyes shut. His heart was shuddering. He willed himself to take a deep breath, but he could barely manage to breathe at all. There was not an ounce of stillness left inside him. No peace. Only clarity. Brutal clarity.

"But the peace concert was my idea," Elvis whispered, opening his eyes.

"So you thought," Digby replied softly.

"But Miss Shiva—?"

"She has talent," Digby said. "Real show-biz talent."

Elvis let the booklet drop from his hands. Digby picked it up, rifled through the pages. When he came to the last page, he just stared at it dumbfounded.

"Incredible!" he said. He showed it to Elvis.

In a variety of colored ink were detailed renderings of the Las Vegas Strip as reenvisioned by Tzar, the prophet. The Hacienda Hotel was "The Parmahansa Yogananda Meditation Center." The Sands was labeled, "Tzar's Temple of Peace." And the Sahara had been rechristened "The Elvis Presley World Church of Holy Music." This drawing featured a ten-story-high statue of Elvis where the Sahara's front awning presently existed. In the statue, Elvis was sitting in the lotus position, his eyes closed, his mouth wide open apparently in song. It was the prophet's vision of Utopia rising like a phoenix from the vestiges of Sin City.

Suddenly, Digby picked up a large rock from under one of the trees. He struggled back to the rear of the Hudson and with both hands slammed the rock with all his might onto the trunk. It popped up. He reached inside. He returned to Elvis carrying a .22-gauge rifle and a box of shells.

"The holy ends justify the murderous means," Digby said.

"By God, Manovah *was* his driver," Elvis said. "Drove him on his killing rounds. Probably even drove him for free. All she asked in return was some special treatment of his commissioned victims. Nail the fat lady up on the billboard. Send J. C. Whaley to Howie's show, then turn out the lights and spear him on that steeple. Light the spark of war all over town. Get it blazing for all to see. Get them clamoring for relief and then bring in the peace concert. So of course when it looks like the Owl might trade information about this little plan for some extra cash, she had to shoot him."

"It's Joan of Arc all over again," Digby said.

"They'd . . . They'd shoot Shiva, too, if . . . if they thought she'd tell," Elvis stammered.

"They might," Digby said. "Let's hope she hasn't said anything that would make them think she'd talk."

Elvis sprang out of the car. "We got to get her out of there."

Digby hesitated a moment. Then he stuffed *The Utopian Manifesto* into his back pocket, loaded the gun, and led the way through the woods to the Center of the Light.

32

Serendipity-doo!

They stopped at the cyclone fence. Elvis could just make out the main gate through the dense underbrush fifty feet or so to his left. Mufah and the other bearded guard were standing in front of it; they looked like they were playing a game of hopscotch on the gravel in front of the gate.

"I'll never get my fat ass over this thing," Digby whispered, gesturing to the fence. "Looks like we'll have to go in like civilized folk."

Before Elvis could reply—before he even understood what Digby meant—Digby was charging through the brush toward the front gate with the rifle jutting in front of him.

"Hands up!" he shouted. Then he called over his shoulder to Elvis, "Man, I have wanted to say that since I was a kid!"

Mufah laughed. But he immediately stopped when Digby pressed the tip of the barrel into his gut.

"Open the gate," Digby said.

Elvis came panting up beside him. "Listen, Digby, I'm not sure we should be doing this this way," he said.

"Of course not," Mufah said gently. "We are all men of peace, aren't we?"

The man sounded like he really meant it. And that is all it took for Elvis to make up his mind. "You heard him—*Open the gate!*" Elvis snapped.

Mufah unlocked the gate and swung it open, Digby's gun following him every step of the way. Elvis grabbed the other bearded man and put him in a full nelson.

"Now strip! Both of you!" Digby barked.

The two man lifted off their yoga togas. As was the commune's custom, neither wore underwear.

"Rip those things into strips," Digby ordered.

The men did as they were told, not saying a word. Elvis knew what to do next: using the cloth strips, he bound both men, hand and foot, then gagged them, leaving them by the side of the driveway looking like plucked chickens all trussed up for Sunday dinner.

As Elvis and Digby walked through the gate, Digby said, "I call this chapter, 'Naked Lunch.' "

They came to a halt at the edge of the clearing.

About a dozen men, women, and children were bathing and frolicking in the glacial pond. Elvis could hear their laughter, the simple joy in their voices as they called to one another. Over at the garden it was planting time. One group was sowing seeds the old-fashioned way, swinging their hands to seed bags slung over their shoulders, grabbing a handful, then swinging their hands back, tossing the seeds into the open furrows. Following behind them, men and women raked the furrows over. There was an ethereal rhythm to the whole operation. A natural dance. The peaceful kingdom.

Elvis took a single step out into the clearing. At the foot of the garden, someone wearing a DON'T BE CRUEL CONCERT T-shirt was sitting cross-legged on a small Indian rug playing a guitar. Elvis shaded his eyes with one hand. It was Tzar and the guitar was that pot-bellied Oriental instrument that he played to accompany Shiva's dance at the Sahara. Elvis could now hear its sweet whiny sound; he was setting the rhythm for the planters. Standing behind Tzar, Manovah was fussing with the prophet's hair, dipping her hands into a bowl, then fussing with his hair again.

Next to Elvis, Digby said, "Get a load of that. She annointeth his head with oil."

"I don't see Shiva anywhere," Elvis whispered. "Kali neither."

Both men surveyed the entire grounds again, face by face.

"Good," Digby said. "They got out."

"I hope," Elvis said, then, "Follow me."

Elvis stepped back into the pine woods, then started in a long arc to where the red stone ledge met the clearing. When they were no more than twenty feet away, he heard the panther growl. And then he heard Shiva's voice: "It's okay. It's okay. Quiet, Abu. Be still now."

Two more steps and Elvis saw them—Shiva, Kali, and Abu inside the circus cage, the cage's gate bolted and locked. Shiva was standing, her long arms around the animal's neck as she tried to soothe him. Kali sat in the corner of the cage, hugging herself.

"Shiva!" Elvis called in a hoarse whisper.

The panther growled again, louder. Shiva stroked its neck. "Shhh, Abu," she cooed. "Elvis is our friend."

"The key. Where's the key?" Elvis said, in front of the cage now, Digby behind him.

"They took it," Shiva said.

"Manovah? Manovah and Tzar?"

"Yes."

"Why . . . why did they lock you up?" Elvis said.

Digby had set down the rifle and was closely inspecting the cage lock in both his hands.

"Because I told them we were leaving. Going to you," Shiva said.

"And?"

"And that is all I want, Elvis," Shiva said. She let go of the animal and grabbed a cage bar in each of her hands, her face pressed between them. "It's true. That is *all* I want. To be with you forever."

"Maybe now, Miss Shiva," Elvis murmured. He could barely look up at her, barely look into her soulful dark eyes. "Maybe that is what you want now, but not before. Not when you were hunting me . . . seducing me at their bidding. To get me to sing their song for them."

Digby was rooting around in the pine grove to the right of the cage. He leaned over and, struggling, lifted a small boulder.

"I thought it was the right thing to do, Elvis," Shiva whispered imploringly.

"Right for who?"

"For the world."

"And for me, Miss Shiva? Right for me too?"

"I . . . I thought it was . . . bigger than us. Than just our lives," Shiva said.

Digby grunted for Elvis to move aside. He knocked the huge stone against the lock. The panther yelped. The cage rattled. Digby cursed. The lock remained fastened.

"Shhh," Shiva whispered. "They'll hear you."

Digby raised the stone high and slammed it down against the lock. Abu yelped again, louder.

"Can't risk it!" Elvis hissed to Digby.

Digby let the stone fall to the ground. The front of his Hawaiian shirt was ripped, his plump pink belly flopping out over the waist-band of his pants. Suddenly, he ran over to the rifle, leaned down, and seized it in both hands.

"I'll blow the lock off," Digby said. "Blow it and we run." He swiveled his head back and forth, then pointed into the woods. "That way. The car's that way."

Elvis raised his forefinger, holding Digby off.

"I need to know something, Miss Shiva," Elvis said. "This beautiful child here, Kali. Who's her daddy?"

Shiva shut her eyes. Tears slipped from the corners onto her cheeks. "Tzar," she whispered.

Elvis drew in his breath, kept going. "You knew everything that Manovah was up to, didn't you?"

"No," Shiva said. "None of us did at first."

"But later."

"Yes. After the murders, I knew."

"But before the Owl was shot."

"Yes."

"You told Manovah about that meeting with Howie, didn't you? Out in the desert. So she could stop him."

"Yes."

Tears sprang into Elvis's eyes. "You have shamed us both, Miss Shiva," he said, softly.

Suddenly Elvis turned to Digby. "Do it! We'll all run together! *Do it now!*"

Shiva ran to the corner of the cage, taking Kali in her arms. The panther stood directly in front of them. Digby pressed the muzzle of the gun against the keyhole of the lock. He fired.

The sound of the lock clanging against the bars resonated louder than the shot itself. A shout from the clearing. The lock was spinning in the gate. Another shout, coming closer. The lock took its last spin—it was still shut.

Digby shucked the spent shell, reloaded, fired at the lock again. It began spinning again.

"Don't ruin everything!" Manovah screamed, charging into the woods toward them. She was holding a Winchester shotgun. She pointed it at Elvis. "You can change the world! It's within our reach!"

Tzar ran up beside Manovah. He stopped and smiled, fixing his impassioned, blue-green eyes on Elvis's. "Do not forsake me, Elvis," the young prophet said. "We need each other."

The lock suddenly flew off the cage door, landing just in front of Manovah.

"Go!" Elvis shouted at Shiva.

"Don't!" Tzar screamed. "I forbid it!"

Elvis turned, grabbed the cage door, yanked it open. "Go! *Now!*"

All that followed happened in less than a second: Manovah pressing on the trigger; Digby diving in front of Elvis and taking the rain of shot that had been aimed at him; Shiva, Kali, and Abu racing out of the cage and disappearing into the woods.

Digby lay on the ground, the rifle clutched in his hands. Buckshot had entered his neck, chest, and belly like splattered black paint, but only the neck wound spouted blood—squirted it out like a broken pipe with each heartbeat.

Elvis had caught one piece of shot in his shoulder, but that is not why he dropped to his knees and draped his body over the fallen man's. The pain in Elvis's soul had submerged anything he could possibly feel in his flesh.

"Don't move, Elvis!" Tzar barked.

Elvis raised his head. Tzar and Manovah were walking slowly toward him, the shotgun still pointed at Elvis. Underneath Elvis, Digby squirmed. The tip of the .22 suddenly pushed out directly under Elvis's nose.

Digby Ferguson's first shot got Manovah directly in the heart. How he managed to reload and get off his second and final shot, Elvis would never know. That bullet lodged itself between Tzar's luminous eyes. Both Manovah and Tzar were dead before they hit the ground.

Elvis rolled off of Digby. He propped the young man's head against his leg.

By now, most of the denizens of the Center of the Light had crept up to the edge of the clearing. None was armed. Their fresh, sunburned faces were contorted in horror. To Elvis at that moment, every one of them looked like a child. A terrifyingly ignorant child.

"Got 'em both, Big Guy," Digby was gurgling in Elvis's arms, drops of blood spraying from his mouth. *"Serendipity-doo!"*

33

Amen

I am the resurrection and the life,' sayeth the Lord. 'Those who believe in me, even though they die, will live, and everyone who lives and believes in me will never die.' "

"Amen."

"We have come here today to remember before God our brother, Digby Ferguson; to give thanks for his life; to commend him to God our merciful redeemer and judge; to commit his body to be cremated, and to comfort one another in our grief."

"Amen."

Next to Elvis in the front pew of St. James Episcopal Church, Digby's dad and mom looked reverently up at Father Macie, although the minister must have been difficult to see through their tears.

Elvis had made sure that he was the first to bring the awful news to Paddy and Lil Ferguson in their four-room row house on the edge of North Vegas. They had taken it bravely. In truth, they had been expecting it for a long time now, ever since Digby had returned home after his year at Harvard Divinity School. But it was not the drugs that made them expect their son's death, it was his loss of faith. Faith had sustained the boy during the whole time he grew up in this terrible city.

" 'God of all consolation, your Son Jesus Christ was moved to tears at the grave of Lazarus, his friend. Look with compassion on your children in their loss; give to troubled hearts the light of hope and strengthen in us the gift of faith, in Jesus Christ our Lord.' "

"Amen."

Elvis shifted his weight to his left side. Although the doctor had easily been able to remove the shot from his right shoulder, streaks of pain still radiated down his back. He wondered what Digby would have made of this service, back in the church where he had taken his first communion. The fact is, stoned or straight, Digby would have had a big laugh at the whole shebang.

"Since we believe that Jesus died and rose again, even so, through Jesus, God will bring with him those who have died. So we will be with the Lord forever. Therefore encourage one another with these words."

"Amen."

Behind him, Elvis could make out some familiar voices in those "Amens": Gus, Miss Kathy, Howie Pickles, Luke de Luca, Candy Kane, Rabbi Kurtzman, Joby, and Little Timmy. And this last time somewhere in there Elvis heard the sonorous "Amen" of Sheriff Reginald Turtleff.

Turtleff had been on the TV news almost nonstop for the past twenty-four hours reporting his brilliant resolution of the murders, of Manovah and Tzar's conspiracy to foment turf wars, and of their deaths and Digby's. Each broadcast, Turtleff's rendition of the story became more colorful and dramatic, especially the part about him and his deputies capturing Abu with a net and shipping the animal off to the zoo in Reno. In all, the only unresolved part of the entire case was the whereabouts of a woman named Shirley Lee, also known as Shiva, and her daughter, Kali. Despite an all-points dragnet, the pair had vanished.

"Our hymn is 'Bosom of Abraham,'" Father Macie said. He looked at Elvis and nodded.

Elvis slowly rose to his feet. He had not wanted to do this. Not at all. God knows if he would ever be able to sing gospel again and not feel like a fraud—the dupe of the Don't Be Cruel Concert. But Paddy and Lil Ferguson had prevailed. They had told Elvis how much Digby loved his gospel singing when he grew up. And later too, when he came home. Why, only a few days ago, Digby had told his mother that he thought Elvis had a gift, a simple gift uncomplicated by history and theology. Digby had told her that that was why he wanted to get to know Elvis. He thought he could learn something from him about faith. Elvis turned and faced the congregation.

> *"Rock a my soul in the bosom of Abraham.*
> *Rock a my soul in the bosom of Abraham."*

Vanished. He would never see Shiva again. He knew that.

> *"Oh rock a my soul . . . "*

And God knows, he would never see Digby Ferguson again. In ways that Elvis could not begin to understand, that loss would hurt even more.

> *"That love is*
> *So high you can't get over it.*
> *So low, you can't get under it."*

Tears were flowing freely from Elvis's eyes. Suddenly, an achingly sweet soprano voice rose from the congregation to join his own. It was Little Timmy.

> *"So wide, you can't get around it.*
> *Oh rock a my soul . . . "*

Had Elvis really healed that boy? Or was it that hot-headed doctor down in Tucson? Either way, it was ultimately God who made Timmy well again, wasn't it?

After the last "Amen," Paddy Ferguson reached under his pew and withdrew a cardboard box. Hand-printed on the box's cover, it said, *Viva Las Vengeance, A True Story of Crime and Redemption by Digby Ferguson.*

"It's all in there, Mr. Presley," Digby's father said. "His notebooks, his Polaroids. Everything."

"It would be so good if you could get it published for him, Elvis," Lil Ferguson said. "Digby would be so proud."

Elvis took the box. He kissed them both and then, rushing past all the hands clamoring to touch him, made his way up the aisle to the church's exit and out into the blinding, midday Las Vegas sun.

"Elvis! Over here!" Freddy's voice.

Elvis shaded his eyes. His white Cadillac was idling at the curb in front of St. James Church, Freddy at the wheel. Colonel Tom Parker was sitting in the backseat. Elvis had never hated Parker more than he did at that moment—hated his smugness, hated his soullessness. Hated him for being right.

"Everything's packed," Parker called to Elvis. "We've got a movie to make, son."

Elvis walked slowly to the car.